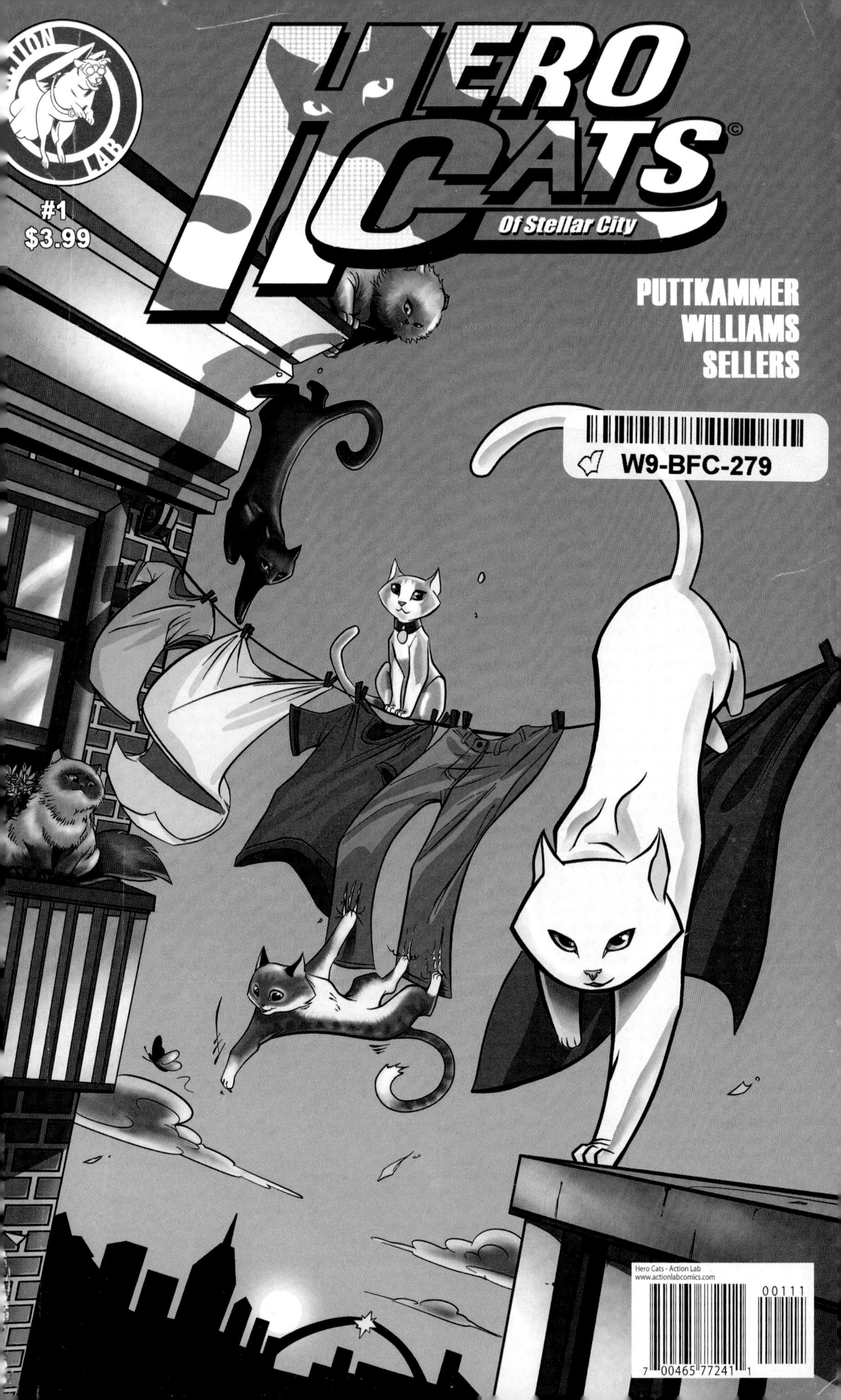

ACTION LAB
#1
$3.99
HERO CATS©
Of Stellar City
PUTTKAMMER
WILLIAMS
SELLERS
W9-BFC-279
Hero Cats - Action Lab
www.actionlabcomics.com

'THE CITY CALLS'

HERO CATS
Of Stellar City

WRITTEN BY KYLE PUTTKAMMER

PENCILS AND COLORS BY MARCUS WILLIAMS

INKS AND POLISH BY RYAN SELLERS

LETTERS BY BRIANA HIGGINS

WWW.HEROCATSCOMIC.COM

Bryan Seaton - Publisher

Kevin Freeman - President

Creative Director - Dave Dwonch

Editor In Chief - Shawn Gabborin

VP Digital Media - Shawn Pryor

Co-Directors of Marketing - Jamal Igle & Kelly Dale

Social Media Director - Jim Dietz

Education Outreach Director - Jeremy Whitley

Associate Editors - Chad Cicconi & Colleen Boyd

HERO CATS #1, August 2014. Copyright Kyle Puttkammer, 2014. Published by Action Lab Entertainment. All rights reserved. All characters are fictional. Any likeness to anyone living or dead is purely coincidental. No part of this publication may be reproduced or transmitted without permission, except for small excerpts for review purposes. Printed in Canada. First Printing.

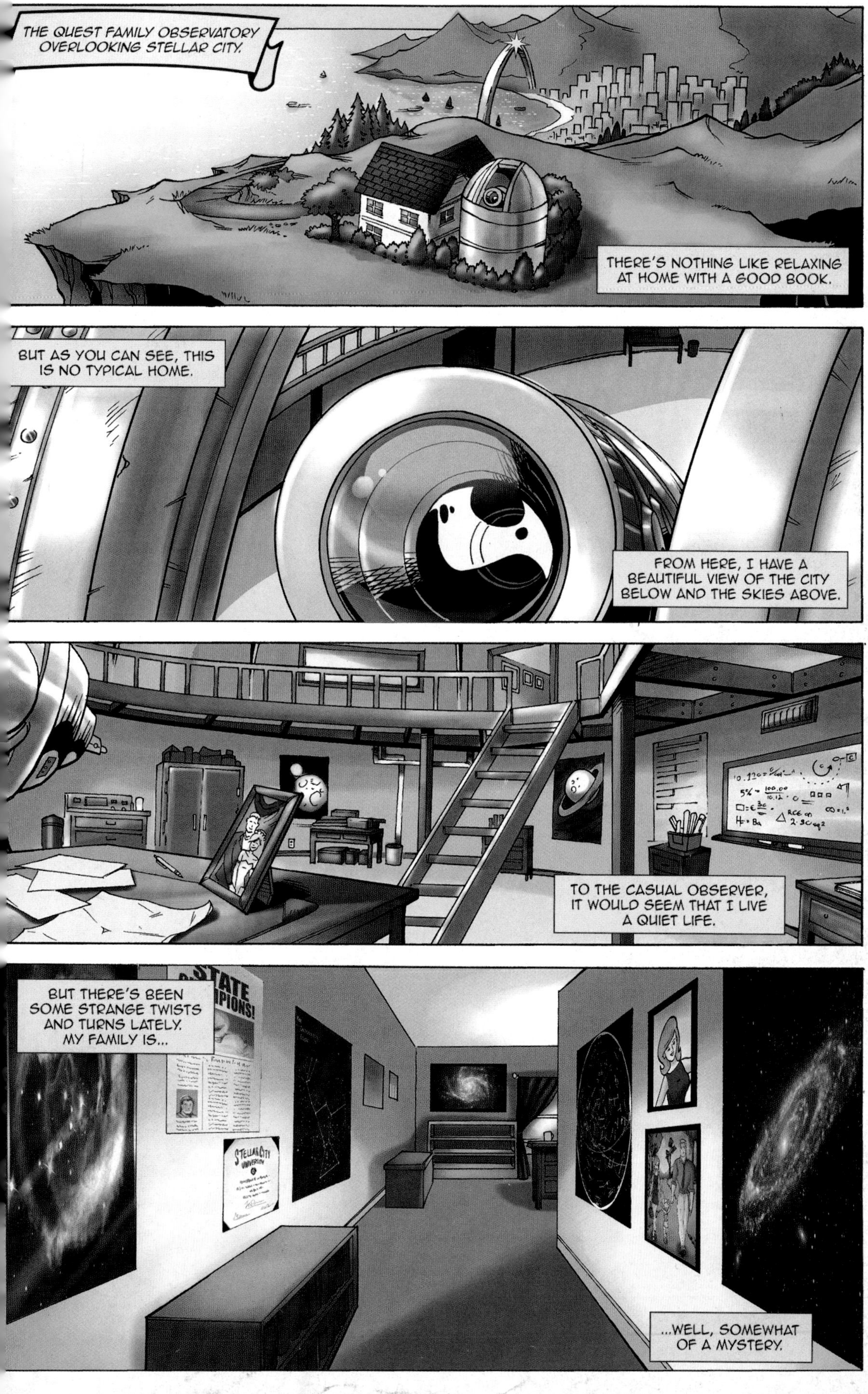
THE QUEST FAMILY OBSERVATORY OVERLOOKING STELLAR CITY.
THERE'S NOTHING LIKE RELAXING AT HOME WITH A GOOD BOOK.
BUT AS YOU CAN SEE, THIS IS NO TYPICAL HOME.
FROM HERE, I HAVE A BEAUTIFUL VIEW OF THE CITY BELOW AND THE SKIES ABOVE.
TO THE CASUAL OBSERVER, IT WOULD SEEM THAT I LIVE A QUIET LIFE.
BUT THERE'S BEEN SOME STRANGE TWISTS AND TURNS LATELY. MY FAMILY IS...
STELLAR CITY UNIVERSITY
...WELL, SOMEWHAT OF A MYSTERY.

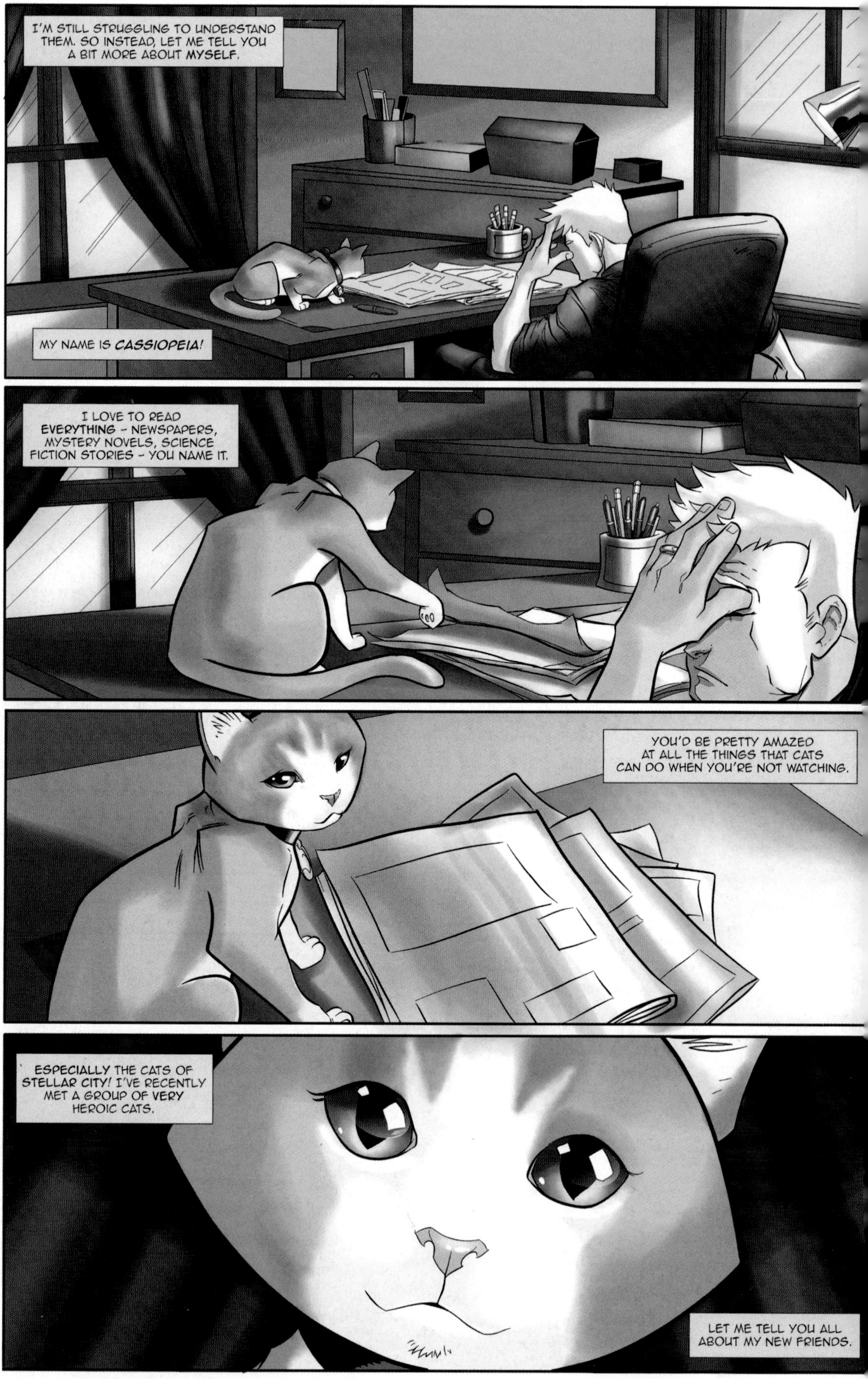
I'M STILL STRUGGLING TO UNDERSTAND THEM. SO INSTEAD, LET ME TELL YOU A BIT MORE ABOUT MYSELF.
MY NAME IS *CASSIOPEIA!*
I LOVE TO READ **EVERYTHING** – NEWSPAPERS, MYSTERY NOVELS, SCIENCE FICTION STORIES – YOU NAME IT.
YOU'D BE PRETTY AMAZED AT ALL THE THINGS THAT CATS CAN DO WHEN YOU'RE NOT WATCHING.
ESPECIALLY THE CATS OF STELLAR CITY! I'VE RECENTLY MET A GROUP OF **VERY** HEROIC CATS.
LET ME TELL YOU ALL ABOUT MY NEW FRIENDS.

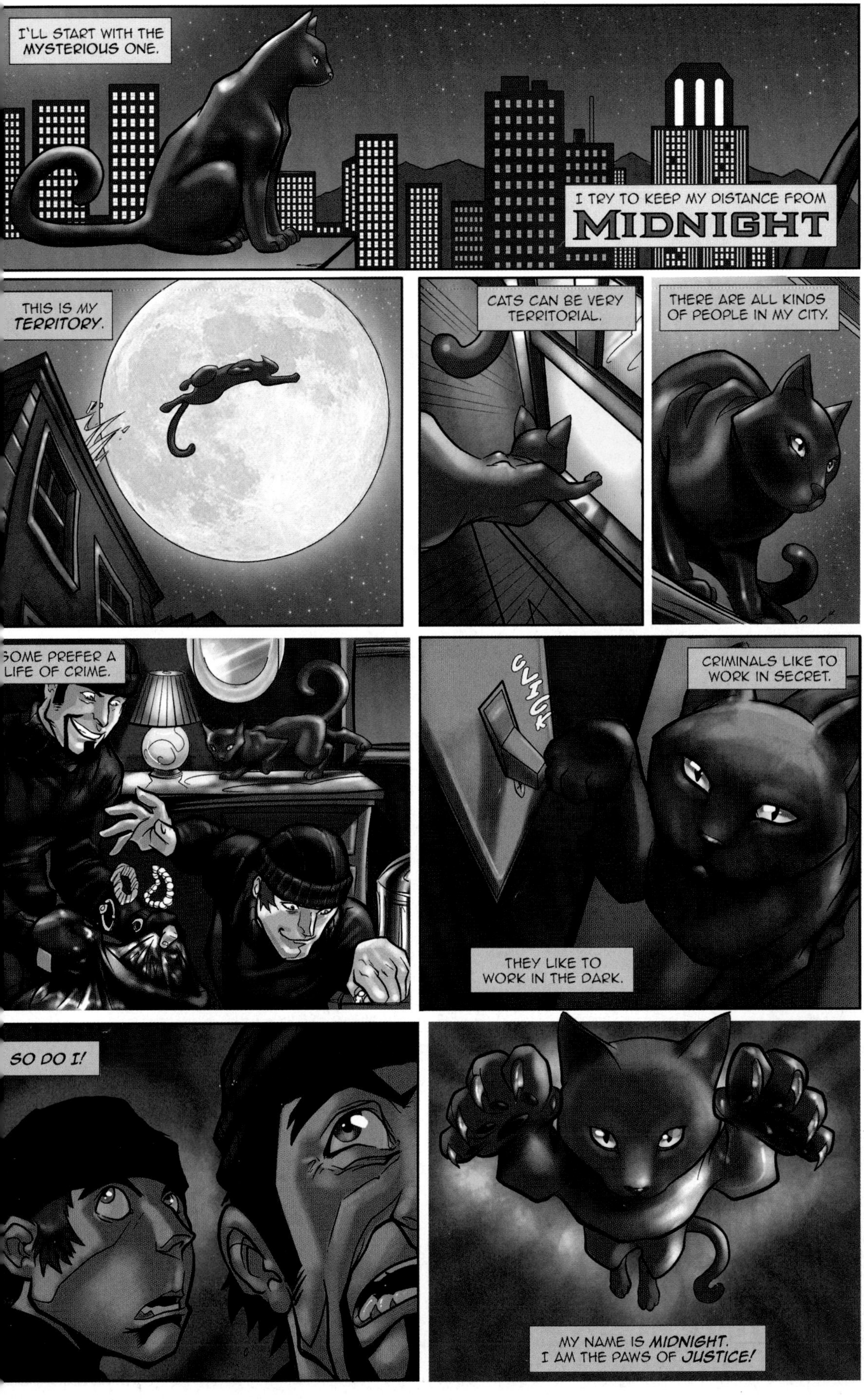

I'LL START WITH THE MYSTERIOUS ONE.
I TRY TO KEEP MY DISTANCE FROM MIDNIGHT
THIS IS MY TERRITORY.
CATS CAN BE VERY TERRITORIAL.
THERE ARE ALL KINDS OF PEOPLE IN MY CITY.
SOME PREFER A LIFE OF CRIME.
CLICK
CRIMINALS LIKE TO WORK IN SECRET.
THEY LIKE TO WORK IN THE DARK.
SO DO I!
MY NAME IS MIDNIGHT. I AM THE PAWS OF JUSTICE!

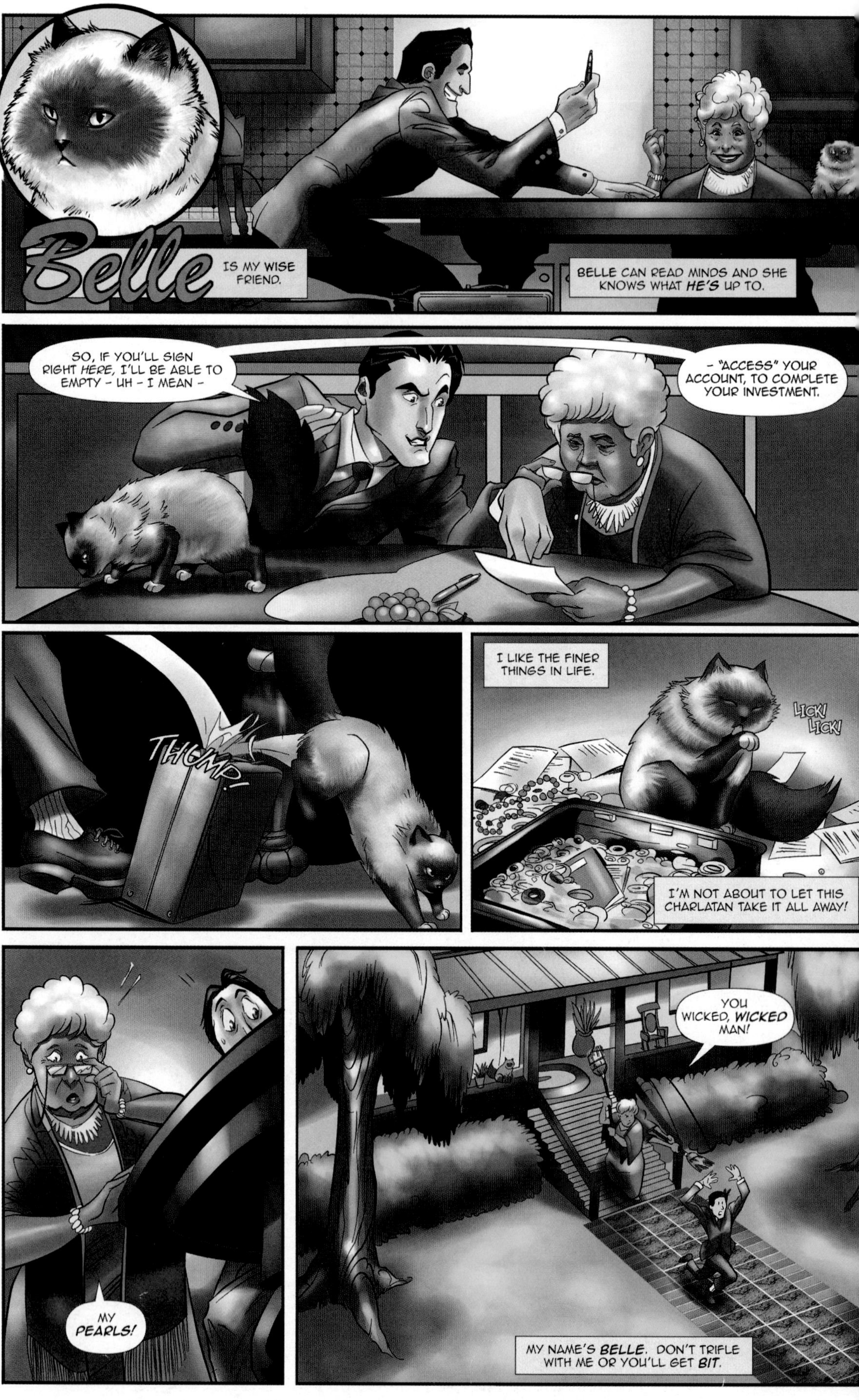

Belle
IS MY WISE FRIEND.
BELLE CAN READ MINDS AND SHE KNOWS WHAT HE'S UP TO.
SO, IF YOU'LL SIGN RIGHT HERE, I'LL BE ABLE TO EMPTY - UH - I MEAN -
- "ACCESS" YOUR ACCOUNT, TO COMPLETE YOUR INVESTMENT.
THUMP!
I LIKE THE FINER THINGS IN LIFE.
LICK! LICK!
I'M NOT ABOUT TO LET THIS CHARLATAN TAKE IT ALL AWAY!
MY PEARLS!
YOU WICKED, WICKED MAN!
MY NAME'S BELLE. DON'T TRIFLE WITH ME OR YOU'LL GET BIT.

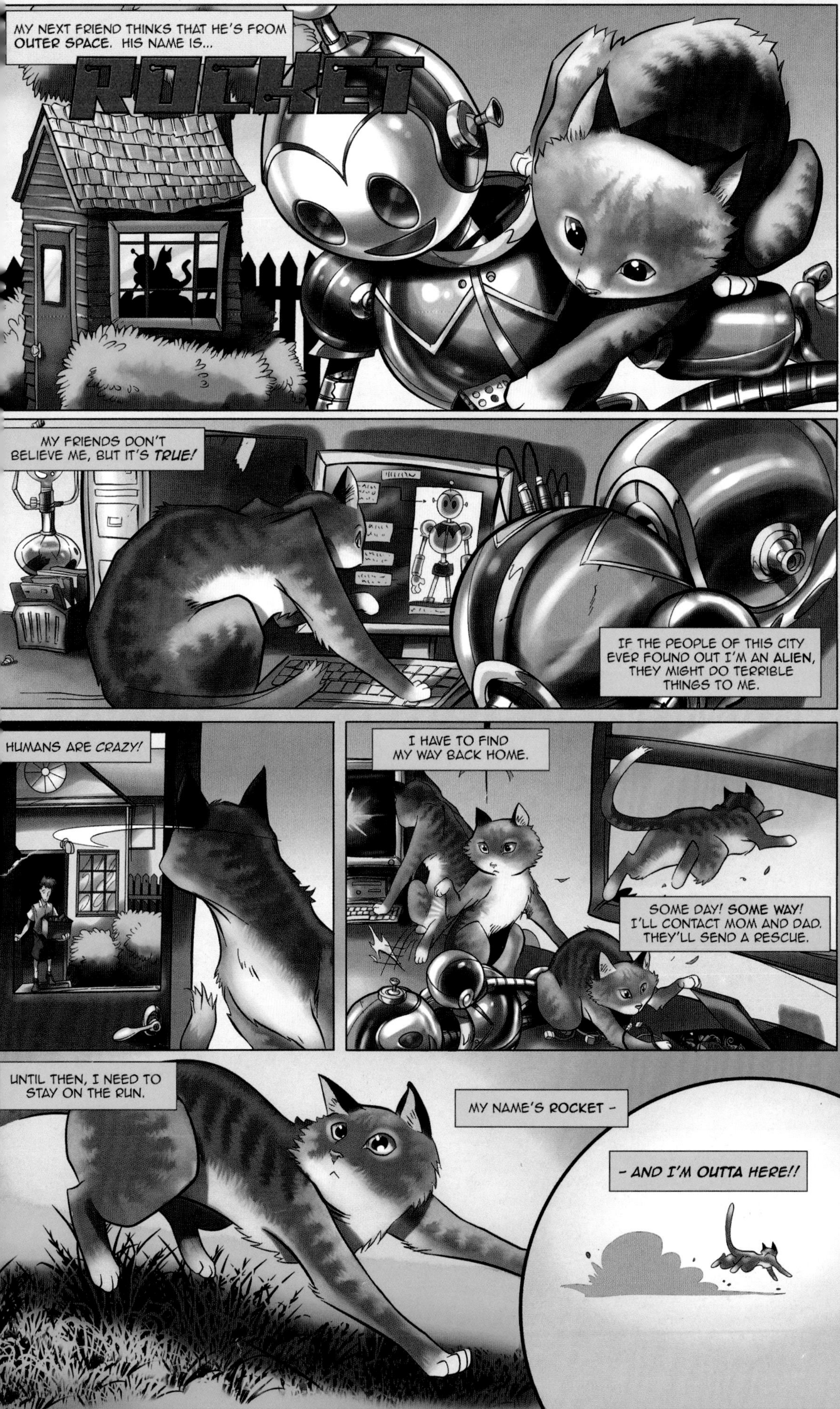
MY NEXT FRIEND THINKS THAT HE'S FROM OUTER SPACE. HIS NAME IS...
ROCKET
MY FRIENDS DON'T BELIEVE ME, BUT IT'S TRUE!
IF THE PEOPLE OF THIS CITY EVER FOUND OUT I'M AN ALIEN, THEY MIGHT DO TERRIBLE THINGS TO ME.
HUMANS ARE CRAZY!
I HAVE TO FIND MY WAY BACK HOME.
SOME DAY! SOME WAY! I'LL CONTACT MOM AND DAD. THEY'LL SEND A RESCUE.
UNTIL THEN, I NEED TO STAY ON THE RUN.
MY NAME'S ROCKET -
- AND I'M OUTTA HERE!!

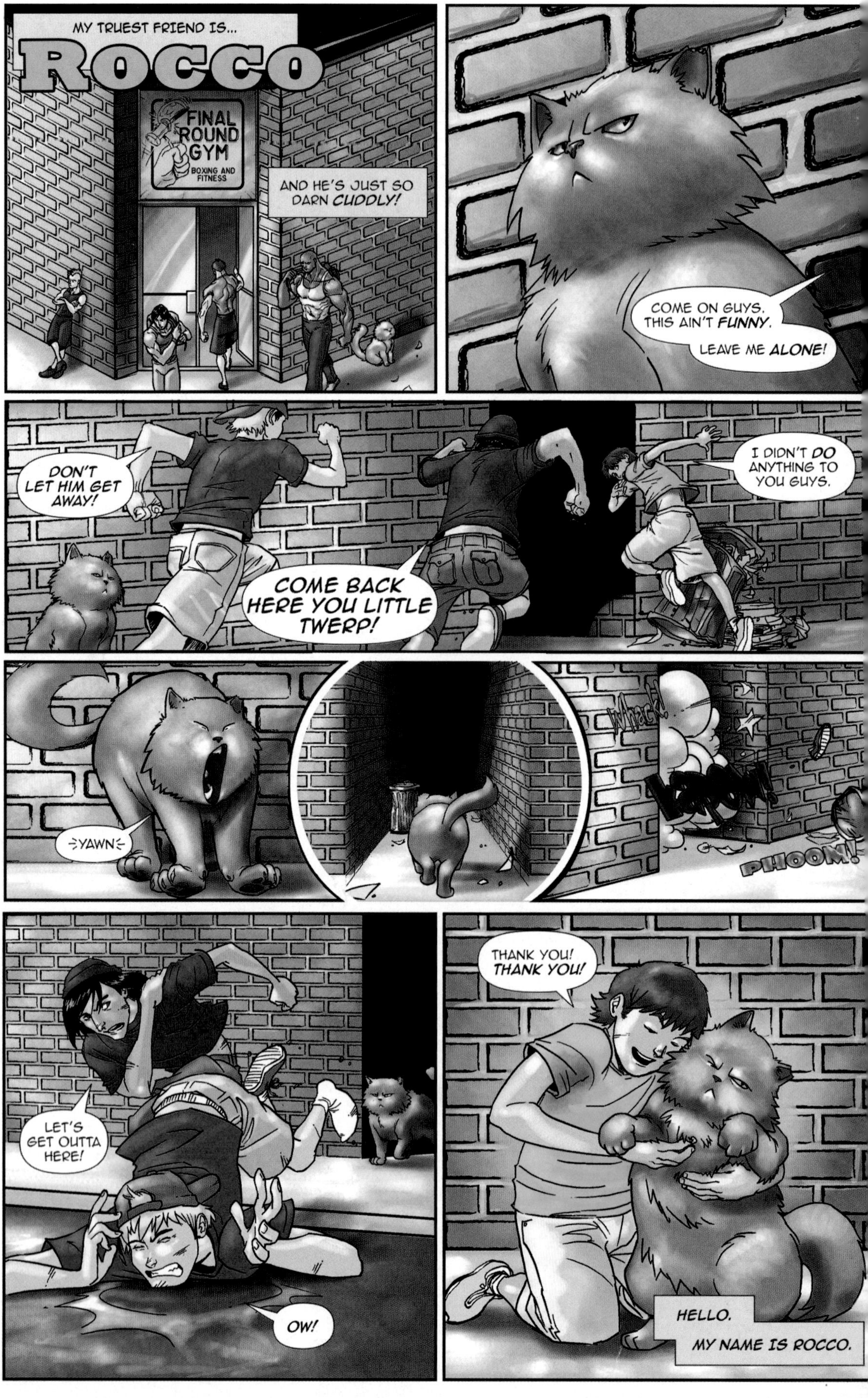
MY TRUEST FRIEND IS...
ROCCO
FINAL ROUND GYM
BOXING AND FITNESS
AND HE'S JUST SO DARN *CUDDLY!*
COME ON GUYS. THIS AIN'T *FUNNY*.
LEAVE ME *ALONE!*
DON'T LET HIM GET AWAY!
COME BACK HERE YOU LITTLE TWERP!
I DIDN'T *DO* ANYTHING TO YOU GUYS.
YAWN
Whack!
PHOOM!
LET'S GET OUTTA HERE!
OW!
THANK YOU! *THANK YOU!*
HELLO.
MY NAME IS ROCCO.

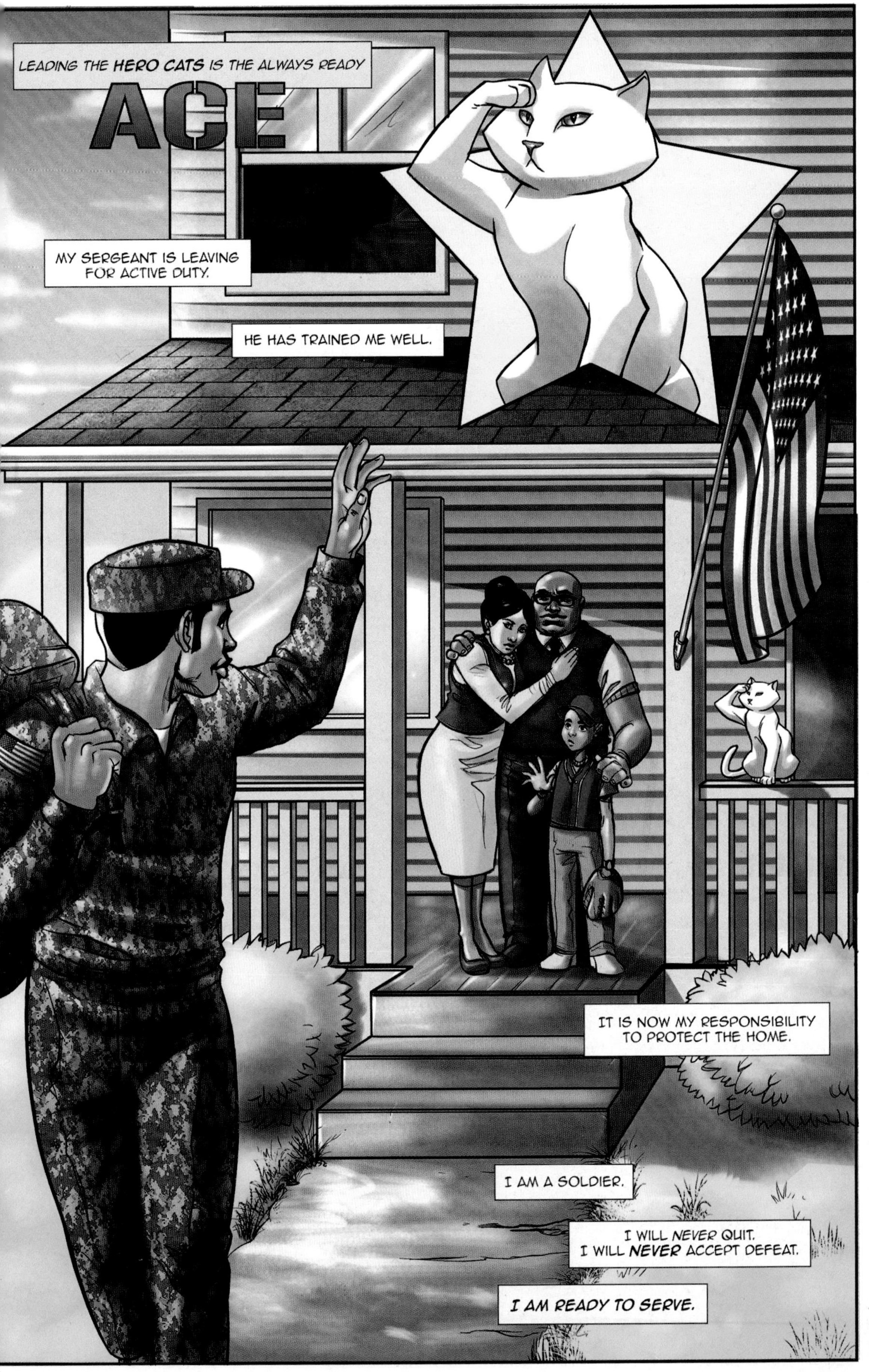
LEADING THE HERO CATS IS THE ALWAYS READY
ACE
MY SERGEANT IS LEAVING FOR ACTIVE DUTY.
HE HAS TRAINED ME WELL.
IT IS NOW MY RESPONSIBILITY TO PROTECT THE HOME.
I AM A SOLDIER.
I WILL NEVER QUIT. I WILL NEVER ACCEPT DEFEAT.
I AM READY TO SERVE.

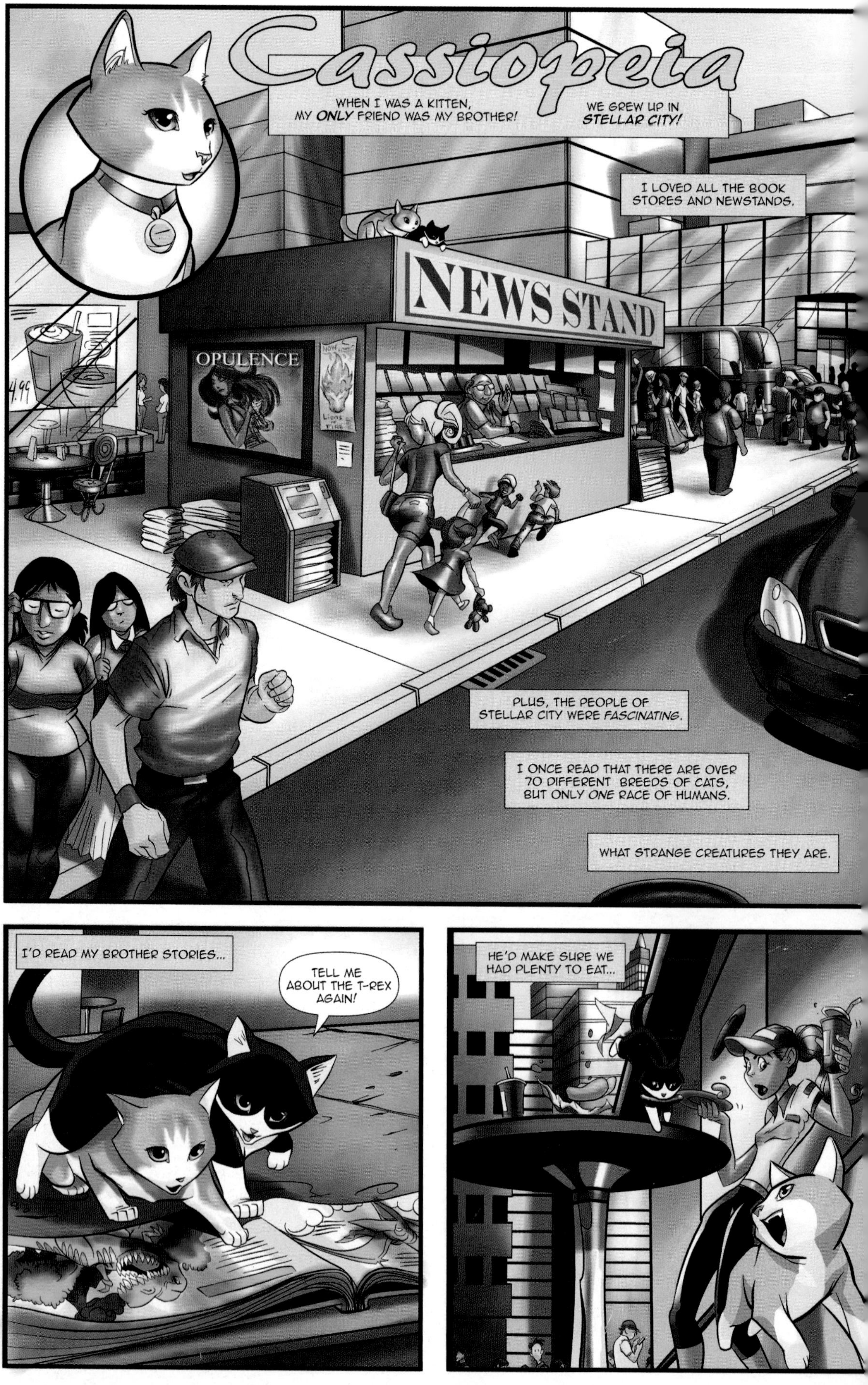

Cassiopeia
WHEN I WAS A KITTEN, MY ONLY FRIEND WAS MY BROTHER!
WE GREW UP IN STELLAR CITY!
I LOVED ALL THE BOOK STORES AND NEWSTANDS.
NEWS STAND
OPULENCE
PLUS, THE PEOPLE OF STELLAR CITY WERE FASCINATING.
I ONCE READ THAT THERE ARE OVER 70 DIFFERENT BREEDS OF CATS, BUT ONLY ONE RACE OF HUMANS.
WHAT STRANGE CREATURES THEY ARE.
I'D READ MY BROTHER STORIES...
TELL ME ABOUT THE T-REX AGAIN!
HE'D MAKE SURE WE HAD PLENTY TO EAT...

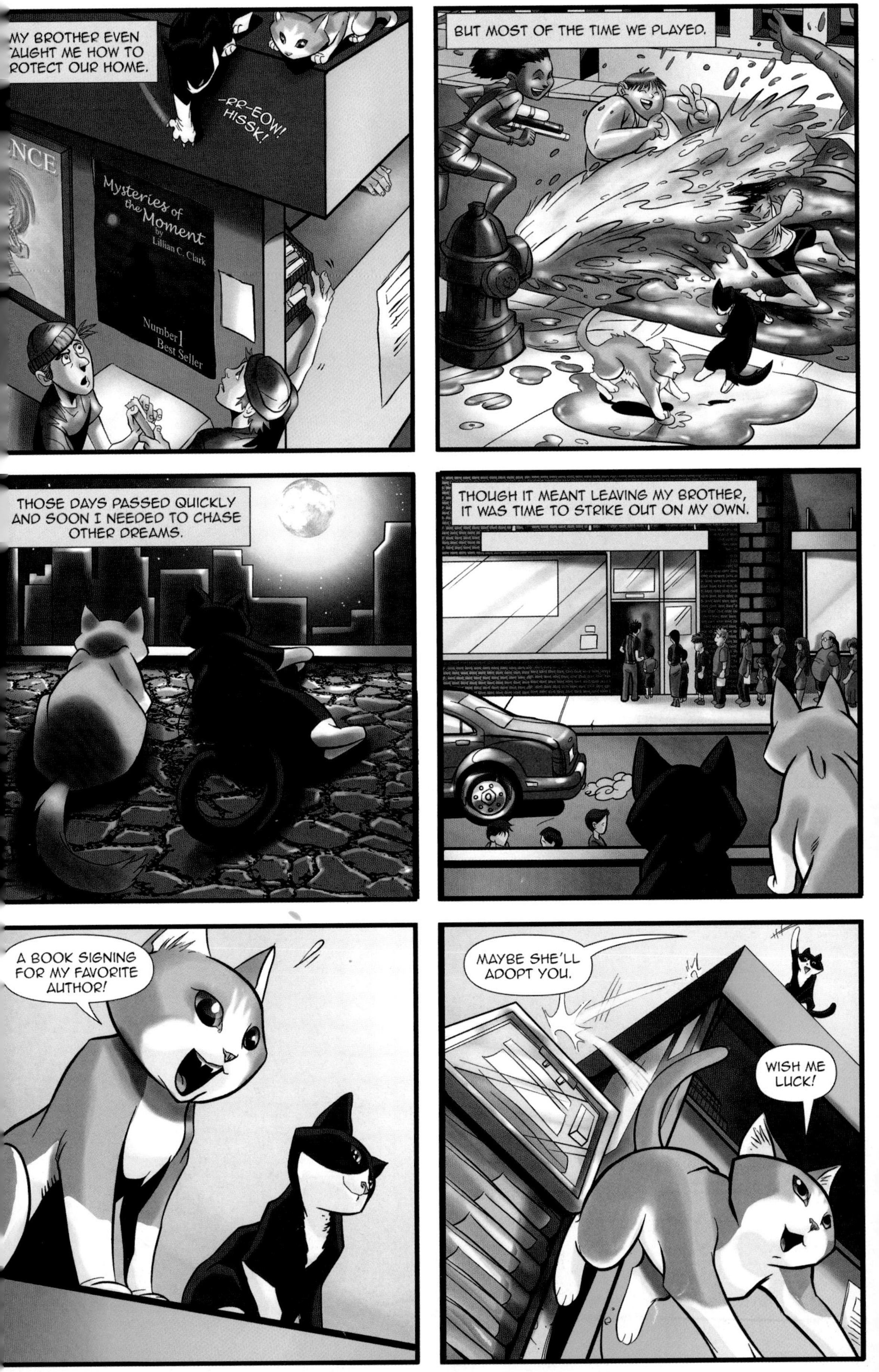
MY BROTHER EVEN TAUGHT ME HOW TO PROTECT OUR HOME.
-RR-EOW! HISSK!
Mysteries of the Moment by Lillian C. Clark
Number 1 Best Seller
BUT MOST OF THE TIME WE PLAYED.
THOSE DAYS PASSED QUICKLY AND SOON I NEEDED TO CHASE OTHER DREAMS.
THOUGH IT MEANT LEAVING MY BROTHER, IT WAS TIME TO STRIKE OUT ON MY OWN.
A BOOK SIGNING FOR MY FAVORITE AUTHOR!
MAYBE SHE'LL ADOPT YOU.
WISH ME LUCK!

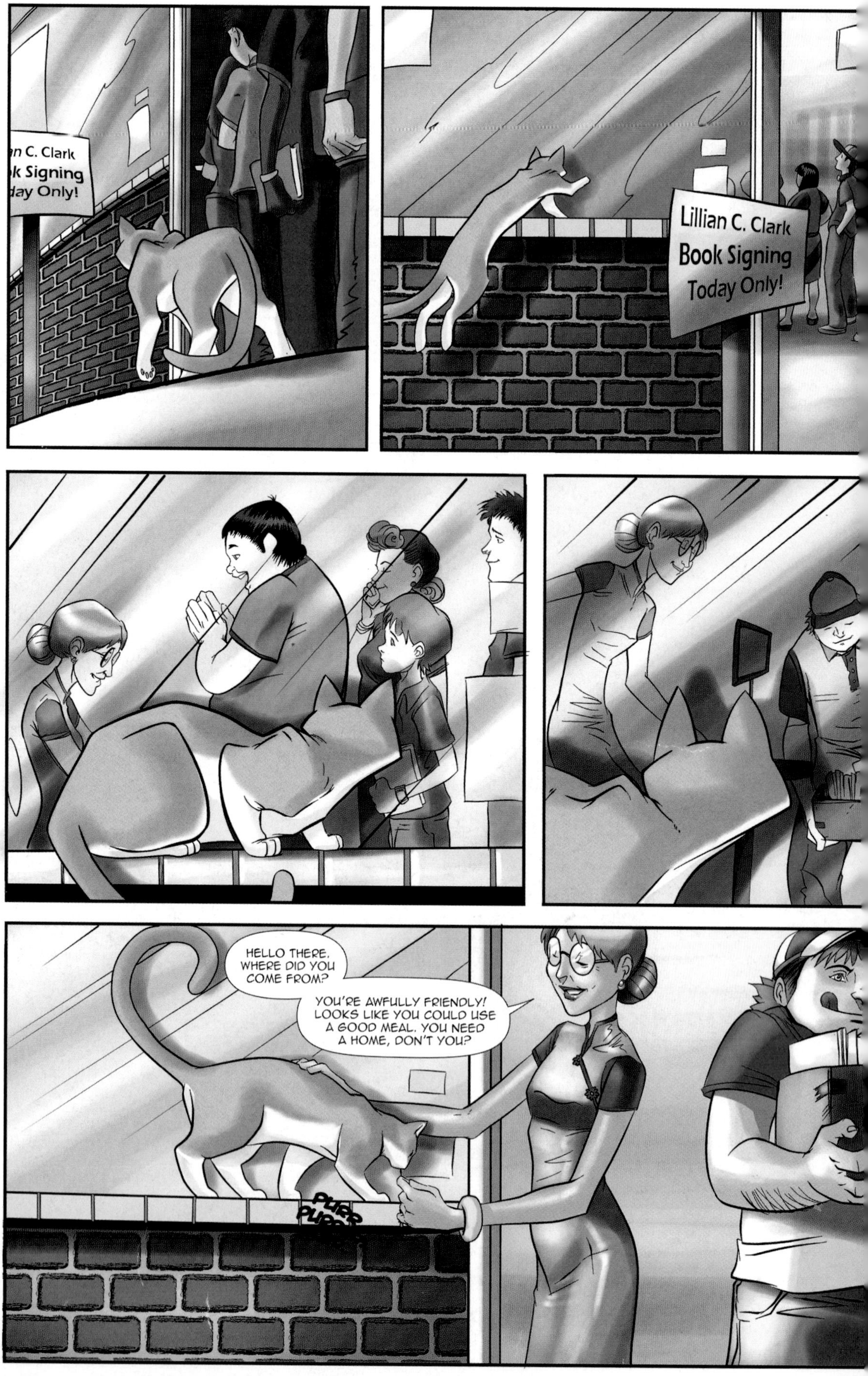
Lillian C. Clark
Book Signing
Today Only!
HELLO THERE, WHERE DID YOU COME FROM?
YOU'RE AWFULLY FRIENDLY! LOOKS LIKE YOU COULD USE A GOOD MEAL. YOU NEED A HOME, DON'T YOU?
PURR

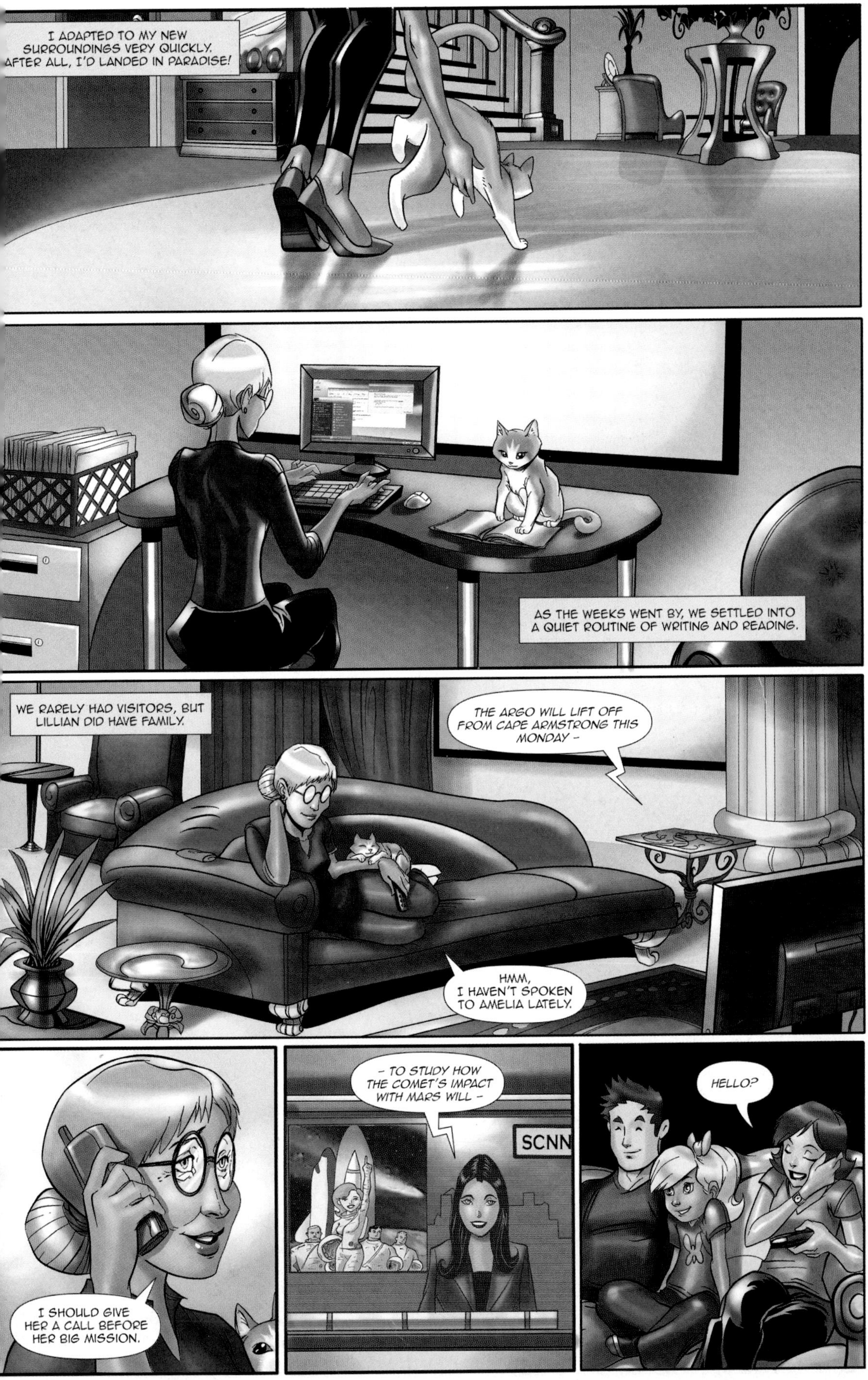
I ADAPTED TO MY NEW SURROUNDINGS VERY QUICKLY. AFTER ALL, I'D LANDED IN PARADISE!
AS THE WEEKS WENT BY, WE SETTLED INTO A QUIET ROUTINE OF WRITING AND READING.
WE RARELY HAD VISITORS, BUT LILLIAN DID HAVE FAMILY.
THE ARGO WILL LIFT OFF FROM CAPE ARMSTRONG THIS MONDAY –
HMM, I HAVEN'T SPOKEN TO AMELIA LATELY.
I SHOULD GIVE HER A CALL BEFORE HER BIG MISSION.
– TO STUDY HOW THE COMET'S IMPACT WITH MARS WILL –
SCNN
HELLO?

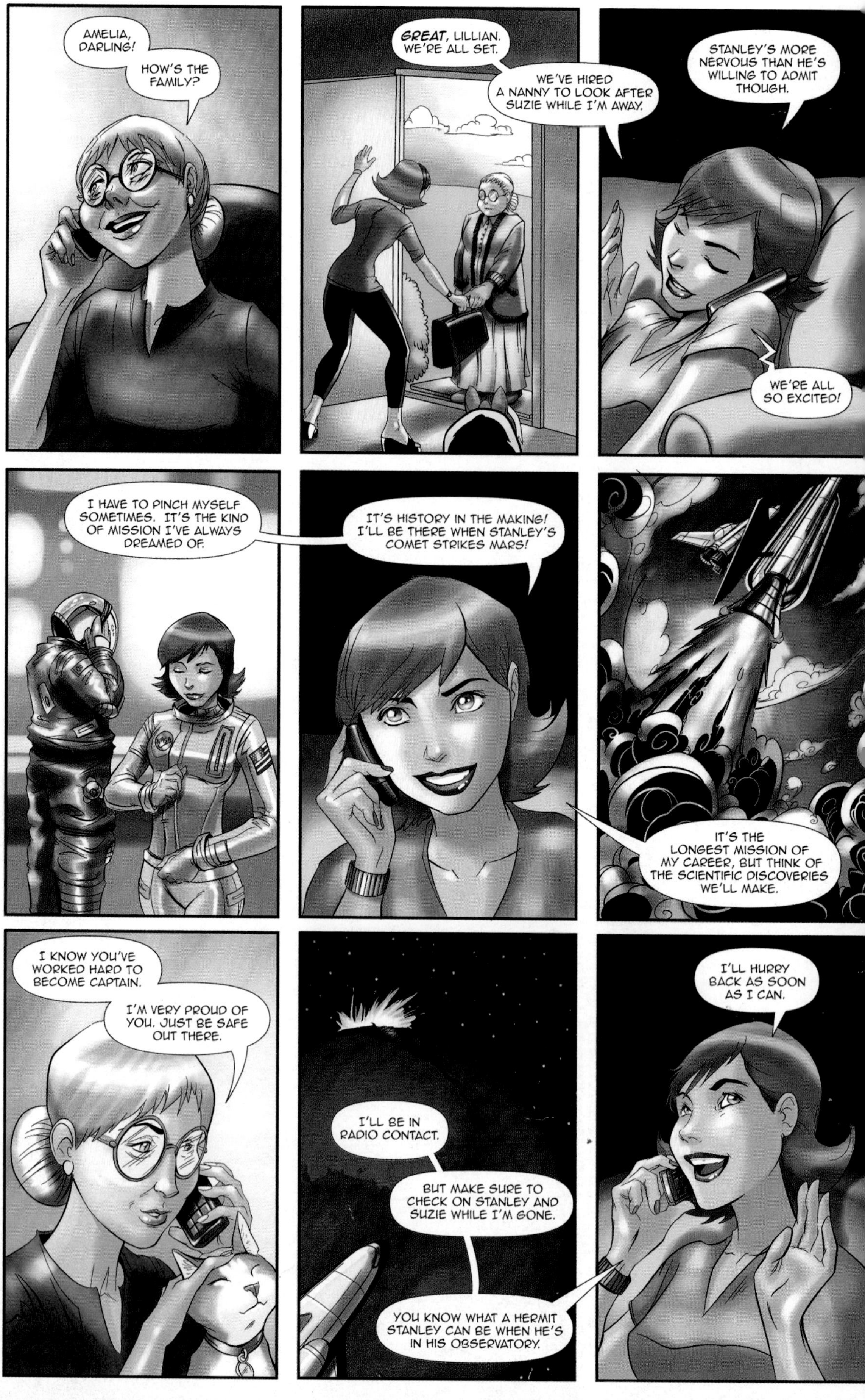
AMELIA, DARLING!
HOW'S THE FAMILY?
GREAT, LILLIAN. WE'RE ALL SET.
WE'VE HIRED A NANNY TO LOOK AFTER SUZIE WHILE I'M AWAY.
STANLEY'S MORE NERVOUS THAN HE'S WILLING TO ADMIT THOUGH.
WE'RE ALL SO EXCITED!
I HAVE TO PINCH MYSELF SOMETIMES. IT'S THE KIND OF MISSION I'VE ALWAYS DREAMED OF.
IT'S HISTORY IN THE MAKING! I'LL BE THERE WHEN STANLEY'S COMET STRIKES MARS!
IT'S THE LONGEST MISSION OF MY CAREER, BUT THINK OF THE SCIENTIFIC DISCOVERIES WE'LL MAKE.
I KNOW YOU'VE WORKED HARD TO BECOME CAPTAIN.
I'M VERY PROUD OF YOU. JUST BE SAFE OUT THERE.
I'LL BE IN RADIO CONTACT.
BUT MAKE SURE TO CHECK ON STANLEY AND SUZIE WHILE I'M GONE.
YOU KNOW WHAT A HERMIT STANLEY CAN BE WHEN HE'S IN HIS OBSERVATORY.
I'LL HURRY BACK AS SOON AS I CAN.

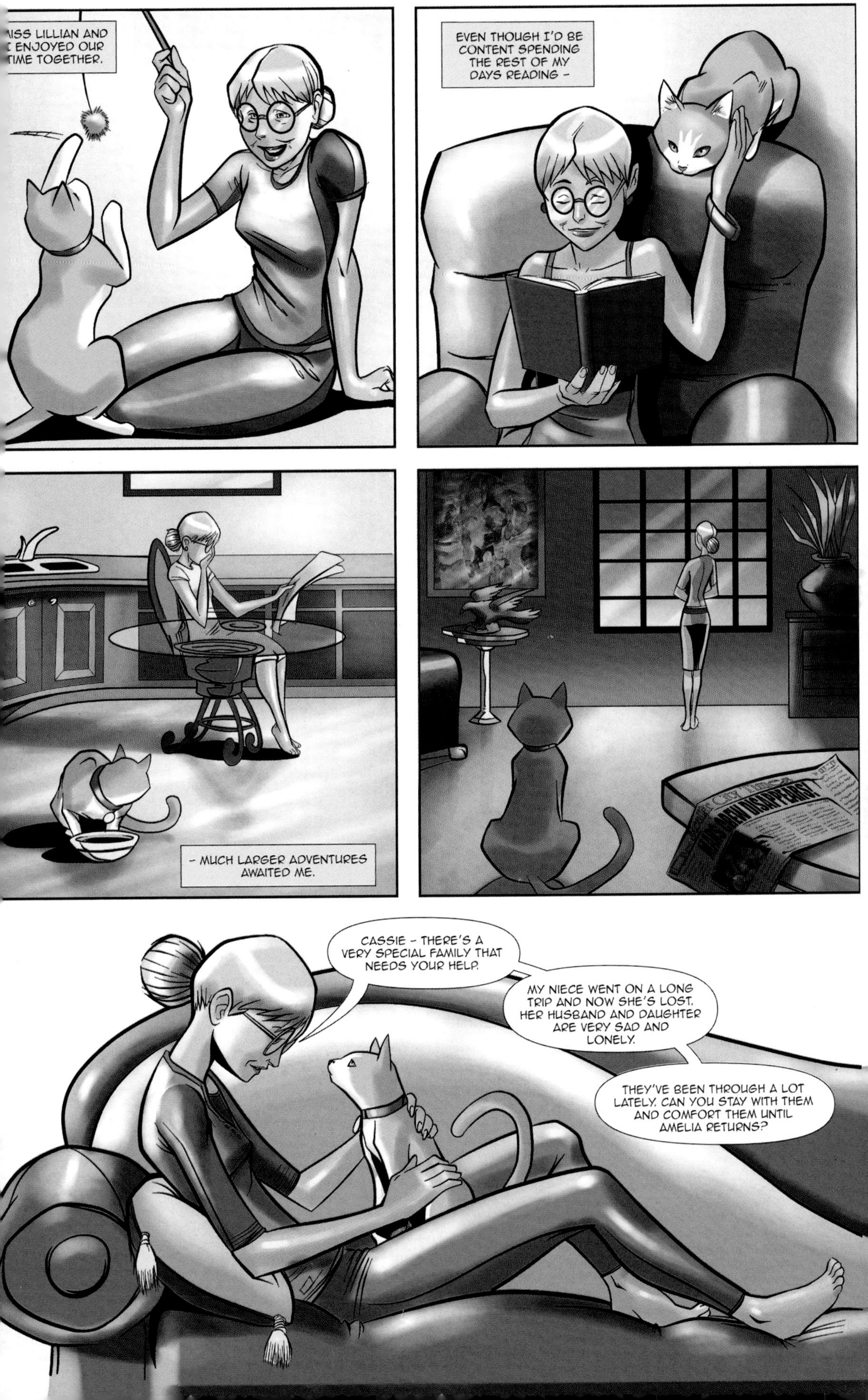
MISS LILLIAN AND I ENJOYED OUR TIME TOGETHER.
EVEN THOUGH I'D BE CONTENT SPENDING THE REST OF MY DAYS READING –
– MUCH LARGER ADVENTURES AWAITED ME.
CASSIE – THERE'S A VERY SPECIAL FAMILY THAT NEEDS YOUR HELP.
MY NIECE WENT ON A LONG TRIP AND NOW SHE'S LOST. HER HUSBAND AND DAUGHTER ARE VERY SAD AND LONELY.
THEY'VE BEEN THROUGH A LOT LATELY. CAN YOU STAY WITH THEM AND COMFORT THEM UNTIL AMELIA RETURNS?

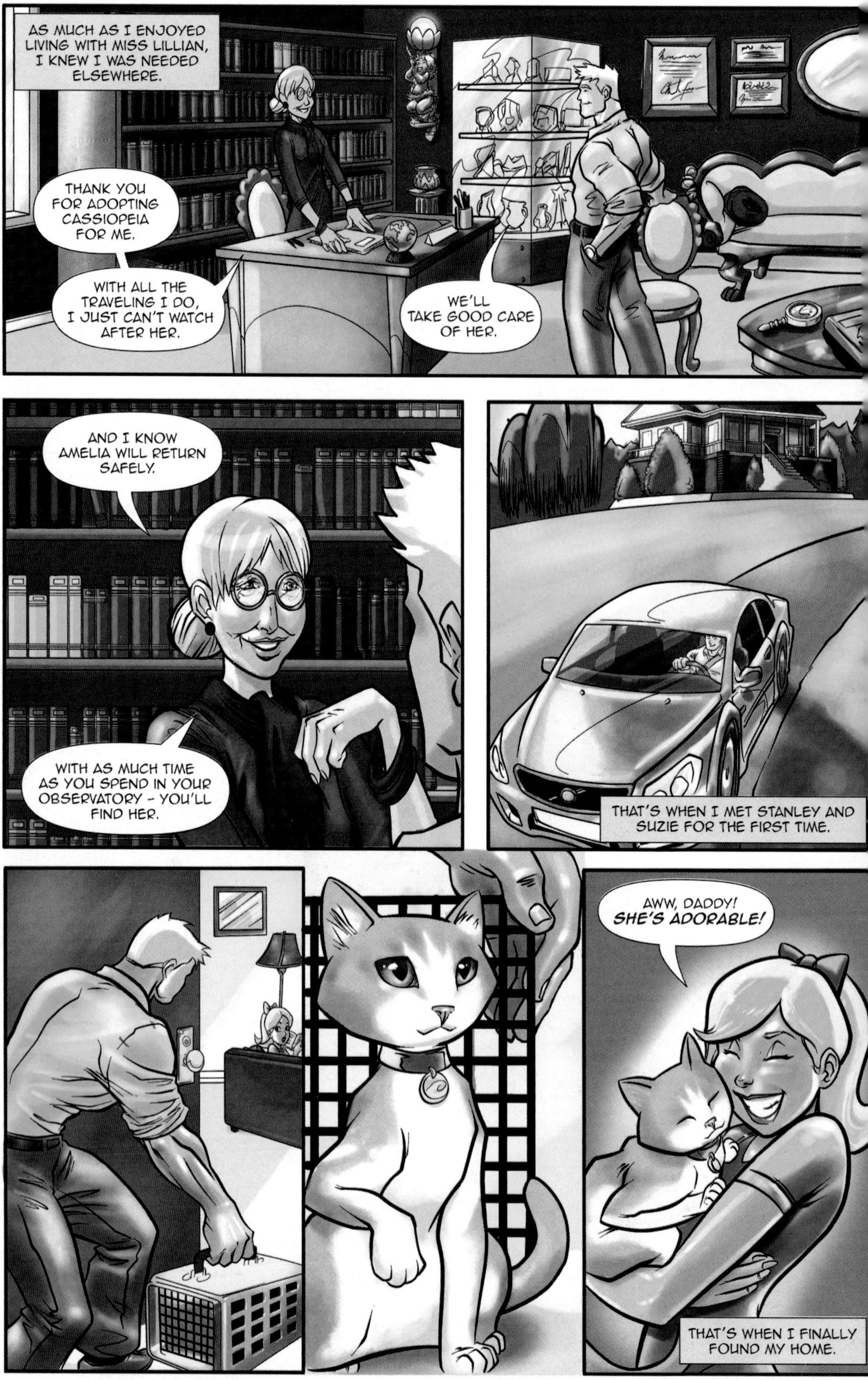
AS MUCH AS I ENJOYED LIVING WITH MISS LILLIAN, I KNEW I WAS NEEDED ELSEWHERE.
THANK YOU FOR ADOPTING CASSIOPEIA FOR ME.
WITH ALL THE TRAVELING I DO, I JUST CAN'T WATCH AFTER HER.
WE'LL TAKE GOOD CARE OF HER.
AND I KNOW AMELIA WILL RETURN SAFELY.
WITH AS MUCH TIME AS YOU SPEND IN YOUR OBSERVATORY - YOU'LL FIND HER.
THAT'S WHEN I MET STANLEY AND SUZIE FOR THE FIRST TIME.
AWW, DADDY! **SHE'S ADORABLE!**
THAT'S WHEN I FINALLY FOUND MY HOME.

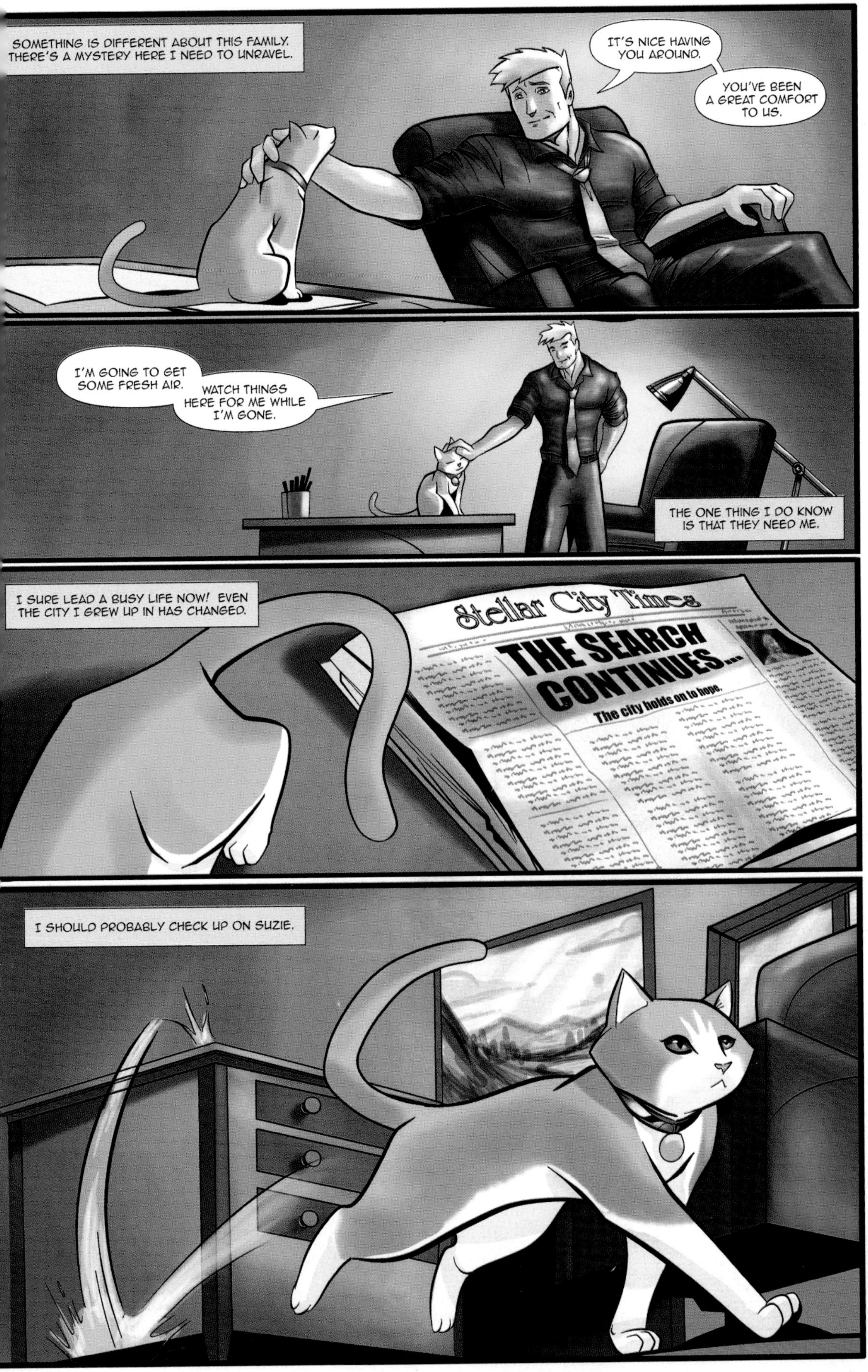
SOMETHING IS DIFFERENT ABOUT THIS FAMILY. THERE'S A MYSTERY HERE I NEED TO UNRAVEL.
IT'S NICE HAVING YOU AROUND.
YOU'VE BEEN A GREAT COMFORT TO US.
I'M GOING TO GET SOME FRESH AIR.
WATCH THINGS HERE FOR ME WHILE I'M GONE.
THE ONE THING I DO KNOW IS THAT THEY NEED ME.
I SURE LEAD A BUSY LIFE NOW! EVEN THE CITY I GREW UP IN HAS CHANGED.
Stellar City Times
THE SEARCH CONTINUES...
The city holds on to hope.
I SHOULD PROBABLY CHECK UP ON SUZIE.

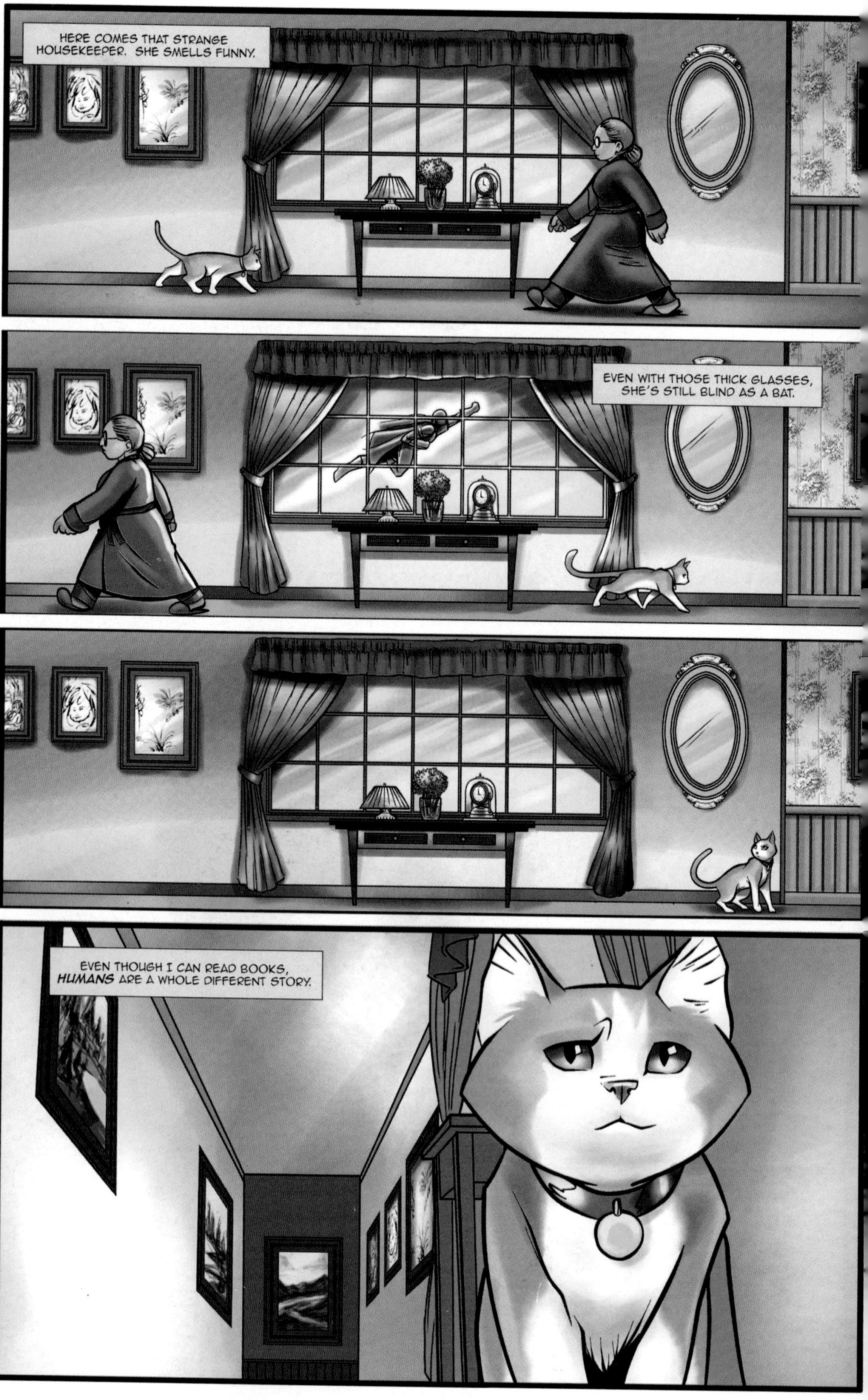
HERE COMES THAT STRANGE HOUSEKEEPER. SHE SMELLS FUNNY.
EVEN WITH THOSE THICK GLASSES, SHE'S STILL BLIND AS A BAT.
EVEN THOUGH I CAN READ BOOKS, *HUMANS* ARE A WHOLE DIFFERENT STORY.

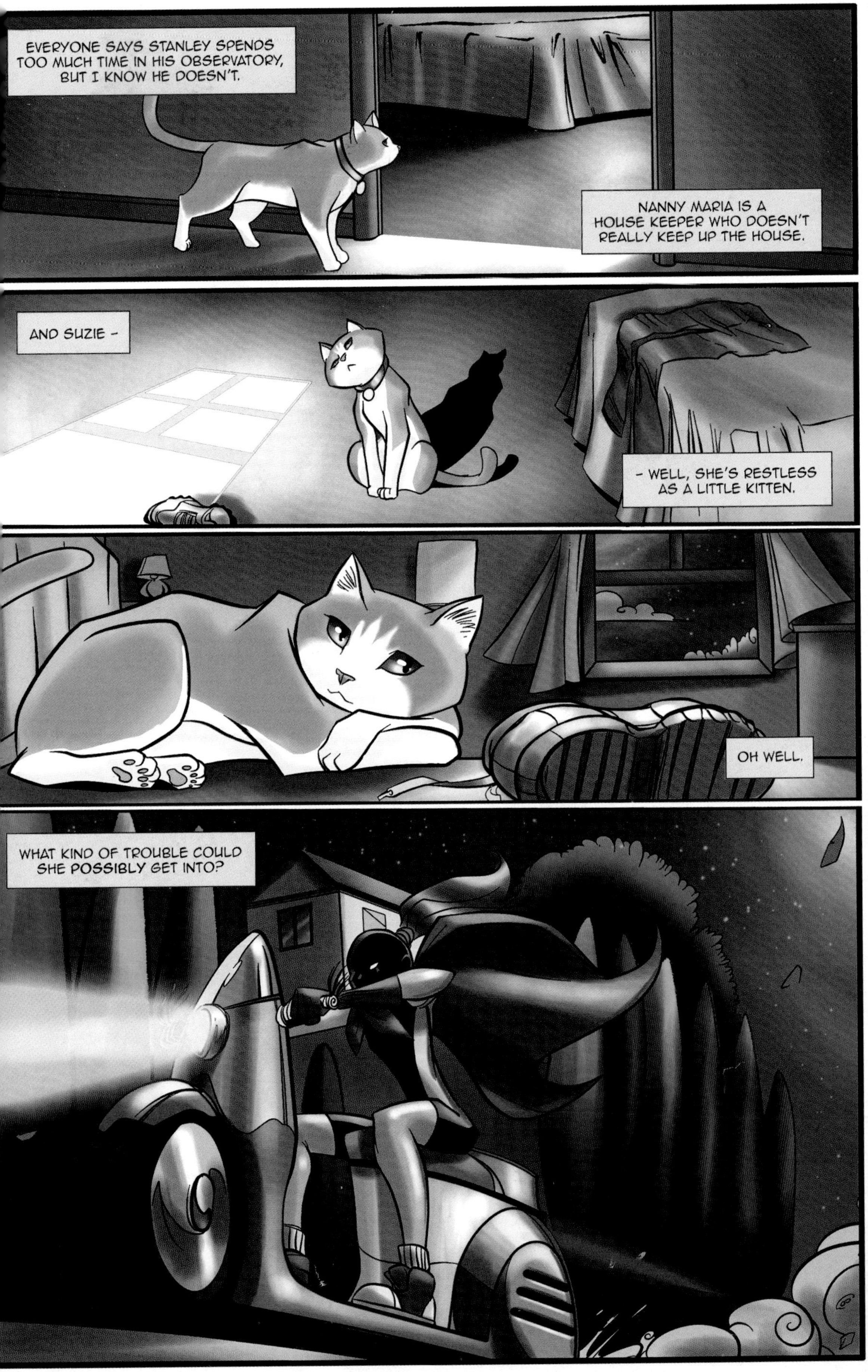
EVERYONE SAYS STANLEY SPENDS TOO MUCH TIME IN HIS OBSERVATORY, BUT I KNOW HE DOESN'T.
NANNY MARIA IS A HOUSE KEEPER WHO DOESN'T REALLY KEEP UP THE HOUSE.
AND SUZIE -
- WELL, SHE'S RESTLESS AS A LITTLE KITTEN.
OH WELL.
WHAT KIND OF TROUBLE COULD SHE POSSIBLY GET INTO?

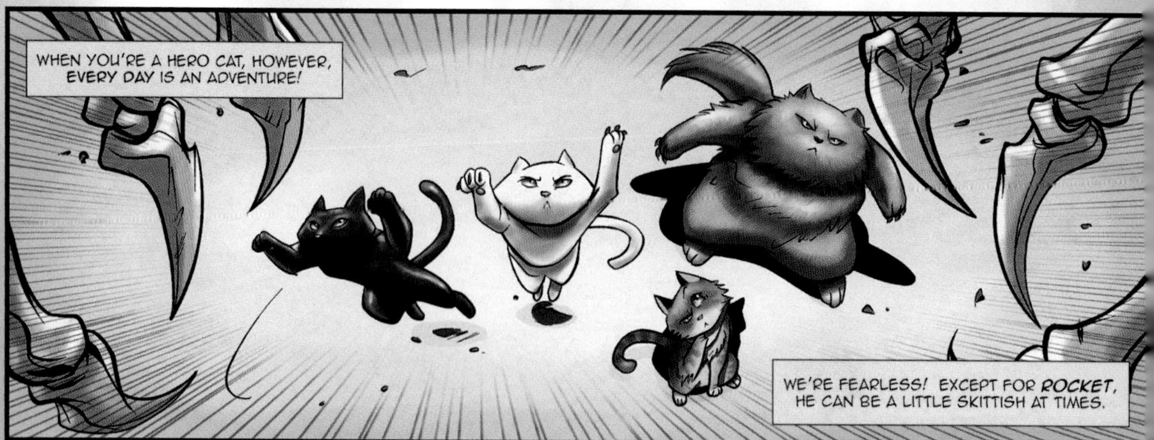
WHEN YOU'RE A HERO CAT, HOWEVER, EVERY DAY IS AN ADVENTURE!
WE'RE FEARLESS! EXCEPT FOR ROCKET, HE CAN BE A LITTLE SKITTISH AT TIMES.

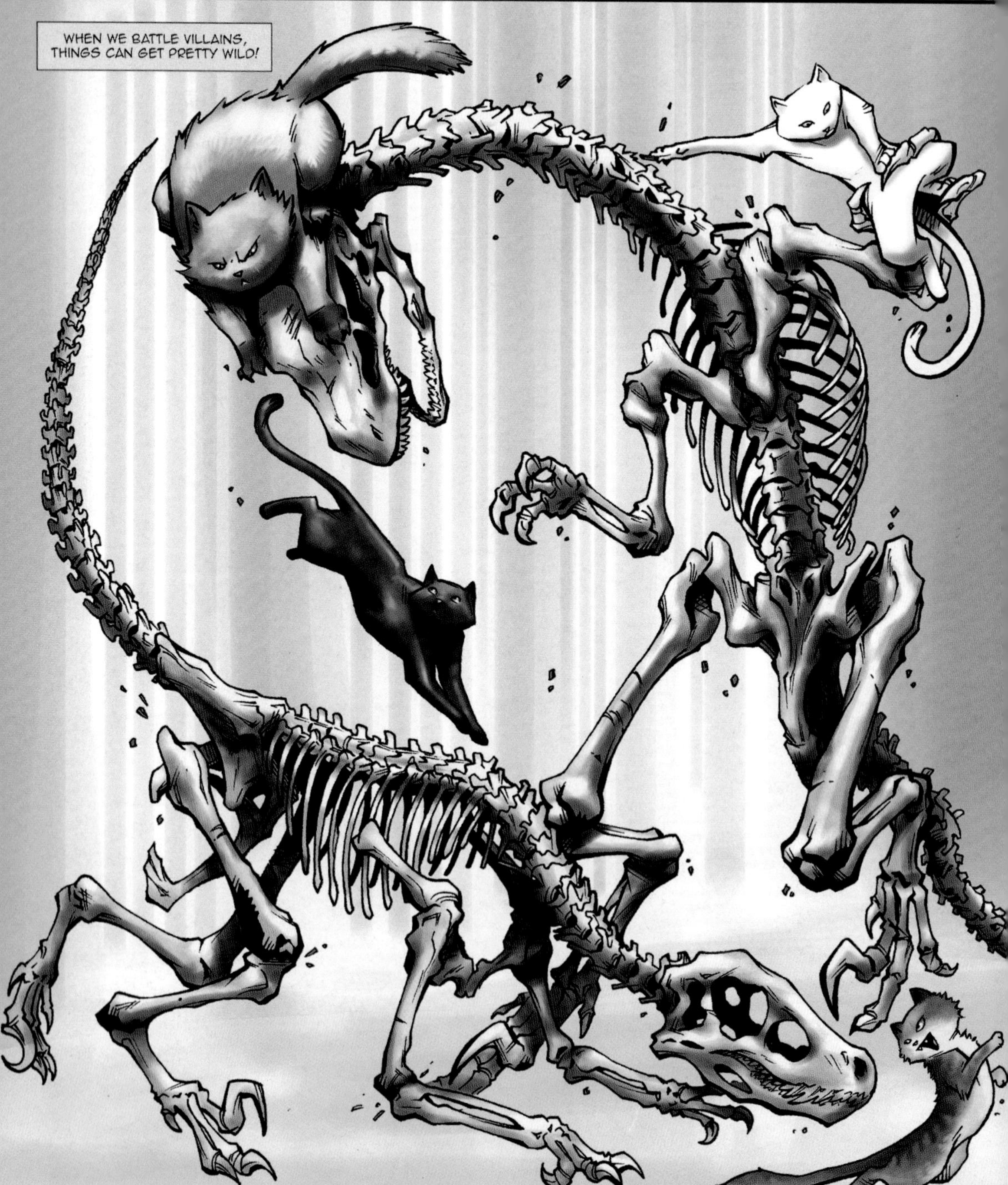
WHEN WE BATTLE VILLAINS, THINGS CAN GET PRETTY WILD!

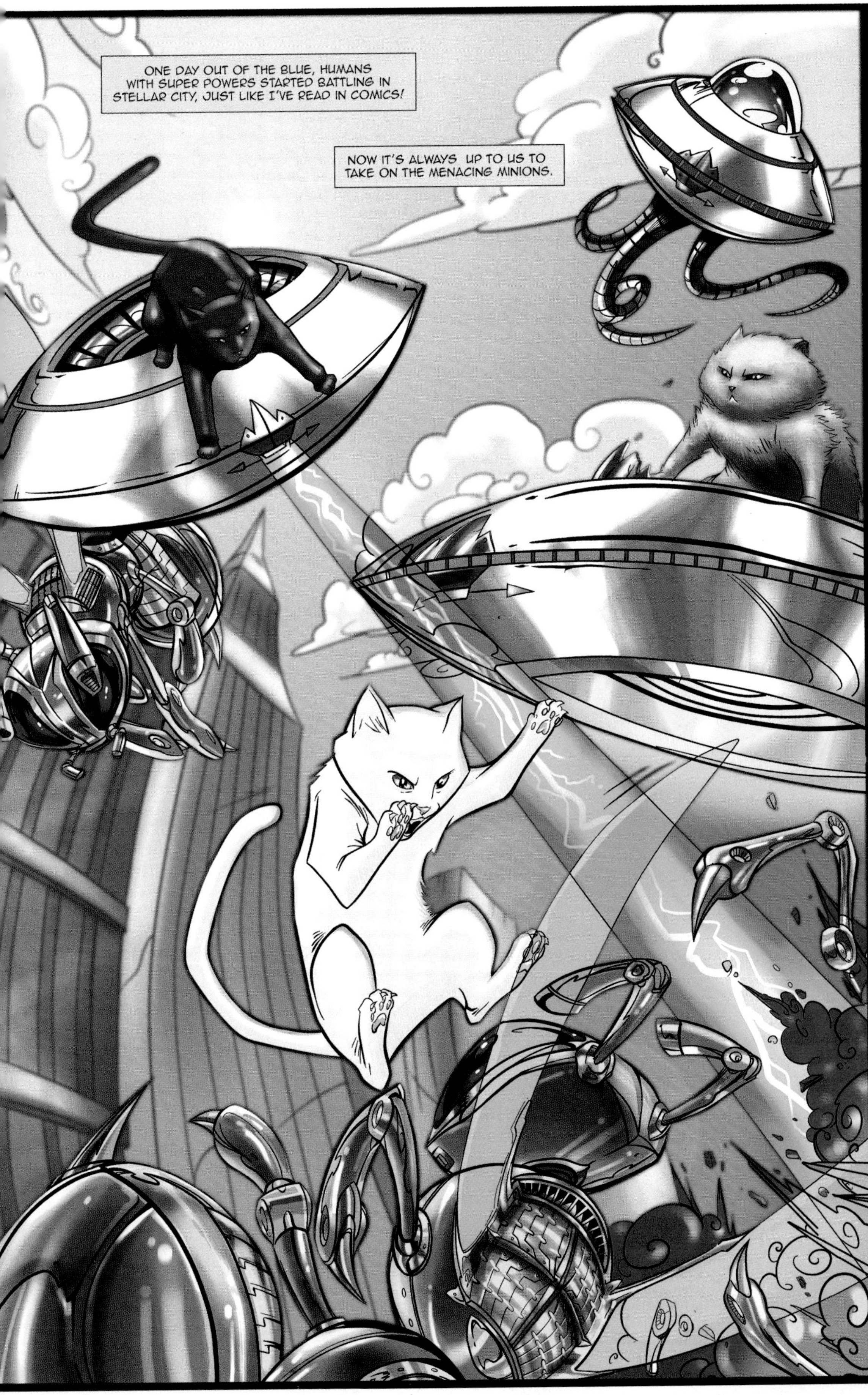
ONE DAY OUT OF THE BLUE, HUMANS WITH SUPER POWERS STARTED BATTLING IN STELLAR CITY, JUST LIKE I'VE READ IN COMICS!
NOW IT'S ALWAYS UP TO US TO TAKE ON THE MENACING MINIONS.

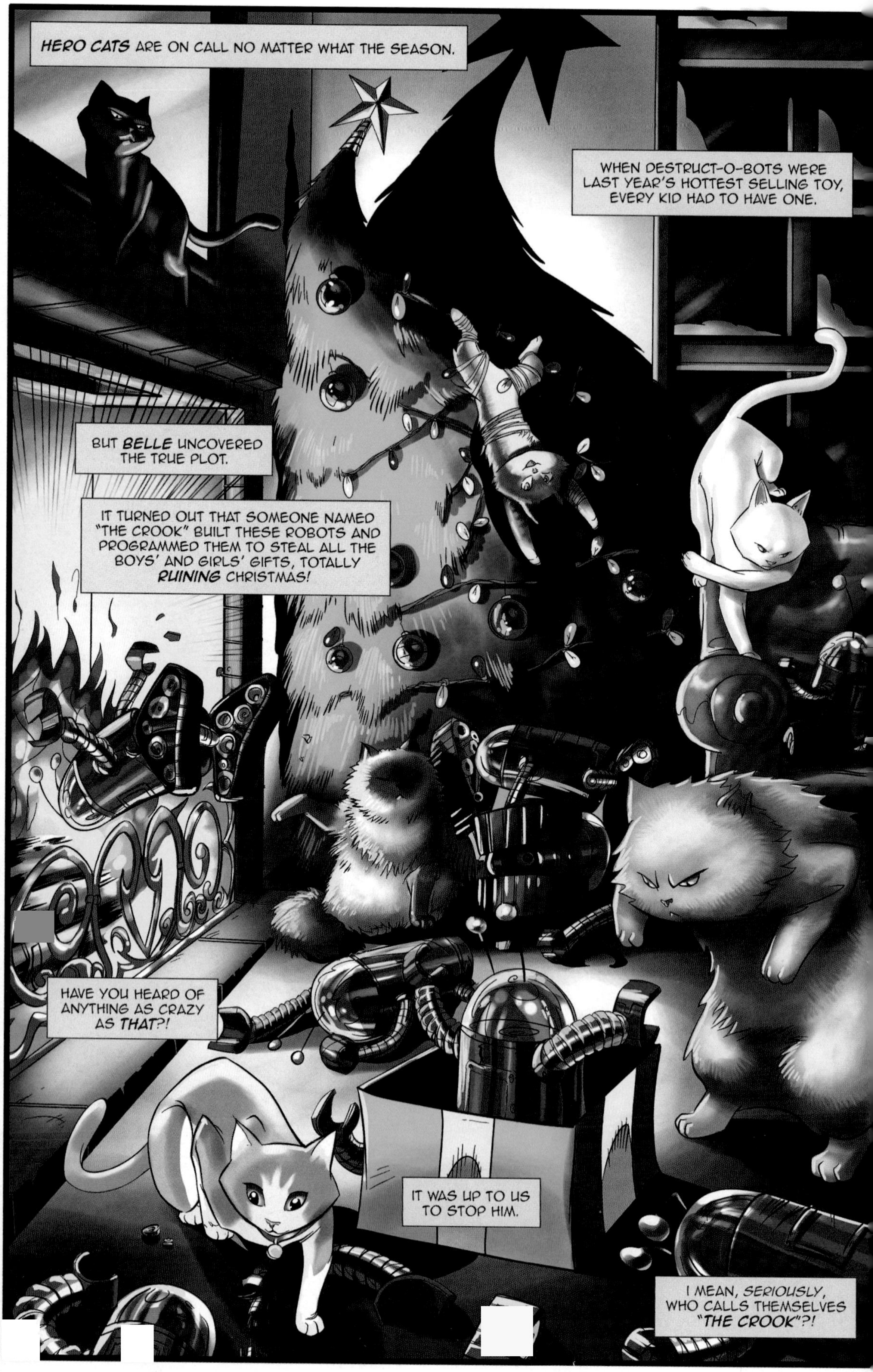
HERO CATS ARE ON CALL NO MATTER WHAT THE SEASON.
WHEN DESTRUCT-O-BOTS WERE LAST YEAR'S HOTTEST SELLING TOY, EVERY KID HAD TO HAVE ONE.
BUT BELLE UNCOVERED THE TRUE PLOT.
IT TURNED OUT THAT SOMEONE NAMED "THE CROOK" BUILT THESE ROBOTS AND PROGRAMMED THEM TO STEAL ALL THE BOYS' AND GIRLS' GIFTS, TOTALLY RUINING CHRISTMAS!
HAVE YOU HEARD OF ANYTHING AS CRAZY AS THAT?!
IT WAS UP TO US TO STOP HIM.
I MEAN, SERIOUSLY, WHO CALLS THEMSELVES "THE CROOK"?!

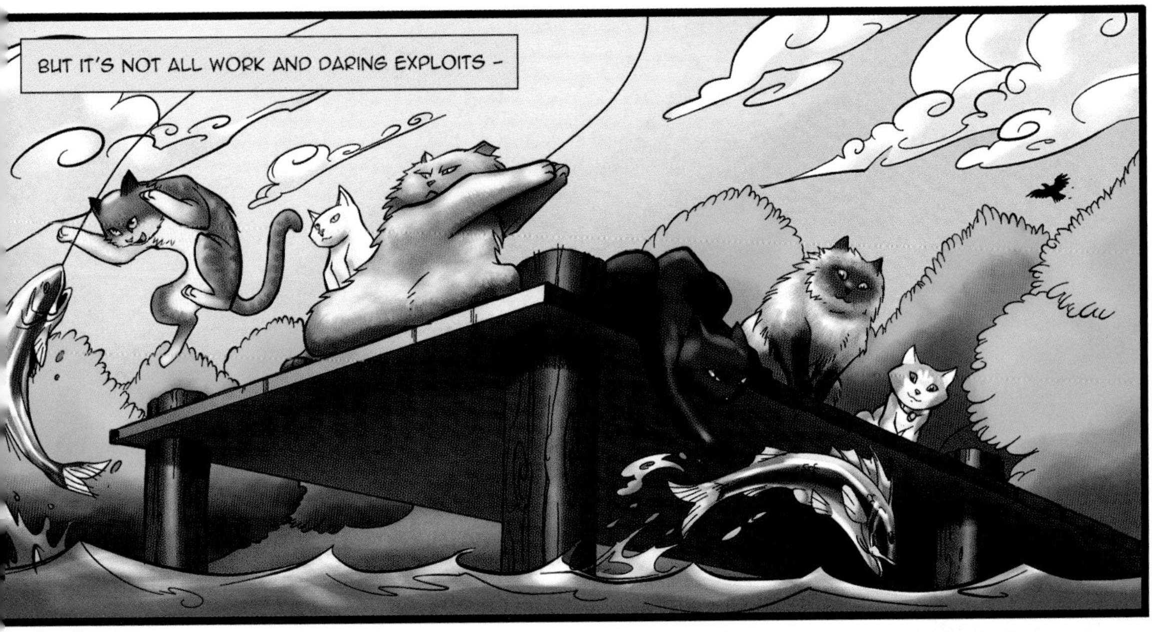
BUT IT'S NOT ALL WORK AND DARING EXPLOITS –

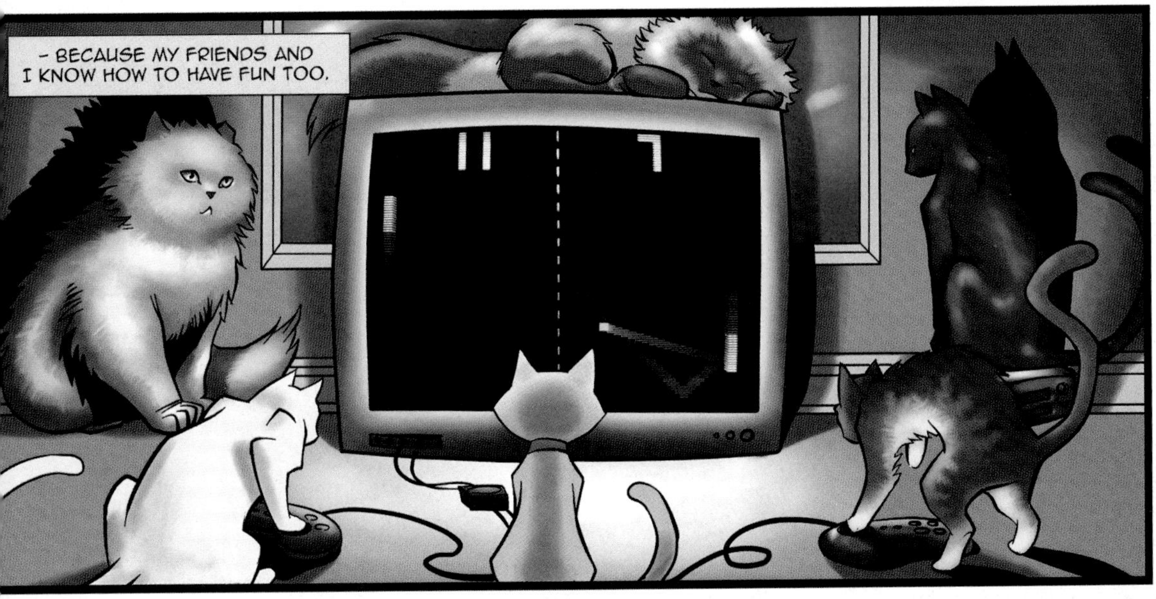
– BECAUSE MY FRIENDS AND I KNOW HOW TO HAVE FUN TOO.

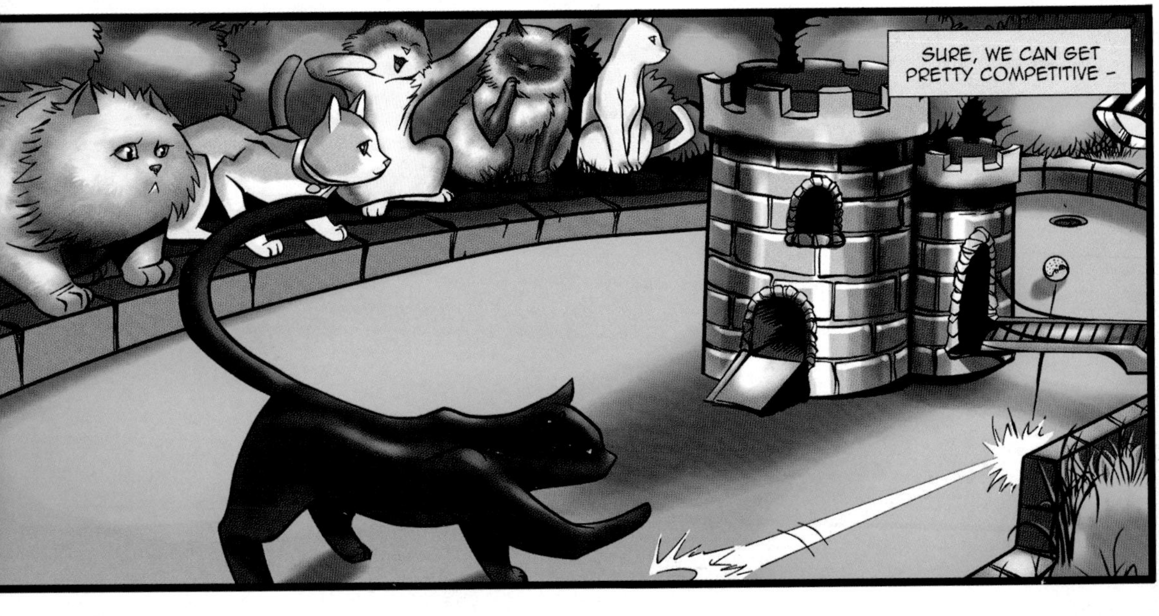
SURE, WE CAN GET PRETTY COMPETITIVE –

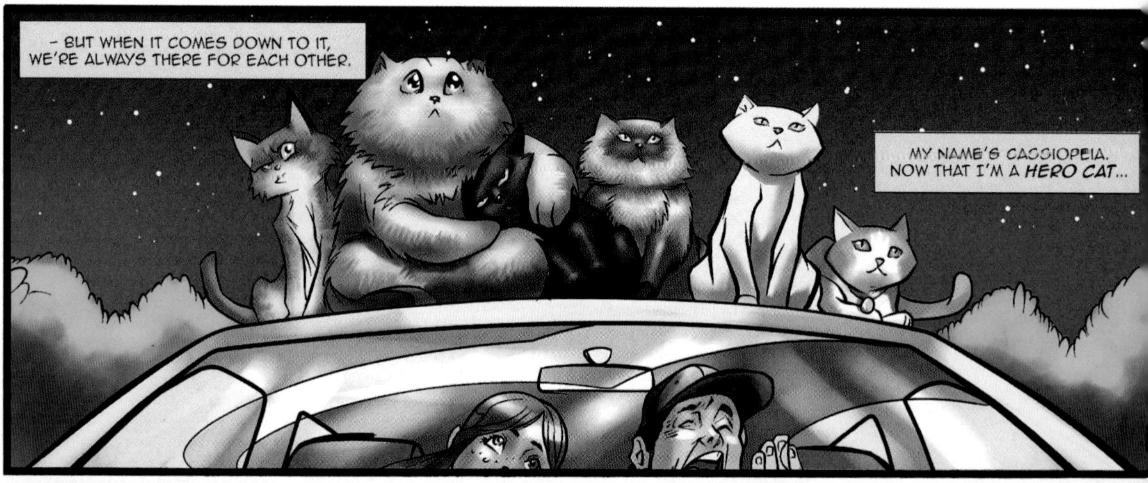

- BUT WHEN IT COMES DOWN TO IT, WE'RE ALWAYS THERE FOR EACH OTHER.
MY NAME'S CASSIOPEIA. NOW THAT I'M A HERO CAT...

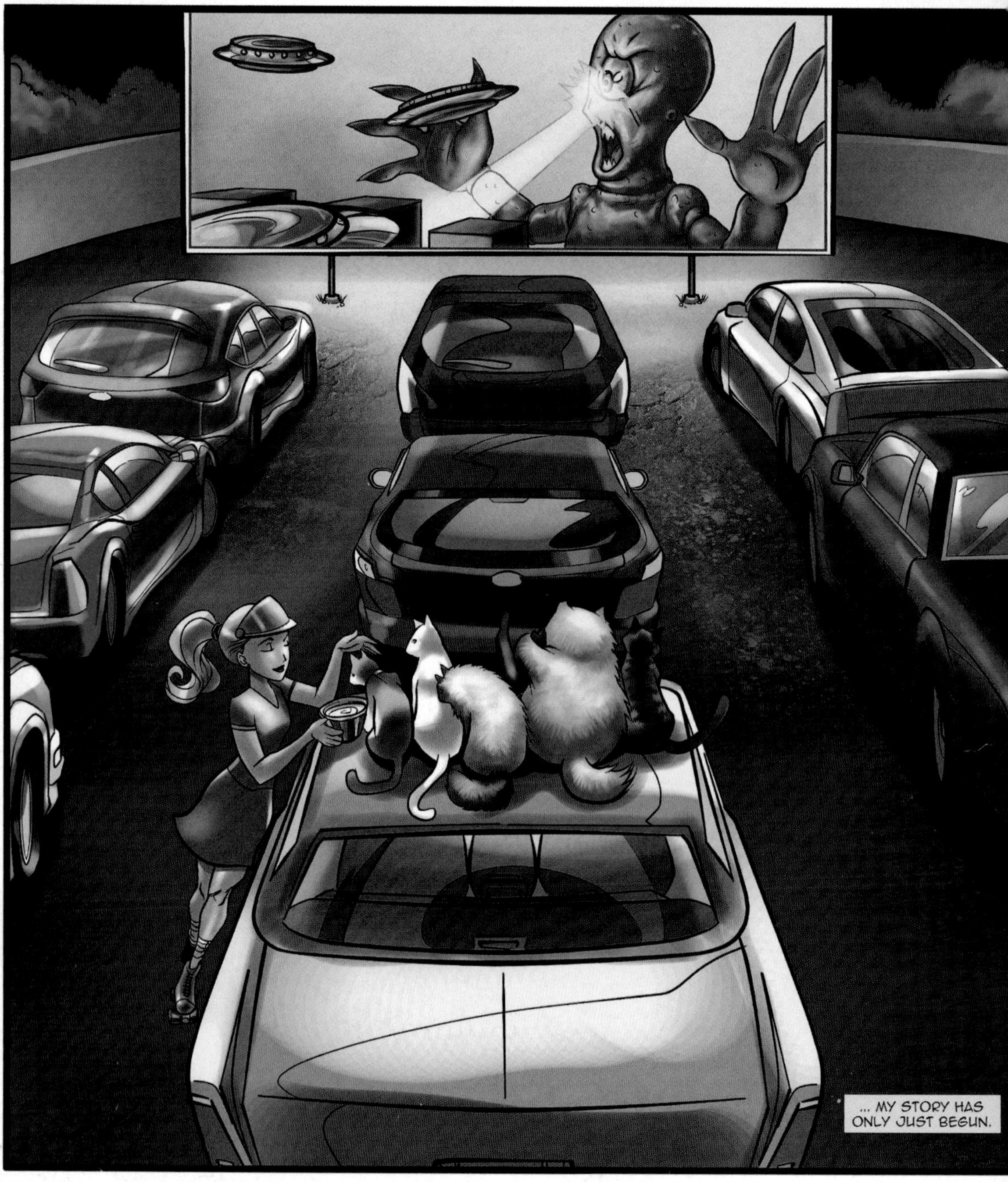

... MY STORY HAS ONLY JUST BEGUN.

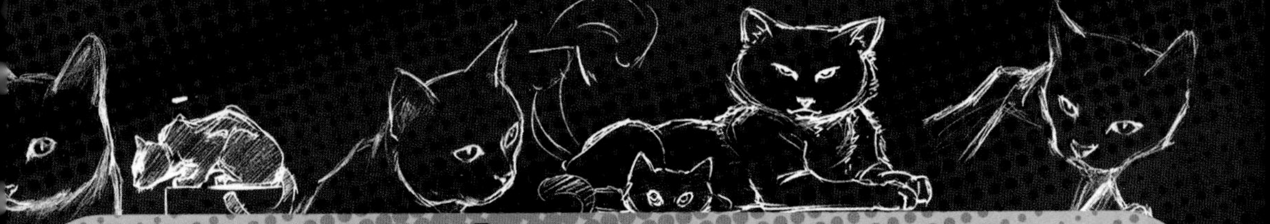

HEROCHAT

I see you've found the first of our many stories. Very good. I'm glad you've learned more about my little sister and her teammates. Their exploits have become somewhat legendary among the cat community. Feel free to share these stories with other humans and any cats who may share your home.

You might be wondering what I've been up to since I was a kitten in Stellar City. Turns out I have the rather special talent of finding hard to acquire items. My skills have taken me to far off lands. But those are stories for another time.

There's still much to tell about these Hero Cats. They can be a bit adventurous, so you'll want to keep up. Your local comic shop will be able to assist you.

For now, you can contact me through my guardian's email. (kyle@galacticquest.com) I look forward to your many questions and comments.

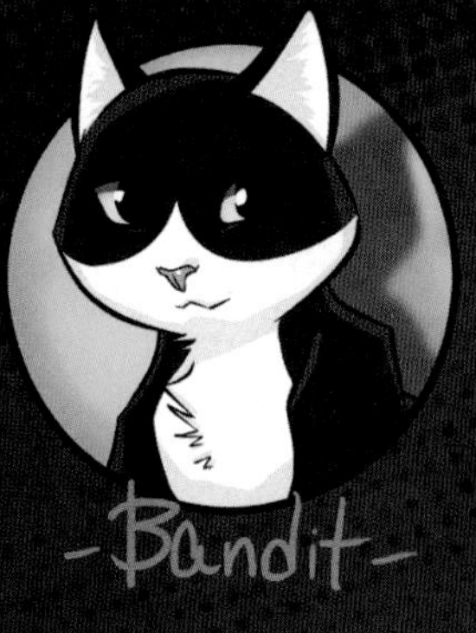
-Bandit-

NEXT UP: THE MENACE OF JOHNNY ARCADO!

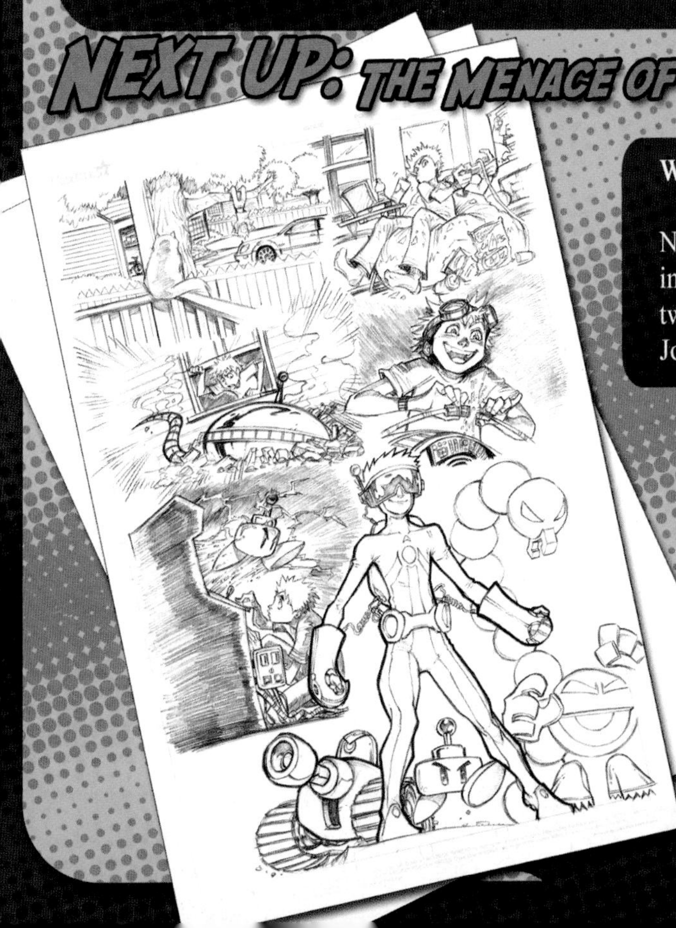

We've barely scratched the surface.

Next up: The Hero Cats are drawn into a dangerous game with the twisted trouble maker, Johnny Arcado!

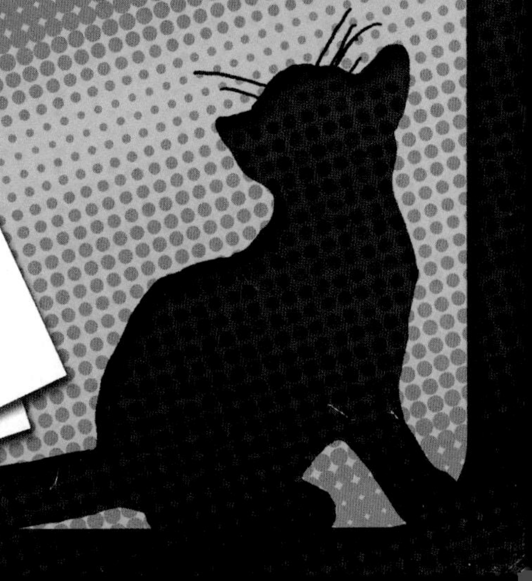

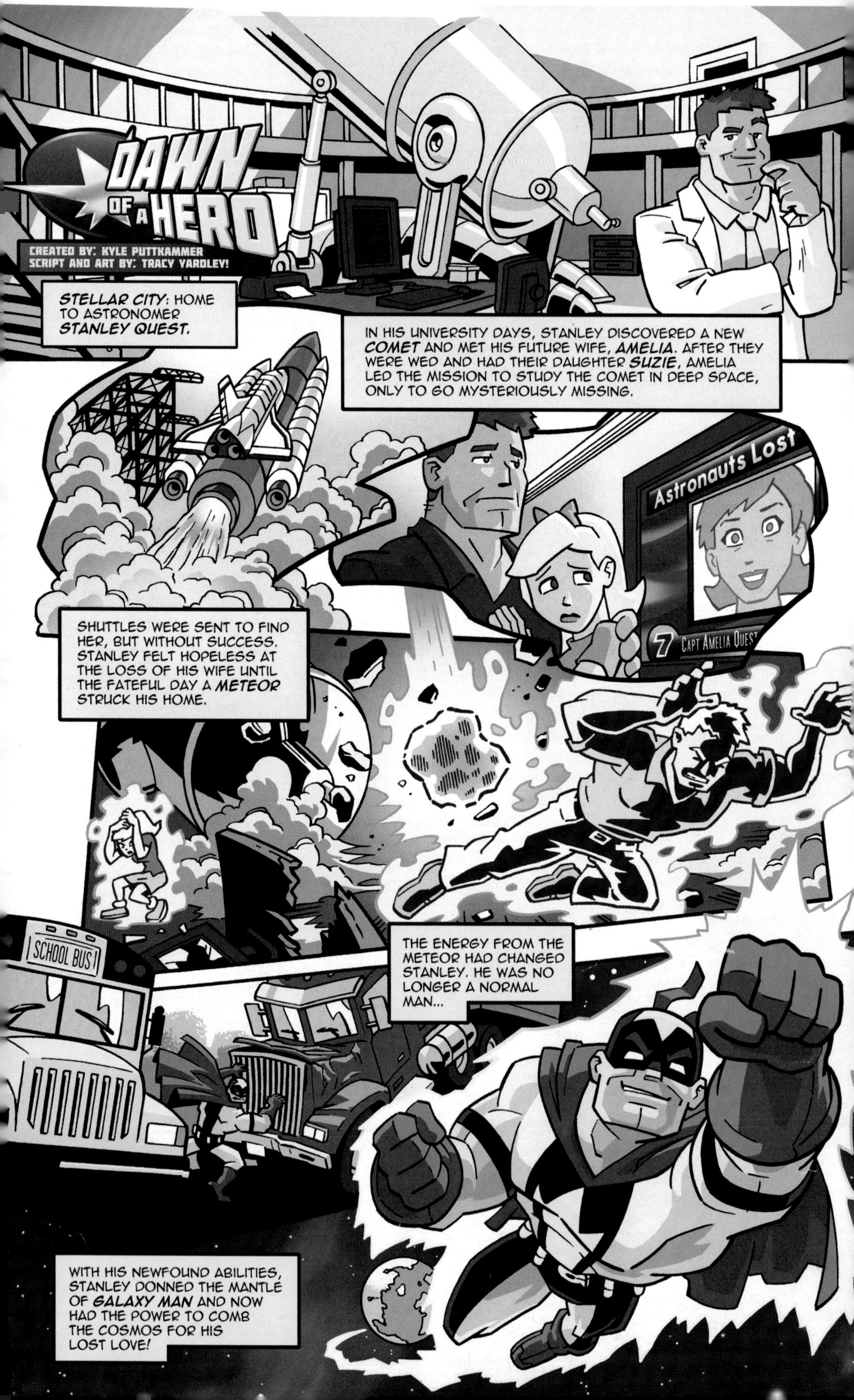
DAWN OF A HERO
CREATED BY: KYLE PUTTKAMMER
SCRIPT AND ART BY: TRACY YARDLEY!
STELLAR CITY: HOME TO ASTRONOMER STANLEY QUEST.
IN HIS UNIVERSITY DAYS, STANLEY DISCOVERED A NEW COMET AND MET HIS FUTURE WIFE, AMELIA. AFTER THEY WERE WED AND HAD THEIR DAUGHTER SUZIE, AMELIA LED THE MISSION TO STUDY THE COMET IN DEEP SPACE, ONLY TO GO MYSTERIOUSLY MISSING.
Astronauts Lost
7 CAPT AMELIA QUEST
SHUTTLES WERE SENT TO FIND HER, BUT WITHOUT SUCCESS. STANLEY FELT HOPELESS AT THE LOSS OF HIS WIFE UNTIL THE FATEFUL DAY A METEOR STRUCK HIS HOME.
SCHOOL BUS
THE ENERGY FROM THE METEOR HAD CHANGED STANLEY. HE WAS NO LONGER A NORMAL MAN...
WITH HIS NEWFOUND ABILITIES, STANLEY DONNED THE MANTLE OF GALAXY MAN AND NOW HAD THE POWER TO COMB THE COSMOS FOR HIS LOST LOVE!

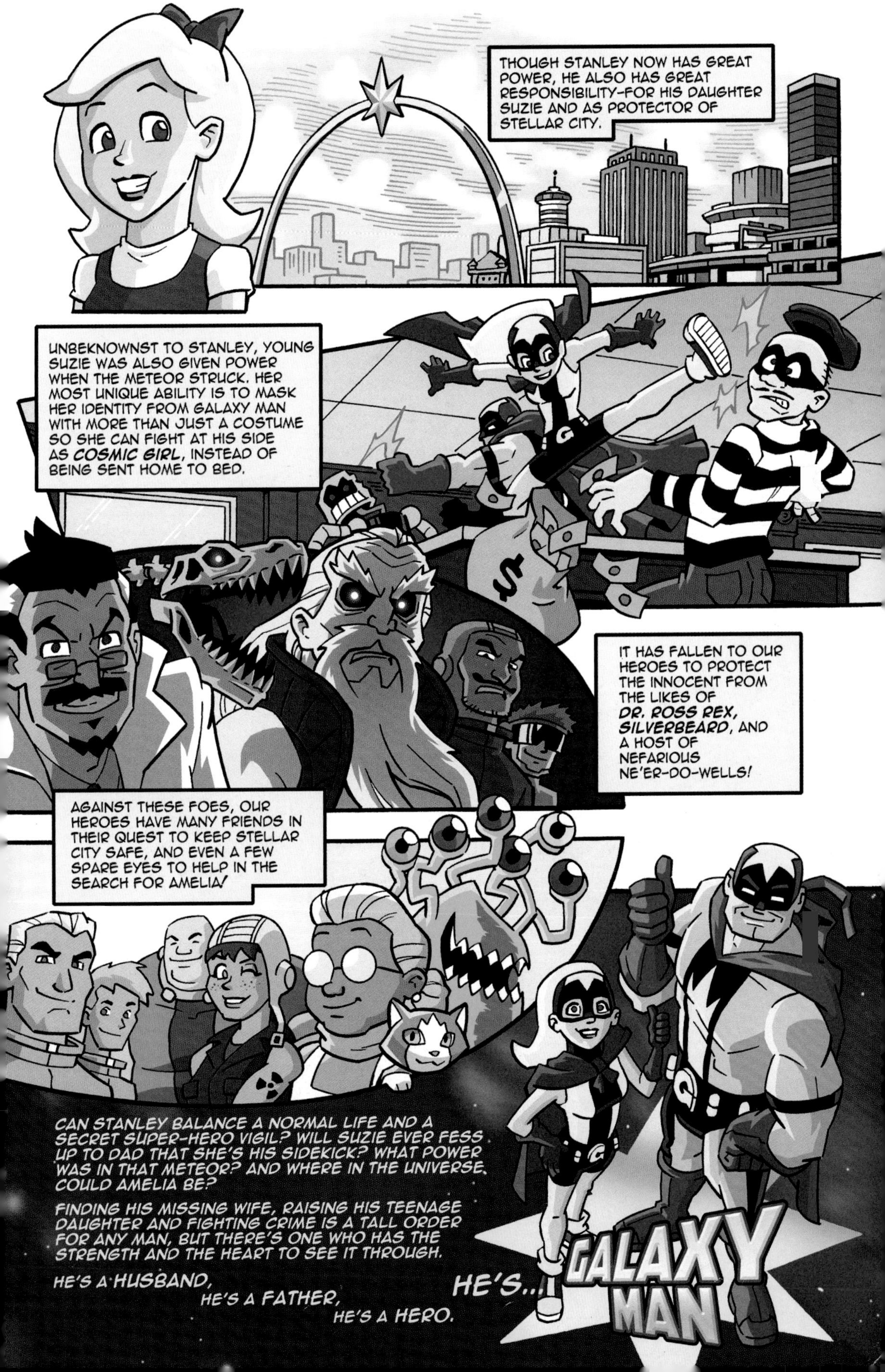
THOUGH STANLEY NOW HAS GREAT POWER, HE ALSO HAS GREAT RESPONSIBILITY–FOR HIS DAUGHTER SUZIE AND AS PROTECTOR OF STELLAR CITY.
UNBEKNOWNST TO STANLEY, YOUNG SUZIE WAS ALSO GIVEN POWER WHEN THE METEOR STRUCK. HER MOST UNIQUE ABILITY IS TO MASK HER IDENTITY FROM GALAXY MAN WITH MORE THAN JUST A COSTUME SO SHE CAN FIGHT AT HIS SIDE AS ***COSMIC GIRL***, INSTEAD OF BEING SENT HOME TO BED.
IT HAS FALLEN TO OUR HEROES TO PROTECT THE INNOCENT FROM THE LIKES OF ***DR. ROSS REX***, ***SILVERBEARD***, AND A HOST OF NEFARIOUS NE'ER-DO-WELLS!
AGAINST THESE FOES, OUR HEROES HAVE MANY FRIENDS IN THEIR QUEST TO KEEP STELLAR CITY SAFE, AND EVEN A FEW SPARE EYES TO HELP IN THE SEARCH FOR AMELIA!
CAN STANLEY BALANCE A NORMAL LIFE AND A SECRET SUPER-HERO VIGIL? WILL SUZIE EVER FESS UP TO DAD THAT SHE'S HIS SIDEKICK? WHAT POWER WAS IN THAT METEOR? AND WHERE IN THE UNIVERSE COULD AMELIA BE?
FINDING HIS MISSING WIFE, RAISING HIS TEENAGE DAUGHTER AND FIGHTING CRIME IS A TALL ORDER FOR ANY MAN, BUT THERE'S ONE WHO HAS THE STRENGTH AND THE HEART TO SEE IT THROUGH.
HE'S A HUSBAND,
HE'S A FATHER,
HE'S A HERO.
HE'S...
GALAXY MAN

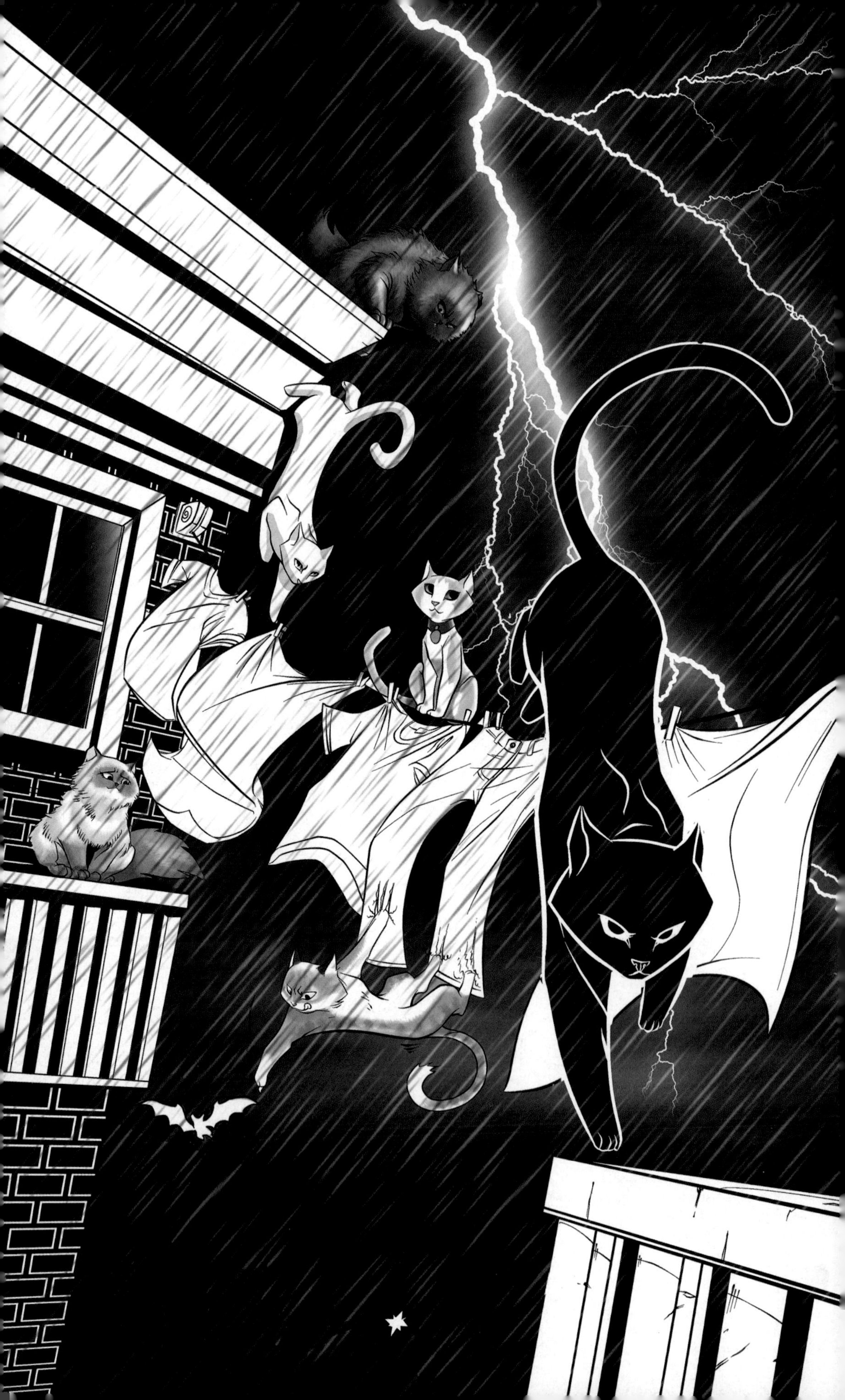

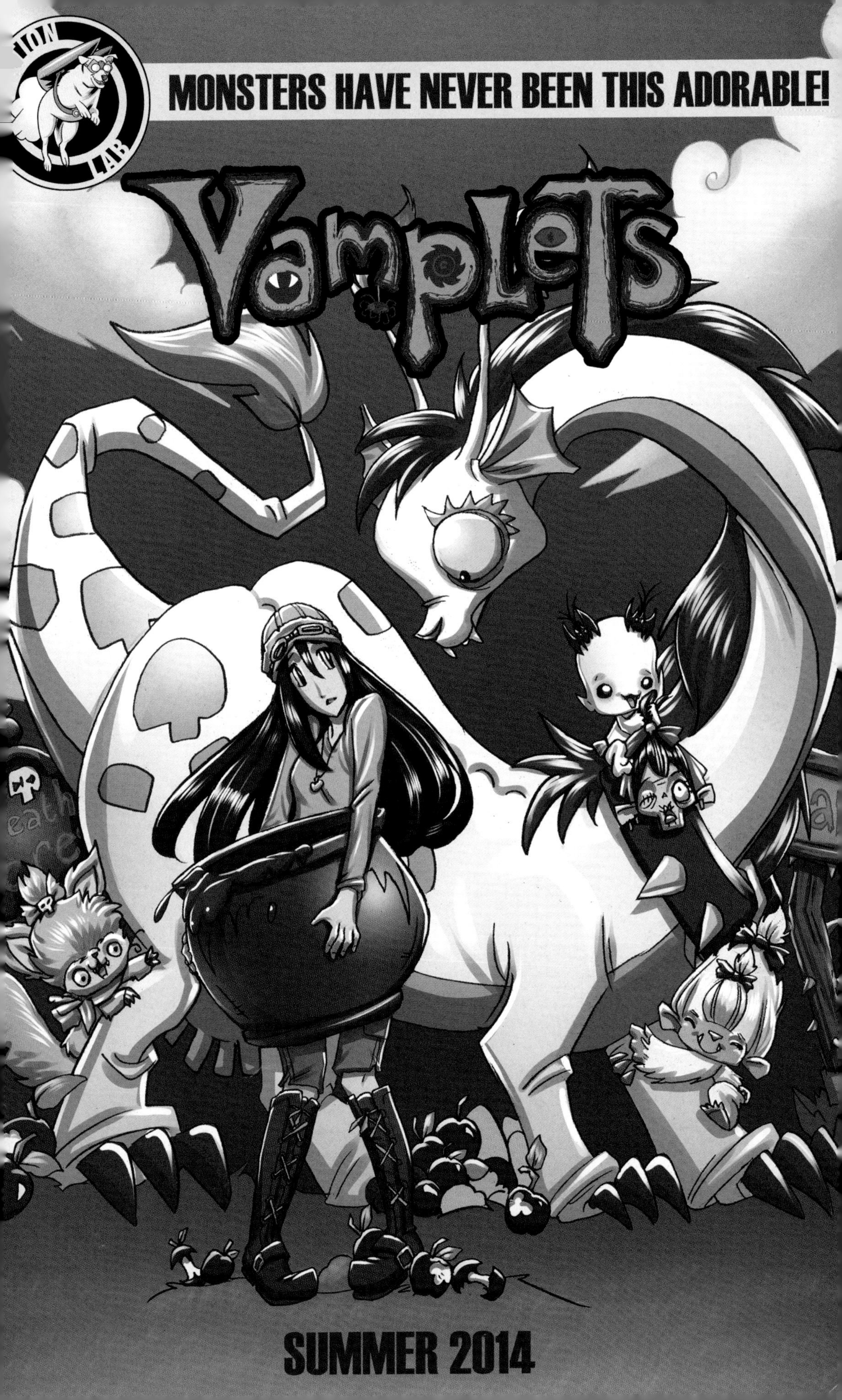

MONSTERS HAVE NEVER BEEN THIS ADORABLE!
Vamplets
SUMMER 2014

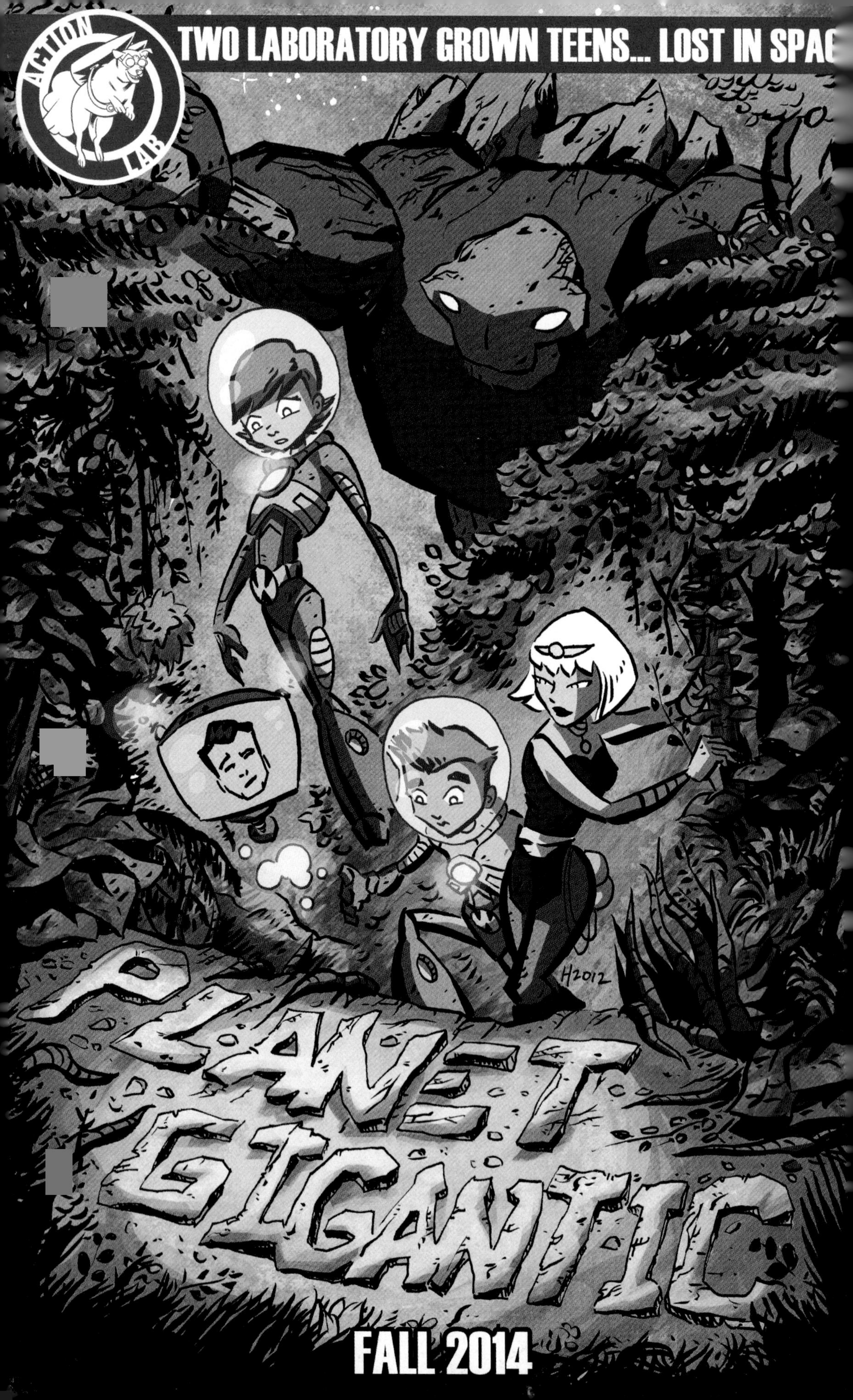
ACTION LAB
TWO LABORATORY GROWN TEENS... LOST IN SPAC
H2012
PLANET GIGANTIC
FALL 2014

Discover your spirit animal and join the quest!

Enter the world of Erdas, where YOU are one of the rare few to summon a spirit animal.

Read the book, then join the adventure at **scholastic.com/spiritanimals**

Use this code to unlock game rewards:
7C81OM6I7C

SPIRIT ANIMALS

BOOK 1
WILD BORN

READ THE BOOK. UNLOCK THE GAME.

BY #1 NEW YORK TIMES BESTSELLING AUTHOR
BRANDON MULL

By the author of the Beyonders and Fablehaven series!

SPIRIT ANIMALS
HUNTED
MAGGIE STIEFVA...

SPIRIT ANIMALS
BLOOD TIES
GARTH NIX & SEAN WILLIAMS

SPIRIT ANIMALS
FIRE AND ICE
SHANNON HALE

NEW

SCHOLASTIC

scholastic.com/spiritanimals

SCHOLASTIC, SPIRIT ANIMALS, and associated logos are trademarks and/or registered trademarks of Scholastic Inc.

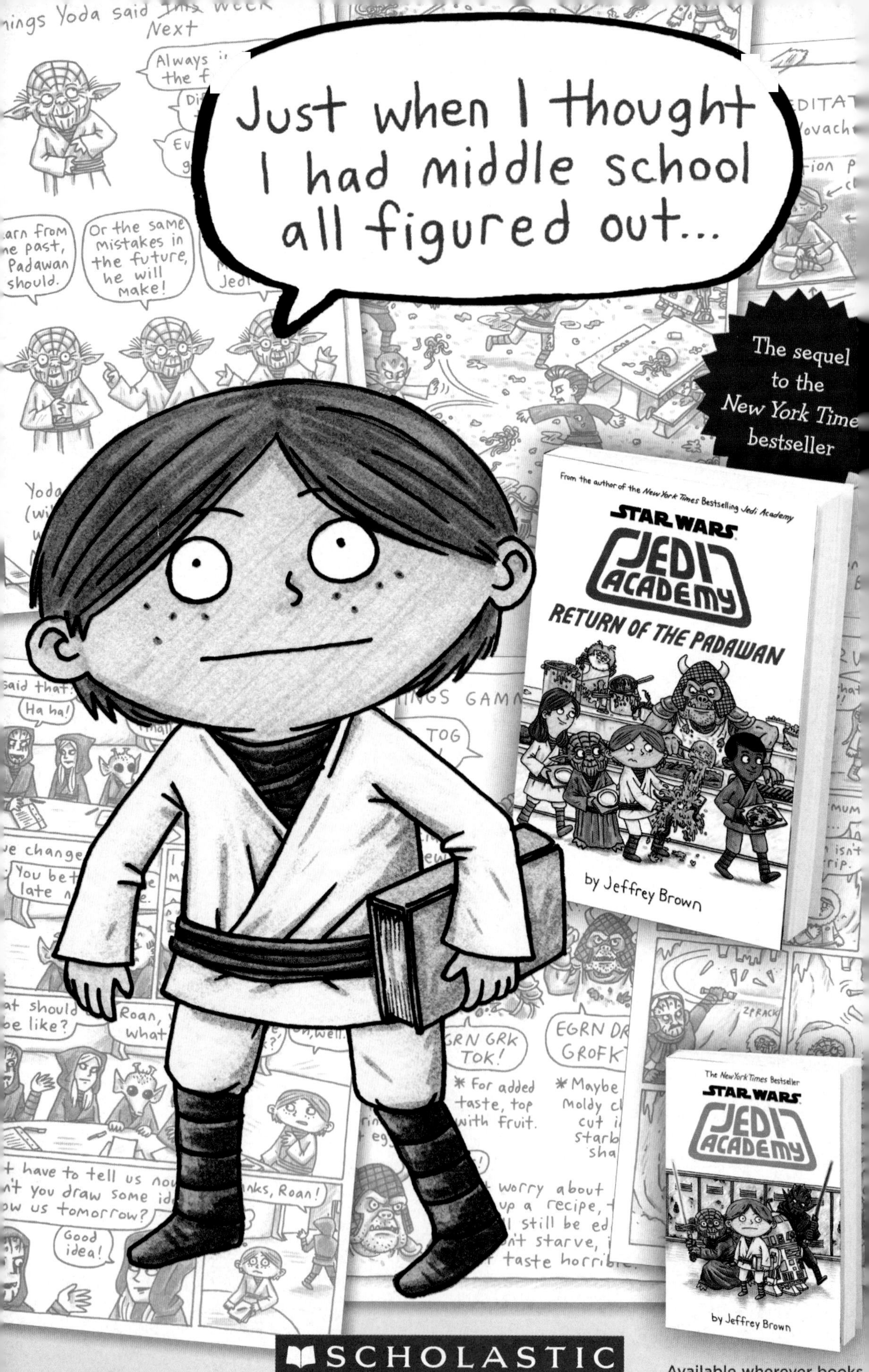
Just when I thought I had middle school all figured out...
The sequel to the New York Times bestseller
From the author of the New York Times Bestselling Jedi Academy
STAR WARS
JEDI ACADEMY
RETURN OF THE PADAWAN
by Jeffrey Brown
The New York Times Bestseller
STAR WARS
JEDI ACADEMY
by Jeffrey Brown
SCHOLASTIC

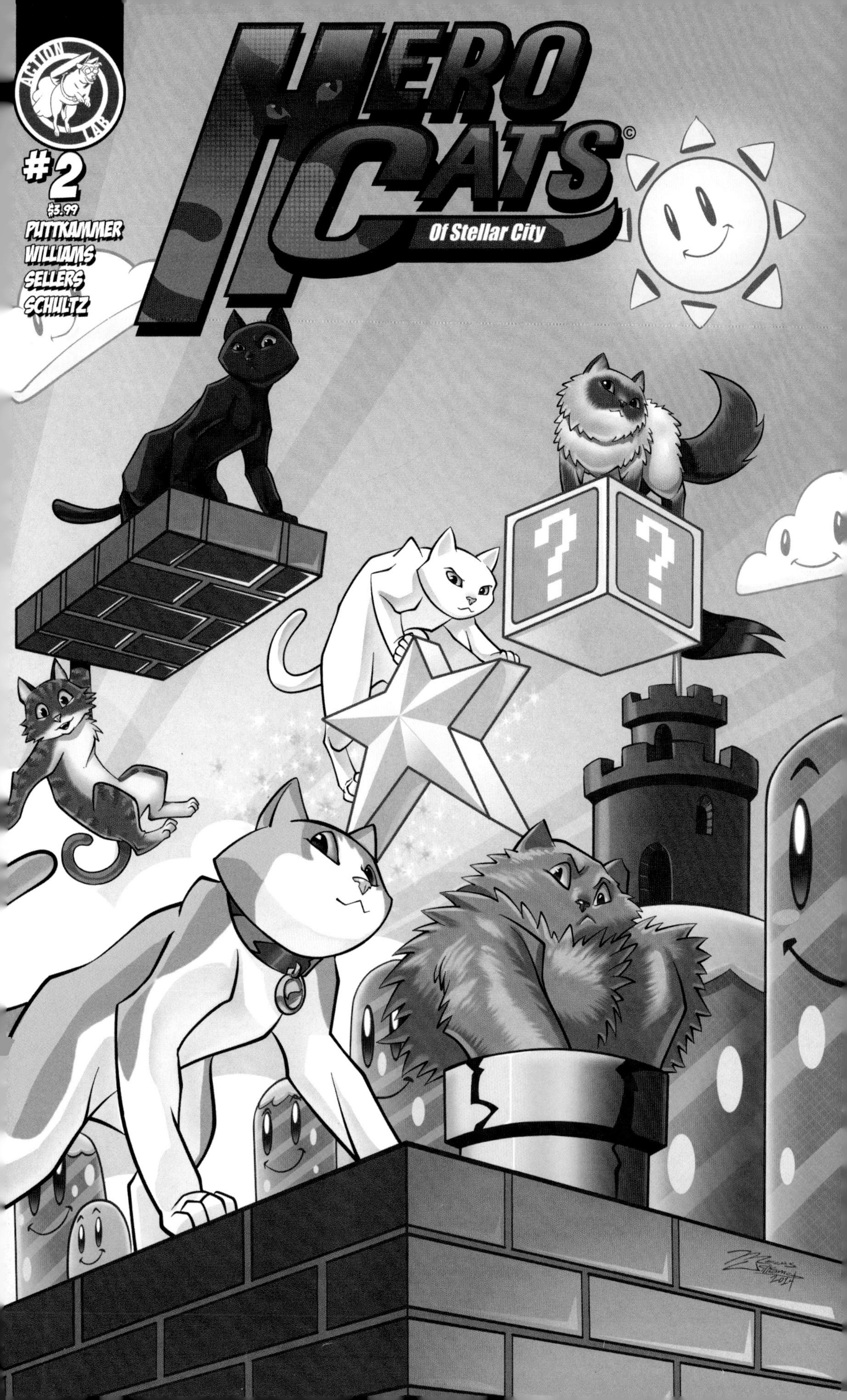

HERO CATS©
Of Stellar City
#2
$3.99
PUTTKAMMER
WILLIAMS
SELLERS
SCHULTZ
ACTION LAB

THE MENACE OF JOHNNY ARCADO!

HERO CATS

Of Stellar City

WRITTEN BY KYLE PUTTKAMMER

PENCILS BY MARCUS WILLIAMS

INKS BY RYAN SELLERS

COLORS BY OMAKA SCHULTZ

LETTERS BY BRIANA HIGGINS

HEROCATSCOMIC.COM

Bryan Seaton - Publisher
Kevin Freeman - President
Creative Director - Dave Dwonch
Editor In Chief - Shawn Gabborin
Co-Directors of Marketing - Jamal Igle & Kelly Dale
Social Media Director - Jim Dietz
Education Outreach Director - Jeremy Whitley
Associate Editors - Chad Cicconi & Colleen Boyd

HERO CATS #2, September 2014. Copyright Kyle Puttkammer, 2014.
Published by Action Lab Entertainment. All rights reserved. All characters
are fictional. Any likeness to anyone living or dead is purely coincidental. No
partof this publication may be reproduced or transmitted without permission,
except for small excerpts for review purposes. Printed in Canada. First Printing.

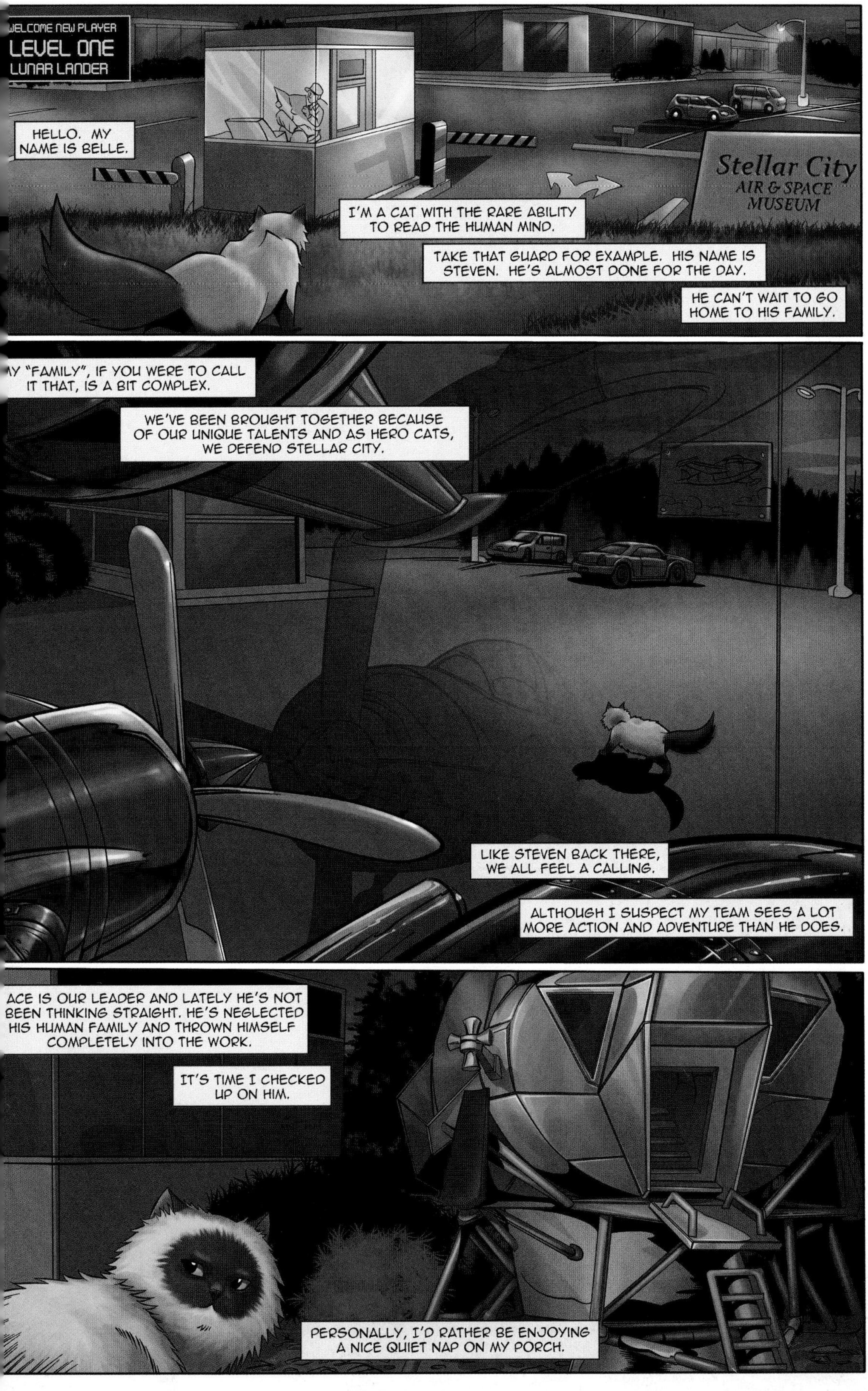
WELCOME NEW PLAYER
LEVEL ONE
LUNAR LANDER
HELLO. MY NAME IS BELLE.
Stellar City AIR & SPACE MUSEUM
I'M A CAT WITH THE RARE ABILITY TO READ THE HUMAN MIND.
TAKE THAT GUARD FOR EXAMPLE. HIS NAME IS STEVEN. HE'S ALMOST DONE FOR THE DAY.
HE CAN'T WAIT TO GO HOME TO HIS FAMILY.
MY "FAMILY", IF YOU WERE TO CALL IT THAT, IS A BIT COMPLEX.
WE'VE BEEN BROUGHT TOGETHER BECAUSE OF OUR UNIQUE TALENTS AND AS HERO CATS, WE DEFEND STELLAR CITY.
LIKE STEVEN BACK THERE, WE ALL FEEL A CALLING.
ALTHOUGH I SUSPECT MY TEAM SEES A LOT MORE ACTION AND ADVENTURE THAN HE DOES.
ACE IS OUR LEADER AND LATELY HE'S NOT BEEN THINKING STRAIGHT. HE'S NEGLECTED HIS HUMAN FAMILY AND THROWN HIMSELF COMPLETELY INTO THE WORK.
IT'S TIME I CHECKED UP ON HIM.
PERSONALLY, I'D RATHER BE ENJOYING A NICE QUIET NAP ON MY PORCH.

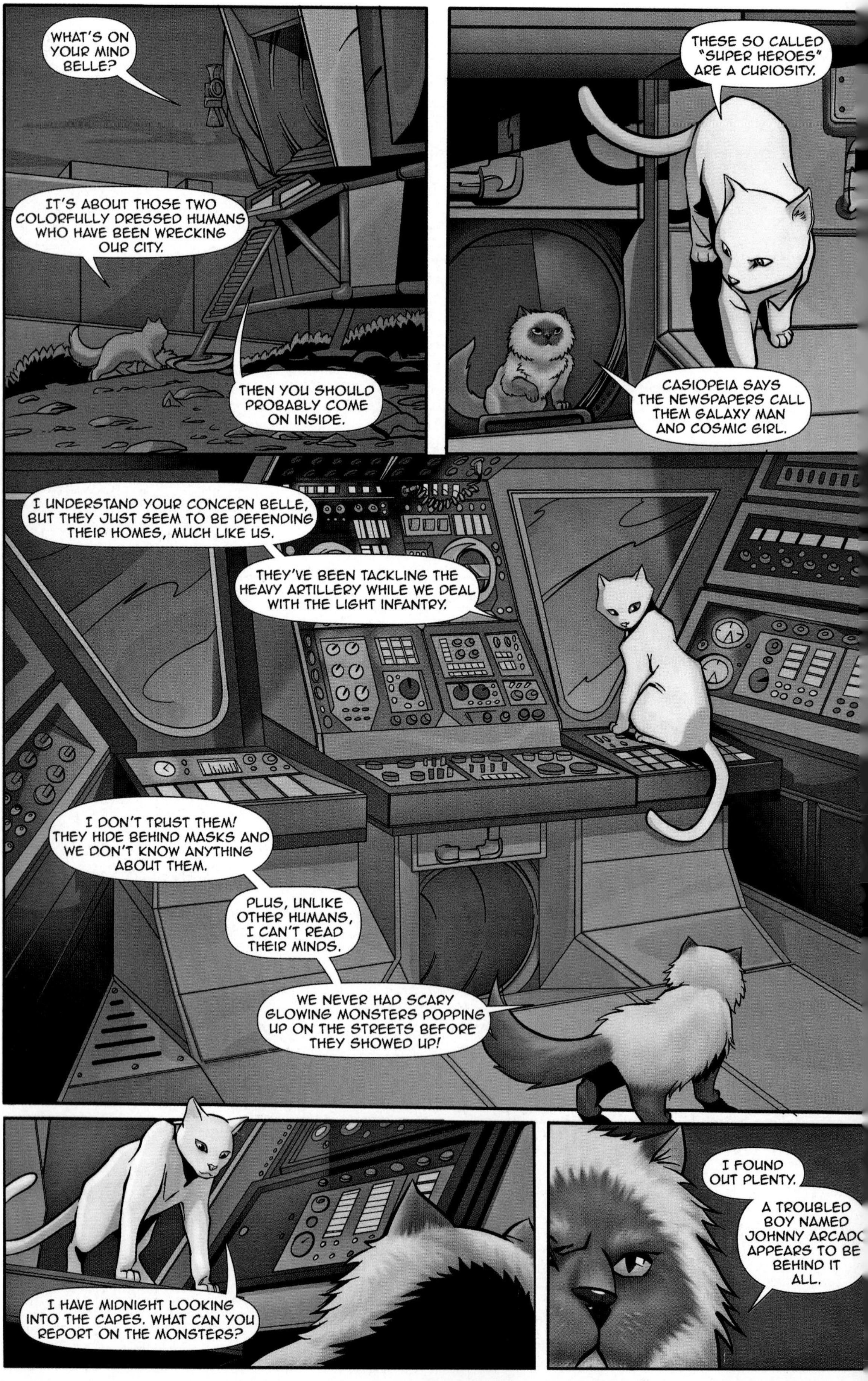
WHAT'S ON YOUR MIND BELLE?
IT'S ABOUT THOSE TWO COLORFULLY DRESSED HUMANS WHO HAVE BEEN WRECKING OUR CITY.
THEN YOU SHOULD PROBABLY COME ON INSIDE.
THESE SO CALLED "SUPER HEROES" ARE A CURIOSITY.
CASIOPEIA SAYS THE NEWSPAPERS CALL THEM GALAXY MAN AND COSMIC GIRL.
I UNDERSTAND YOUR CONCERN BELLE, BUT THEY JUST SEEM TO BE DEFENDING THEIR HOMES, MUCH LIKE US.
THEY'VE BEEN TACKLING THE HEAVY ARTILLERY WHILE WE DEAL WITH THE LIGHT INFANTRY.
I DON'T TRUST THEM! THEY HIDE BEHIND MASKS AND WE DON'T KNOW ANYTHING ABOUT THEM.
PLUS, UNLIKE OTHER HUMANS, I CAN'T READ THEIR MINDS.
WE NEVER HAD SCARY GLOWING MONSTERS POPPING UP ON THE STREETS BEFORE THEY SHOWED UP!
I HAVE MIDNIGHT LOOKING INTO THE CAPES. WHAT CAN YOU REPORT ON THE MONSTERS?
I FOUND OUT PLENTY.
A TROUBLED BOY NAMED JOHNNY ARCADO APPEARS TO BE BEHIND IT ALL.

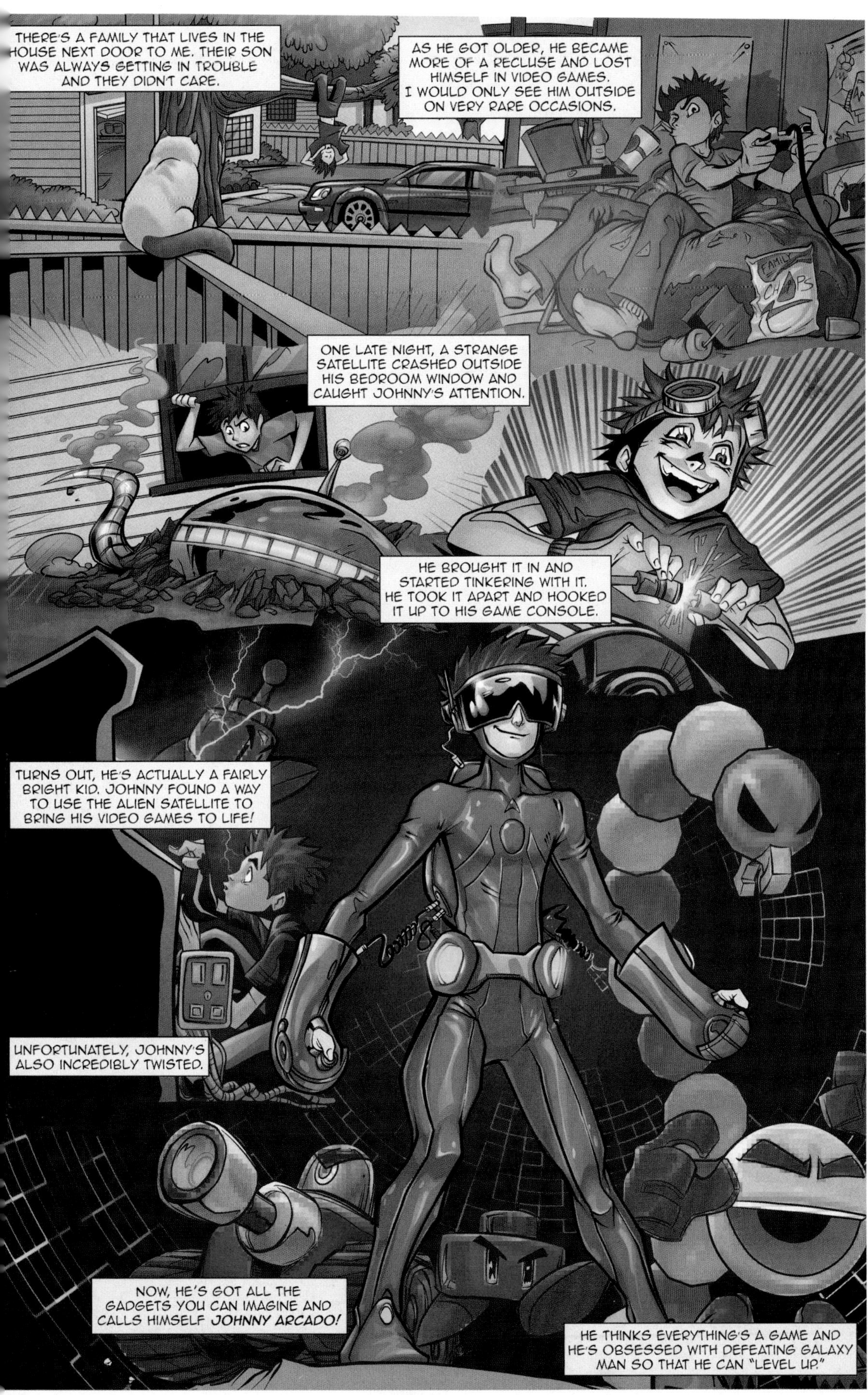

THERE'S A FAMILY THAT LIVES IN THE HOUSE NEXT DOOR TO ME. THEIR SON WAS ALWAYS GETTING IN TROUBLE AND THEY DIDN'T CARE.
AS HE GOT OLDER, HE BECAME MORE OF A RECLUSE AND LOST HIMSELF IN VIDEO GAMES. I WOULD ONLY SEE HIM OUTSIDE ON VERY RARE OCCASIONS.
ONE LATE NIGHT, A STRANGE SATELLITE CRASHED OUTSIDE HIS BEDROOM WINDOW AND CAUGHT JOHNNY'S ATTENTION.
HE BROUGHT IT IN AND STARTED TINKERING WITH IT. HE TOOK IT APART AND HOOKED IT UP TO HIS GAME CONSOLE.
TURNS OUT, HE'S ACTUALLY A FAIRLY BRIGHT KID. JOHNNY FOUND A WAY TO USE THE ALIEN SATELLITE TO BRING HIS VIDEO GAMES TO LIFE!
UNFORTUNATELY, JOHNNY'S ALSO INCREDIBLY TWISTED.
NOW, HE'S GOT ALL THE GADGETS YOU CAN IMAGINE AND CALLS HIMSELF *JOHNNY ARCADO!*
HE THINKS EVERYTHING'S A GAME AND HE'S OBSESSED WITH DEFEATING GALAXY MAN SO THAT HE CAN "LEVEL UP."

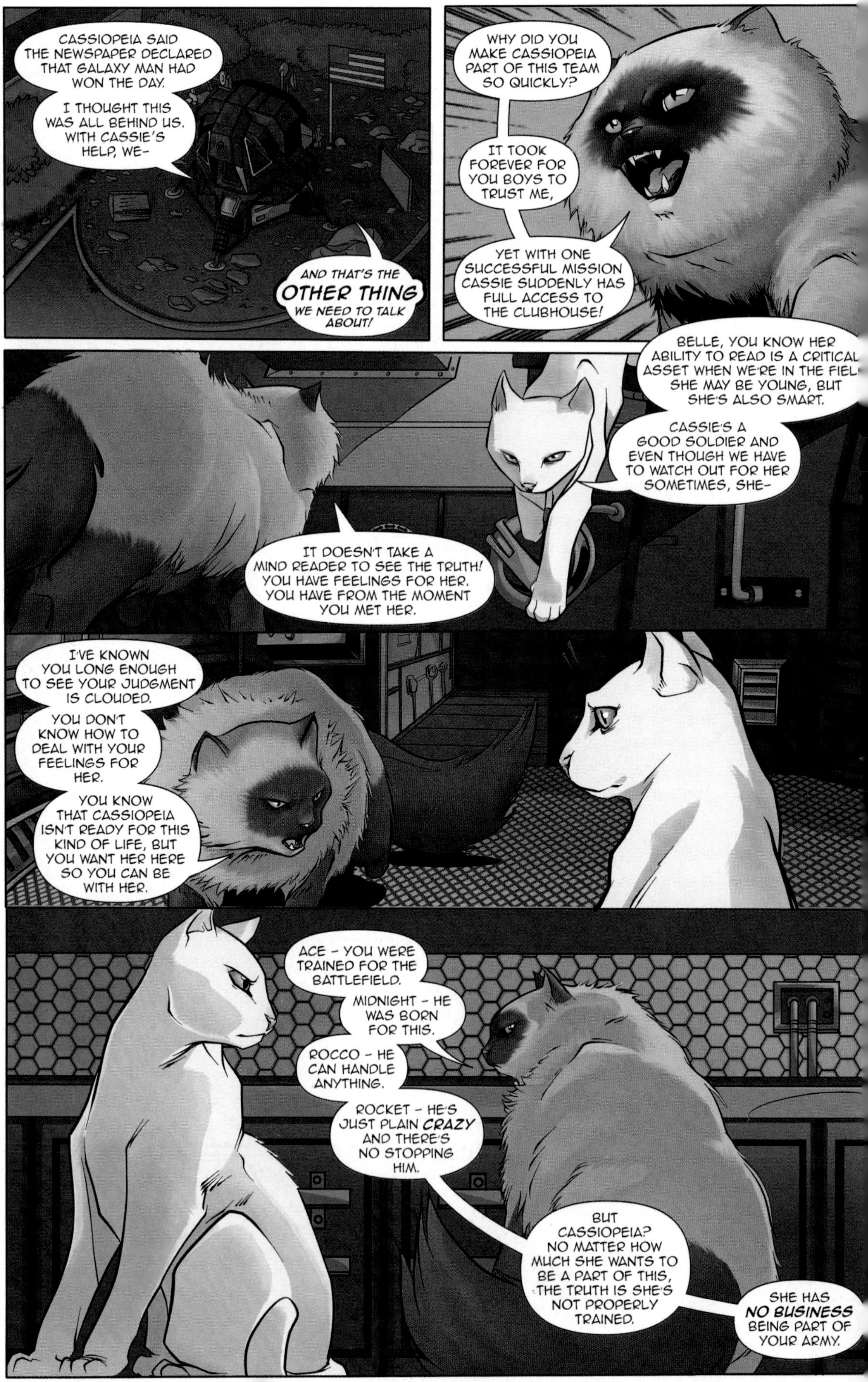
CASSIOPEIA SAID THE NEWSPAPER DECLARED THAT GALAXY MAN HAD WON THE DAY.
I THOUGHT THIS WAS ALL BEHIND US. WITH CASSIE'S HELP, WE-
AND THAT'S THE OTHER THING WE NEED TO TALK ABOUT!
WHY DID YOU MAKE CASSIOPEIA PART OF THIS TEAM SO QUICKLY?
IT TOOK FOREVER FOR YOU BOYS TO TRUST ME,
YET WITH ONE SUCCESSFUL MISSION CASSIE SUDDENLY HAS FULL ACCESS TO THE CLUBHOUSE!
BELLE, YOU KNOW HER ABILITY TO READ IS A CRITICAL ASSET WHEN WE'RE IN THE FIEL SHE MAY BE YOUNG, BUT SHE'S ALSO SMART.
CASSIE'S A GOOD SOLDIER AND EVEN THOUGH WE HAVE TO WATCH OUT FOR HER SOMETIMES, SHE-
IT DOESN'T TAKE A MIND READER TO SEE THE TRUTH! YOU HAVE FEELINGS FOR HER. YOU HAVE FROM THE MOMENT YOU MET HER.
I'VE KNOWN YOU LONG ENOUGH TO SEE YOUR JUDGMENT IS CLOUDED.
YOU DON'T KNOW HOW TO DEAL WITH YOUR FEELINGS FOR HER.
YOU KNOW THAT CASSIOPEIA ISN'T READY FOR THIS KIND OF LIFE, BUT YOU WANT HER HERE SO YOU CAN BE WITH HER.
ACE - YOU WERE TRAINED FOR THE BATTLEFIELD.
MIDNIGHT - HE WAS BORN FOR THIS.
ROCCO - HE CAN HANDLE ANYTHING.
ROCKET - HE'S JUST PLAIN CRAZY AND THERE'S NO STOPPING HIM.
BUT CASSIOPEIA? NO MATTER HOW MUCH SHE WANTS TO BE A PART OF THIS, THE TRUTH IS SHE'S NOT PROPERLY TRAINED.
SHE HAS NO BUSINESS BEING PART OF YOUR ARMY.

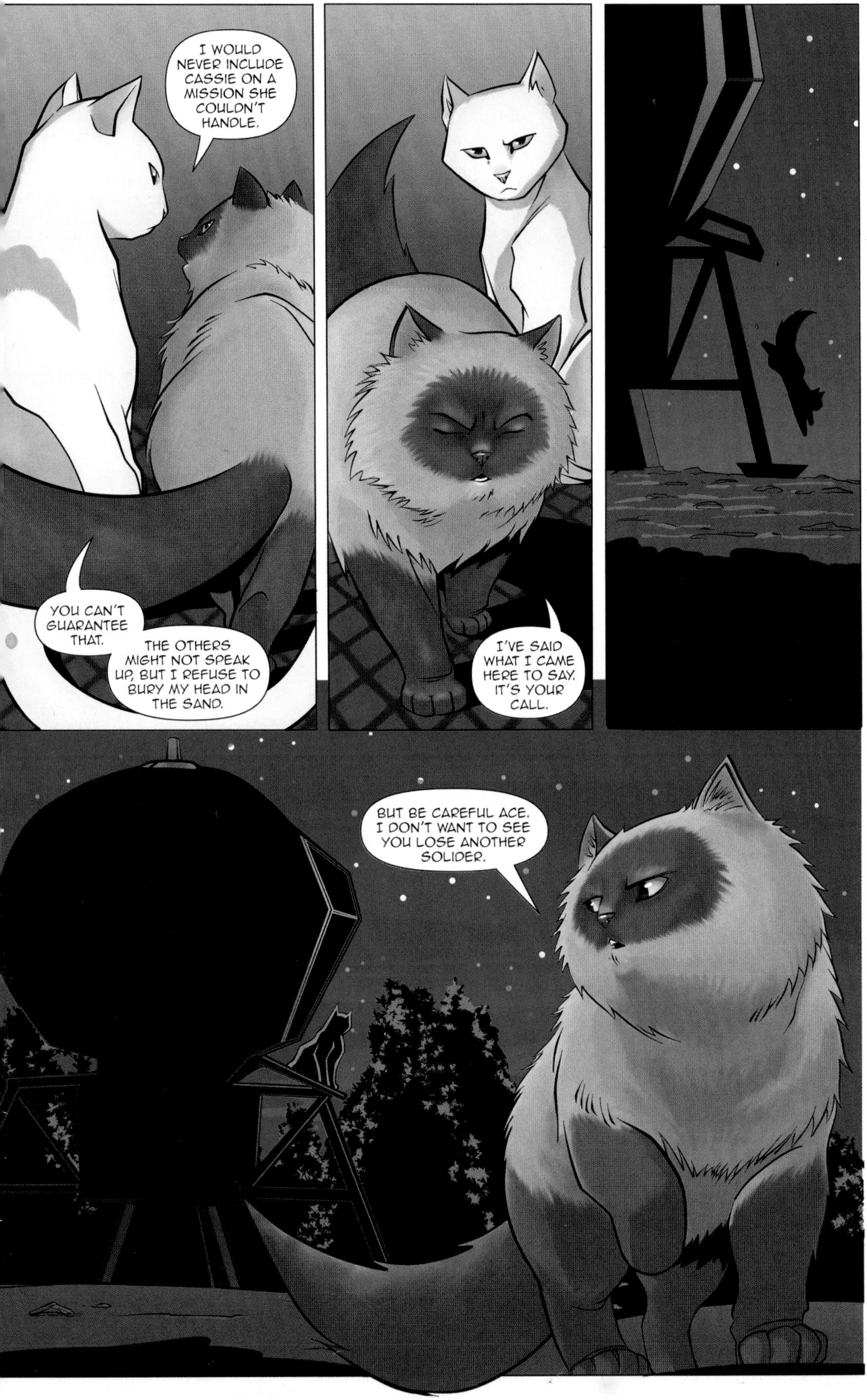
I WOULD NEVER INCLUDE CASSIE ON A MISSION SHE COULDN'T HANDLE.
YOU CAN'T GUARANTEE THAT.
THE OTHERS MIGHT NOT SPEAK UP, BUT I REFUSE TO BURY MY HEAD IN THE SAND.
I'VE SAID WHAT I CAME HERE TO SAY. IT'S YOUR CALL.
BUT BE CAREFUL ACE. I DON'T WANT TO SEE YOU LOSE ANOTHER SOLIDER.

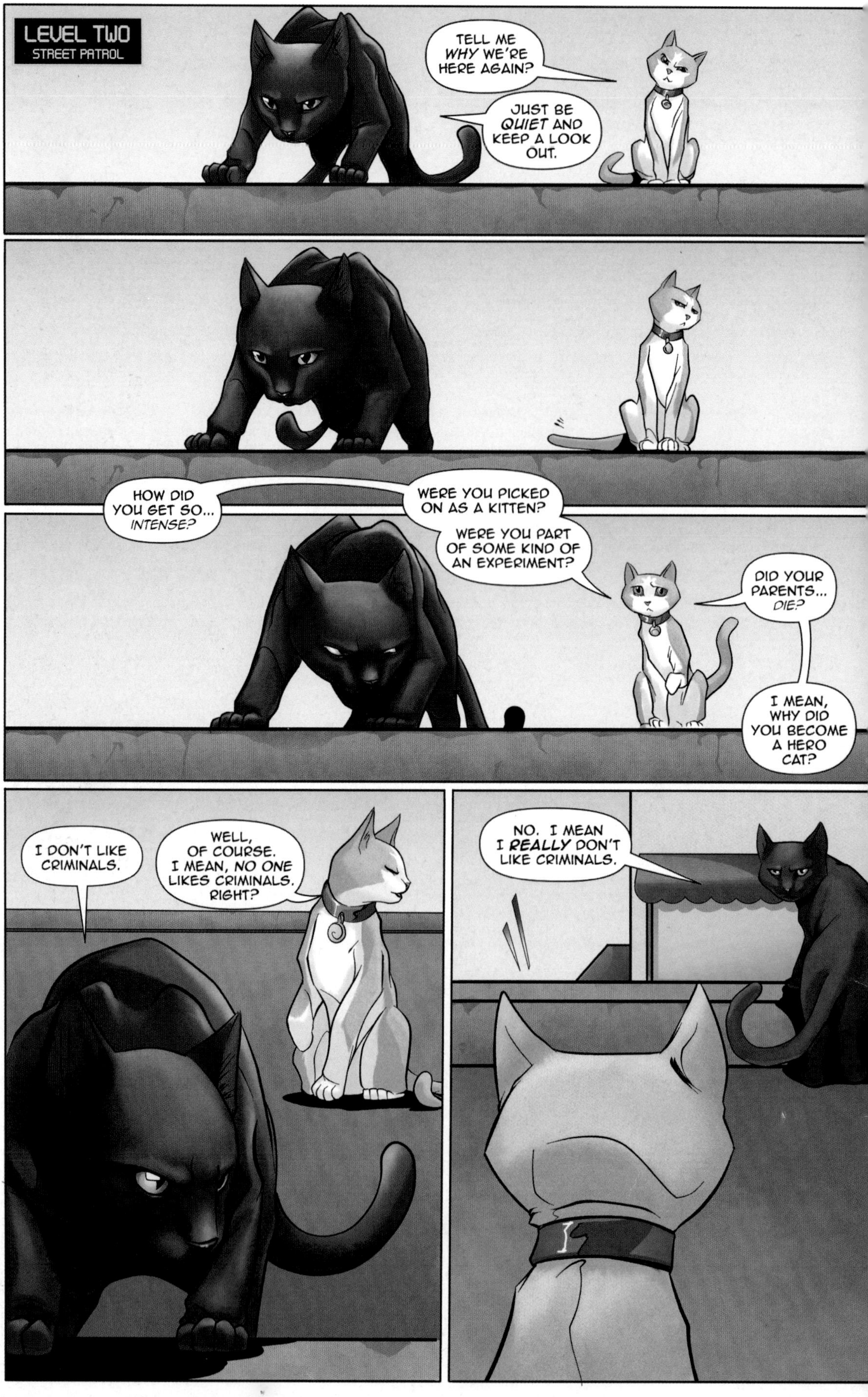
LEVEL TWO
STREET PATROL
TELL ME WHY WE'RE HERE AGAIN?
JUST BE QUIET AND KEEP A LOOK OUT.
HOW DID YOU GET SO... INTENSE?
WERE YOU PICKED ON AS A KITTEN?
WERE YOU PART OF SOME KIND OF AN EXPERIMENT?
DID YOUR PARENTS... DIE?
I MEAN, WHY DID YOU BECOME A HERO CAT?
I DON'T LIKE CRIMINALS.
WELL, OF COURSE. I MEAN, NO ONE LIKES CRIMINALS. RIGHT?
NO. I MEAN I REALLY DON'T LIKE CRIMINALS.

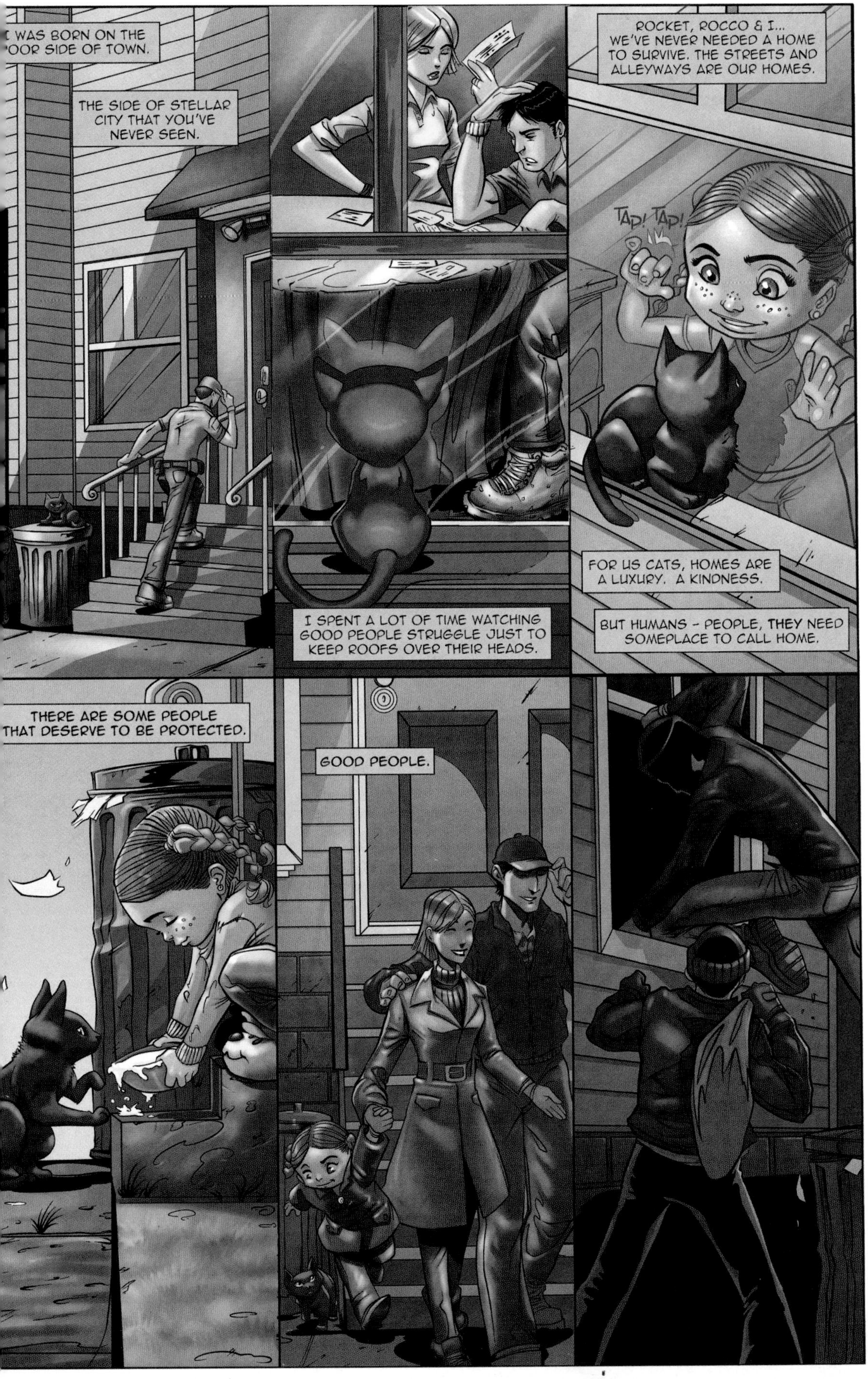
I WAS BORN ON THE POOR SIDE OF TOWN.
THE SIDE OF STELLAR CITY THAT YOU'VE NEVER SEEN.
I SPENT A LOT OF TIME WATCHING GOOD PEOPLE STRUGGLE JUST TO KEEP ROOFS OVER THEIR HEADS.
ROCKET, ROCCO & I... WE'VE NEVER NEEDED A HOME TO SURVIVE. THE STREETS AND ALLEYWAYS ARE OUR HOMES.
TAP! TAP!
FOR US CATS, HOMES ARE A LUXURY. A KINDNESS.
BUT HUMANS - PEOPLE, THEY NEED SOMEPLACE TO CALL HOME.
THERE ARE SOME PEOPLE THAT DESERVE TO BE PROTECTED.
GOOD PEOPLE.

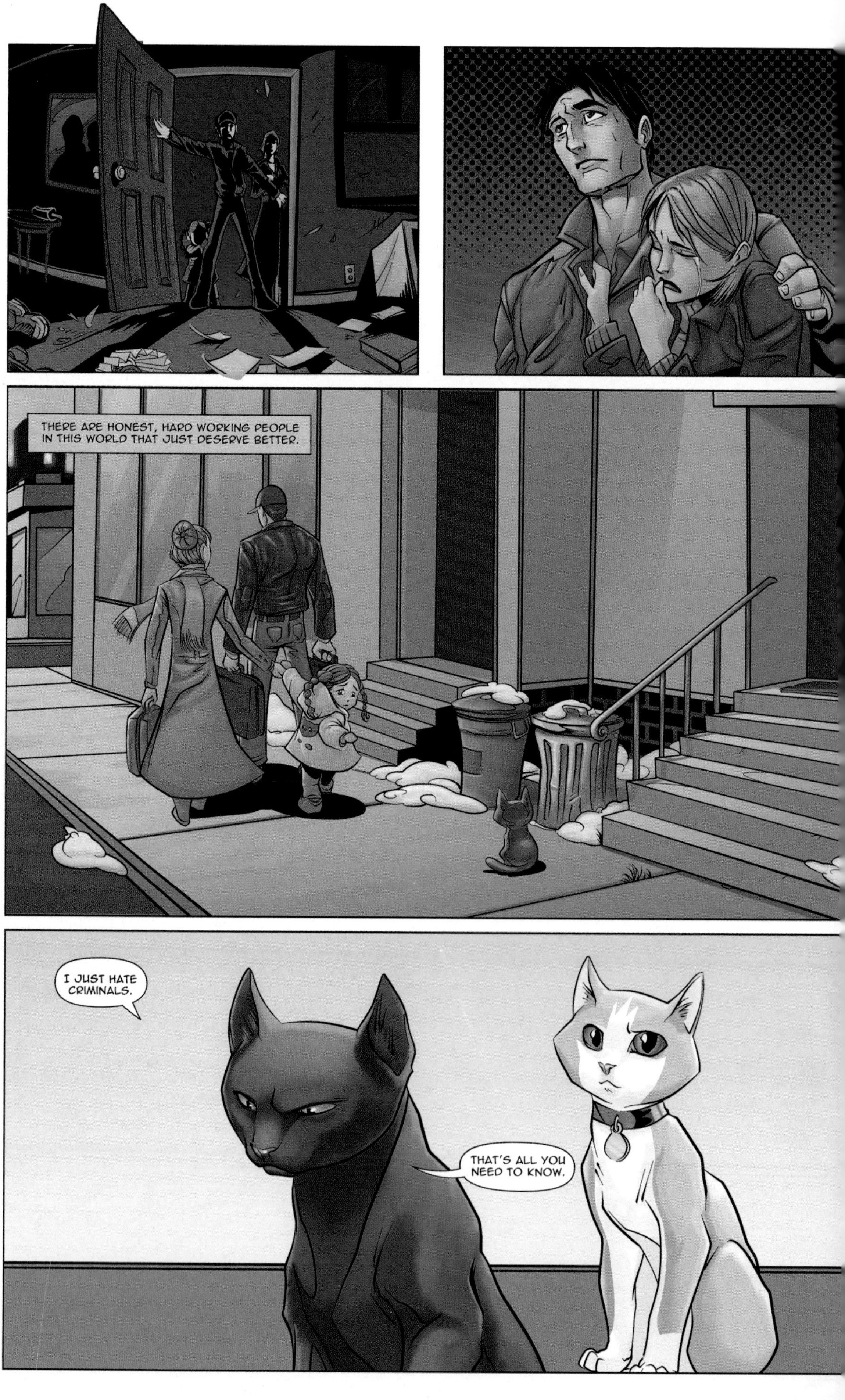
THERE ARE HONEST, HARD WORKING PEOPLE IN THIS WORLD THAT JUST DESERVE BETTER.
I JUST HATE CRIMINALS.
THAT'S ALL YOU NEED TO KNOW.

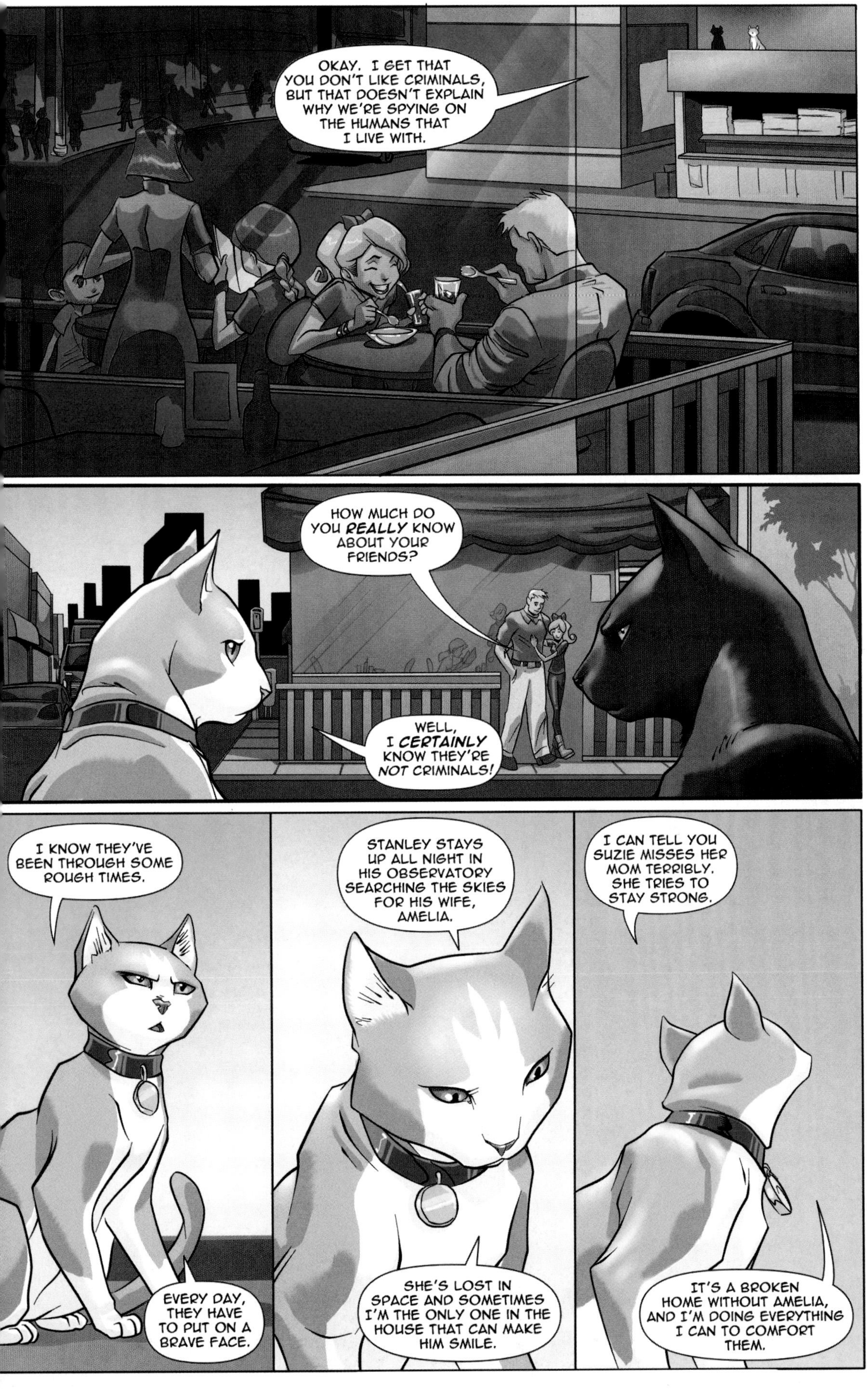
OKAY. I GET THAT YOU DON'T LIKE CRIMINALS, BUT THAT DOESN'T EXPLAIN WHY WE'RE SPYING ON THE HUMANS THAT I LIVE WITH.
HOW MUCH DO YOU REALLY KNOW ABOUT YOUR FRIENDS?
WELL, I CERTAINLY KNOW THEY'RE NOT CRIMINALS!
I KNOW THEY'VE BEEN THROUGH SOME ROUGH TIMES.
EVERY DAY, THEY HAVE TO PUT ON A BRAVE FACE.
STANLEY STAYS UP ALL NIGHT IN HIS OBSERVATORY SEARCHING THE SKIES FOR HIS WIFE, AMELIA.
SHE'S LOST IN SPACE AND SOMETIMES I'M THE ONLY ONE IN THE HOUSE THAT CAN MAKE HIM SMILE.
I CAN TELL YOU SUZIE MISSES HER MOM TERRIBLY. SHE TRIES TO STAY STRONG.
IT'S A BROKEN HOME WITHOUT AMELIA, AND I'M DOING EVERYTHING I CAN TO COMFORT THEM.

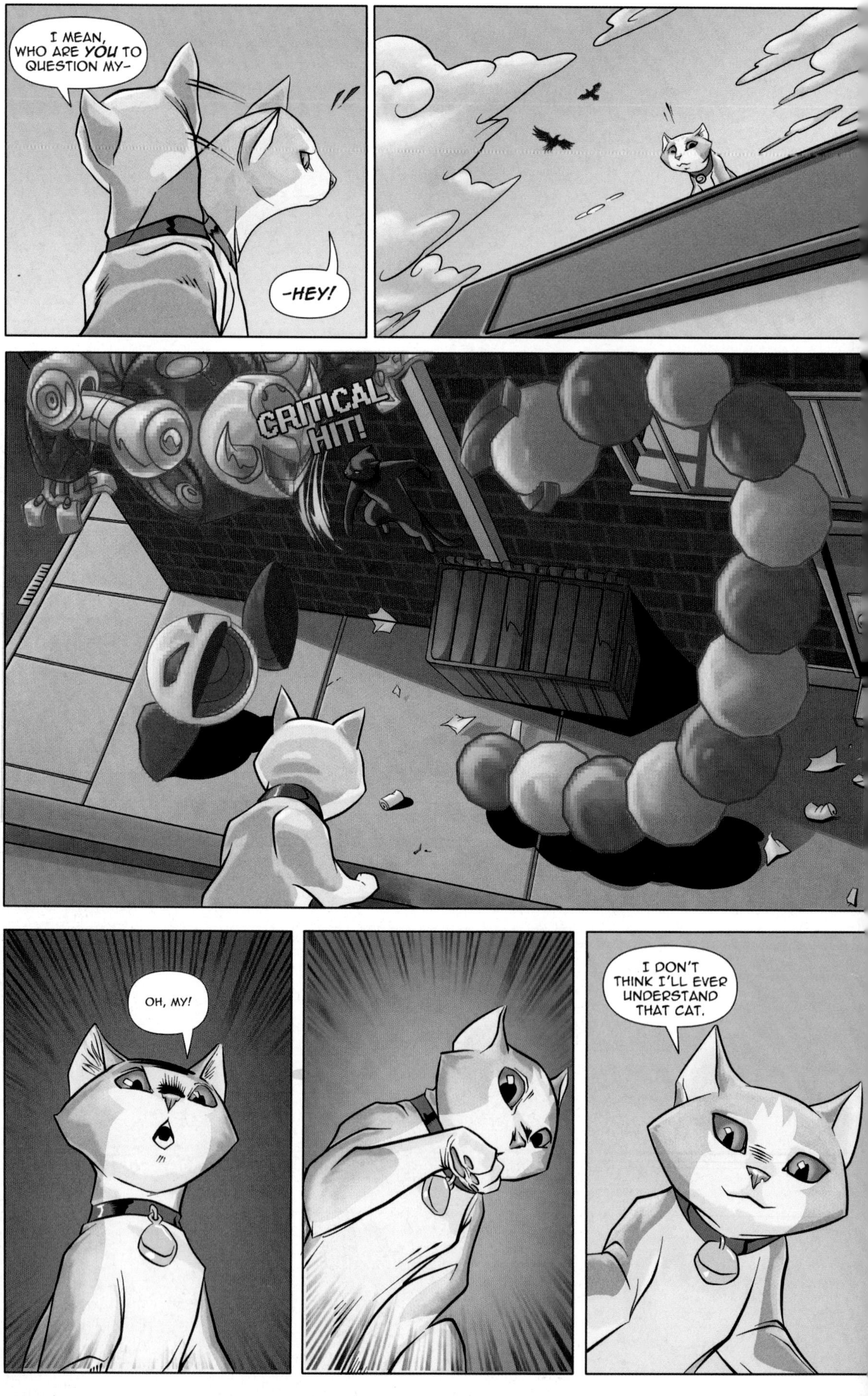
I MEAN, WHO ARE YOU TO QUESTION MY-
-HEY!
CRITICAL HIT!
OH, MY!
I DON'T THINK I'LL EVER UNDERSTAND THAT CAT.

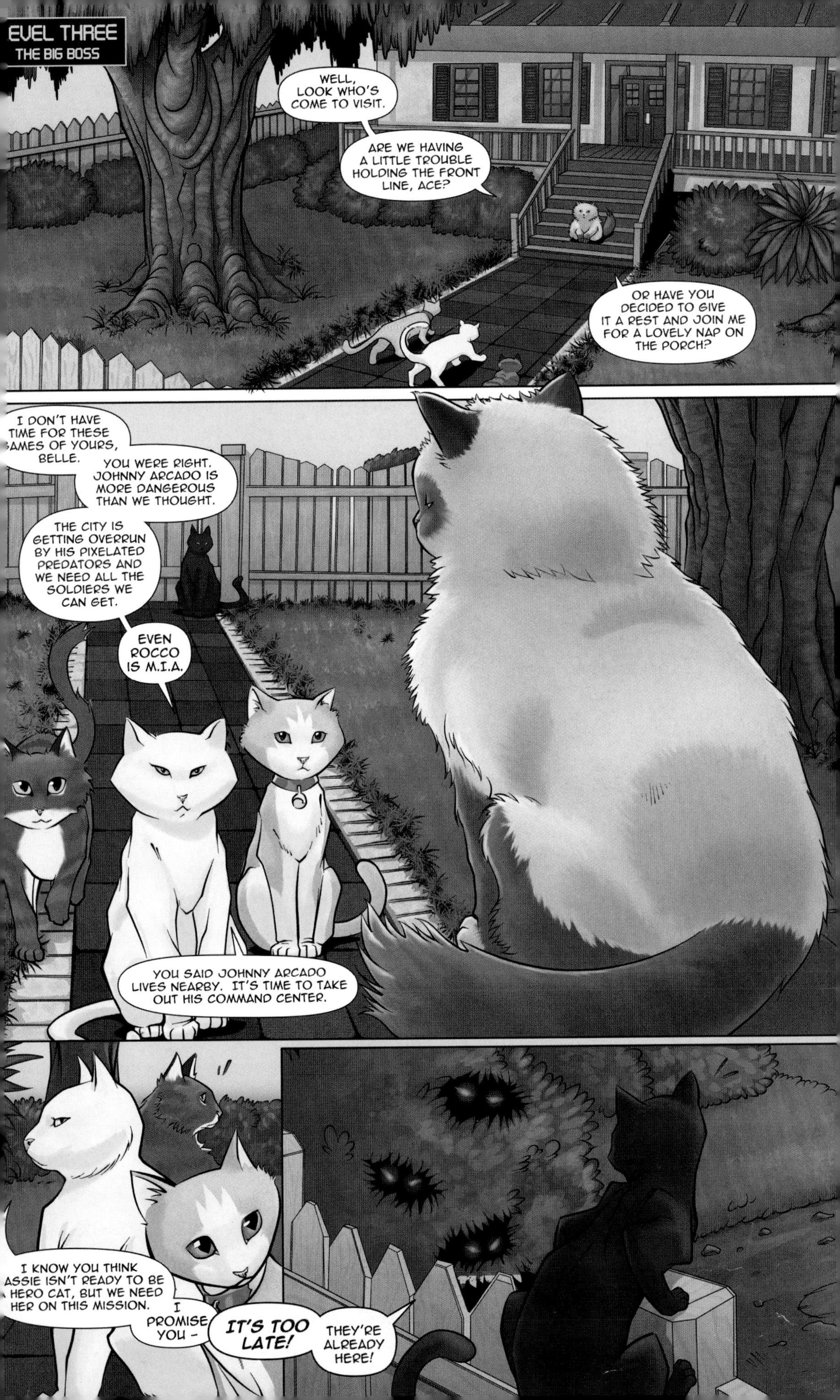

EVEL THREE
THE BIG BOSS
WELL, LOOK WHO'S COME TO VISIT.
ARE WE HAVING A LITTLE TROUBLE HOLDING THE FRONT LINE, ACE?
OR HAVE YOU DECIDED TO GIVE IT A REST AND JOIN ME FOR A LOVELY NAP ON THE PORCH?
I DON'T HAVE TIME FOR THESE GAMES OF YOURS, BELLE.
YOU WERE RIGHT. JOHNNY ARCADO IS MORE DANGEROUS THAN WE THOUGHT.
THE CITY IS GETTING OVERRUN BY HIS PIXELATED PREDATORS AND WE NEED ALL THE SOLDIERS WE CAN GET.
EVEN ROCCO IS M.I.A.
YOU SAID JOHNNY ARCADO LIVES NEARBY. IT'S TIME TO TAKE OUT HIS COMMAND CENTER.
I KNOW YOU THINK ASSIE ISN'T READY TO BE A HERO CAT, BUT WE NEED HER ON THIS MISSION.
I PROMISE YOU -
IT'S TOO LATE!
THEY'RE ALREADY HERE!

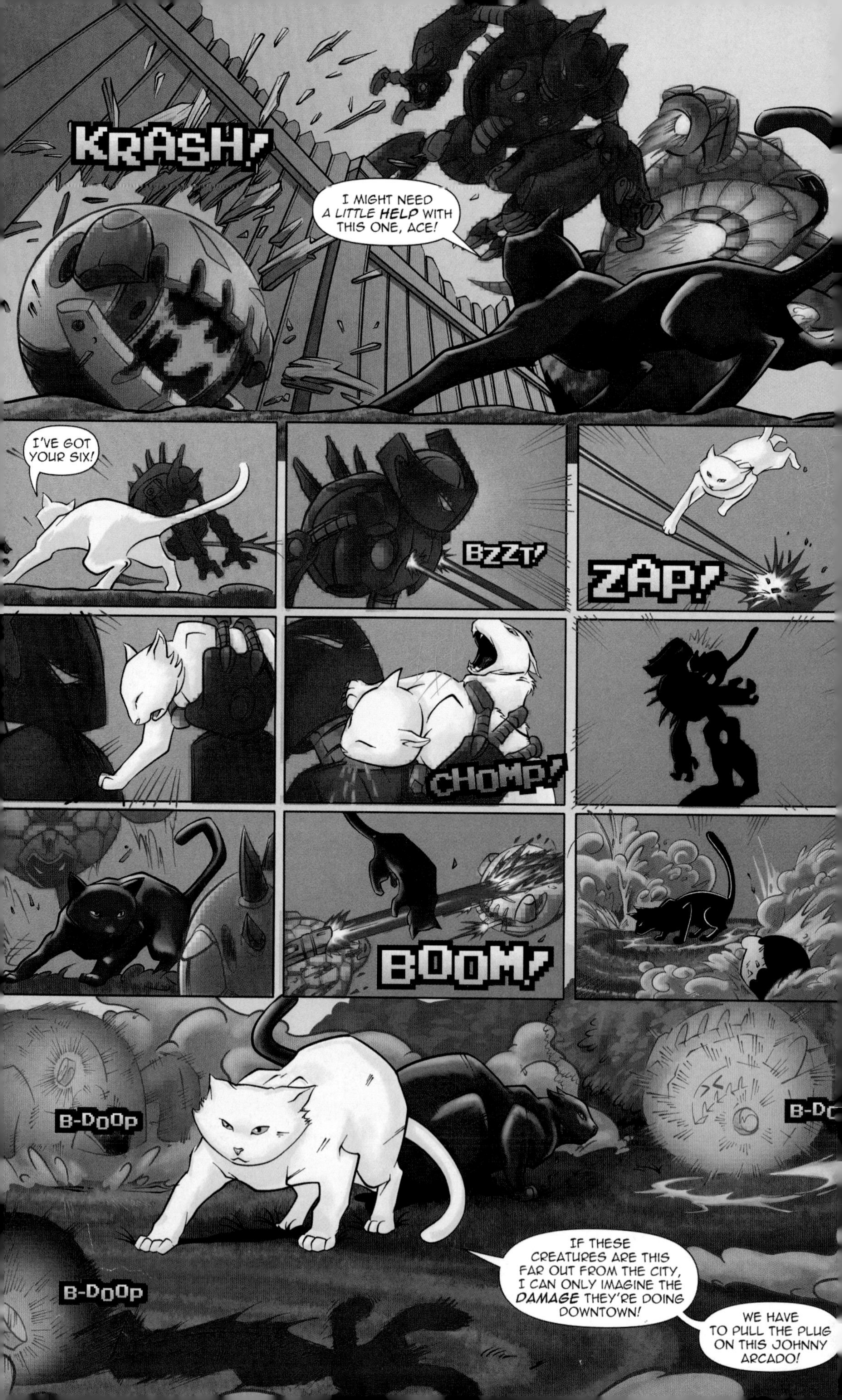
KRASH!
I MIGHT NEED A LITTLE HELP WITH THIS ONE, ACE!
I'VE GOT YOUR SIX!
BZZT!
ZAP!
CHOMP!
BOOM!
B-DOOP
B-DO
B-DOOP
IF THESE CREATURES ARE THIS FAR OUT FROM THE CITY, I CAN ONLY IMAGINE THE DAMAGE THEY'RE DOING DOWNTOWN!
WE HAVE TO PULL THE PLUG ON THIS JOHNNY ARCADO!

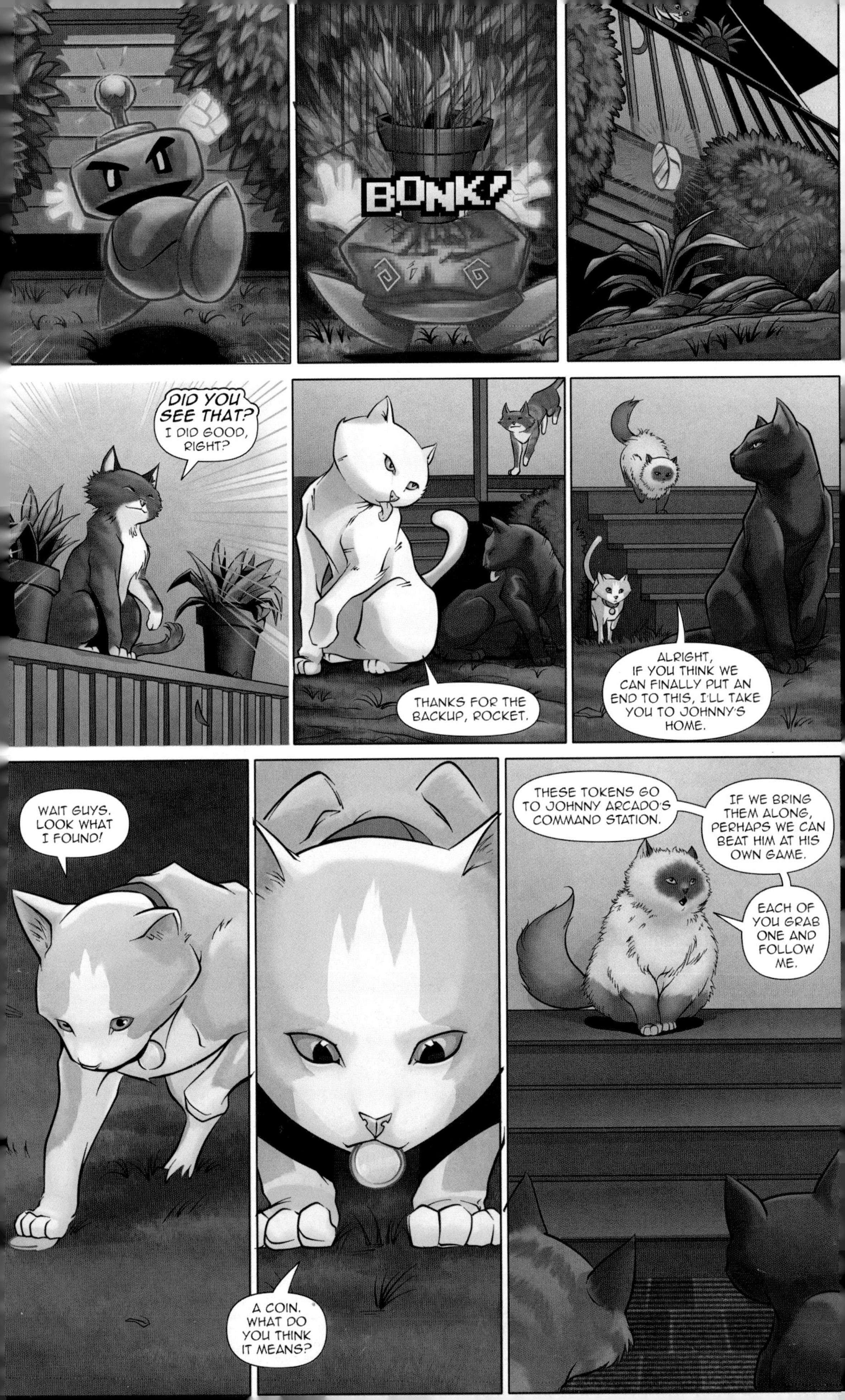
BONK!
DID YOU SEE THAT? I DID GOOD, RIGHT?
THANKS FOR THE BACKUP, ROCKET.
ALRIGHT, IF YOU THINK WE CAN FINALLY PUT AN END TO THIS, I'LL TAKE YOU TO JOHNNY'S HOME.
WAIT GUYS. LOOK WHAT I FOUND!
A COIN. WHAT DO YOU THINK IT MEANS?
THESE TOKENS GO TO JOHNNY ARCADO'S COMMAND STATION.
IF WE BRING THEM ALONG, PERHAPS WE CAN BEAT HIM AT HIS OWN GAME.
EACH OF YOU GRAB ONE AND FOLLOW ME.

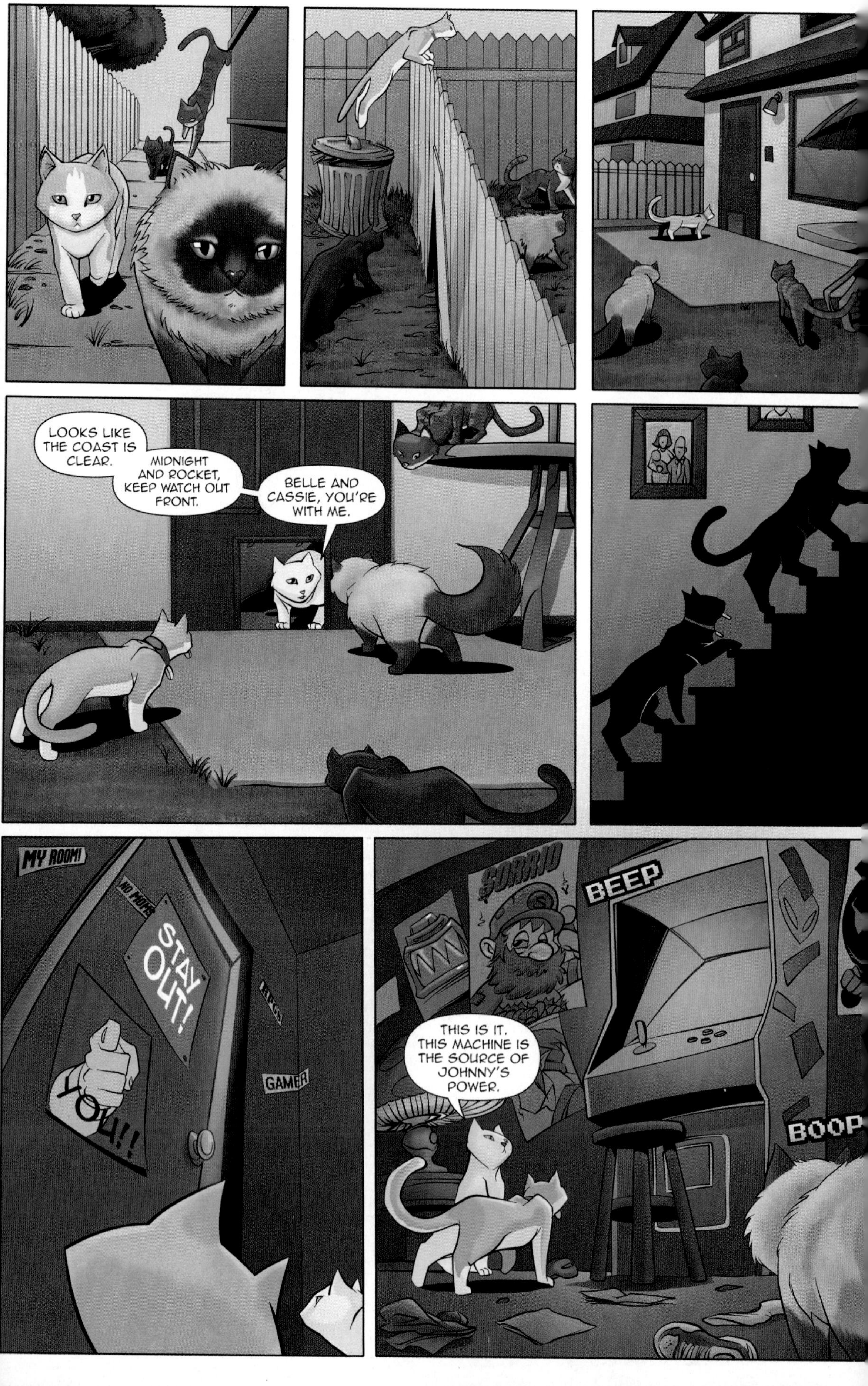
LOOKS LIKE THE COAST IS CLEAR.
MIDNIGHT AND ROCKET, KEEP WATCH OUT FRONT.
BELLE AND CASSIE, YOU'RE WITH ME.
MY ROOM!
NO MOMS
STAY OUT!
YOU!!
GAMER
BEEP
THIS IS IT. THIS MACHINE IS THE SOURCE OF JOHNNY'S POWER.
BOOP

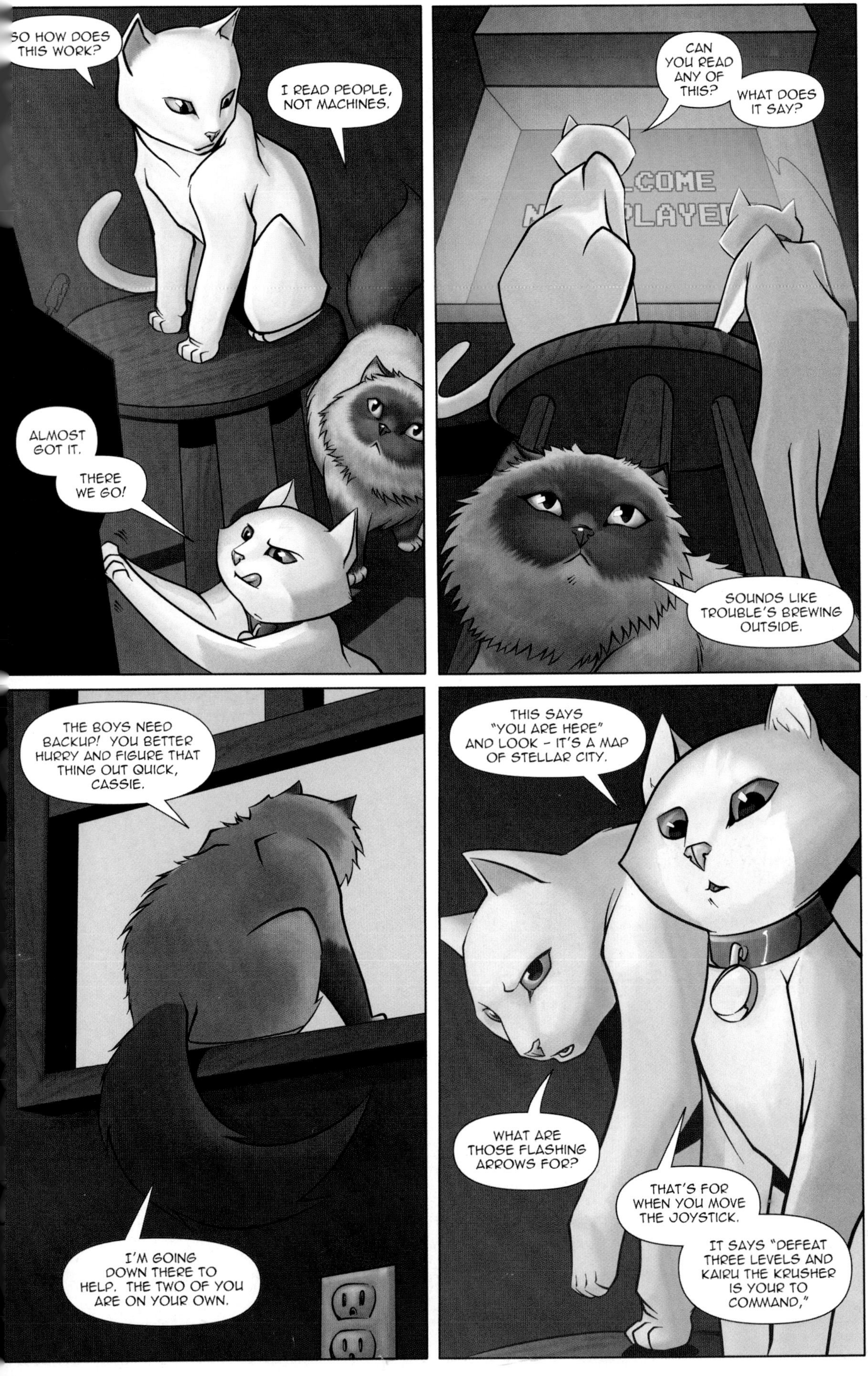
SO HOW DOES THIS WORK?
I READ PEOPLE, NOT MACHINES.
ALMOST GOT IT.
THERE WE GO!
CAN YOU READ ANY OF THIS?
WHAT DOES IT SAY?
SOUNDS LIKE TROUBLE'S BREWING OUTSIDE.
THE BOYS NEED BACKUP! YOU BETTER HURRY AND FIGURE THAT THING OUT QUICK, CASSIE.
I'M GOING DOWN THERE TO HELP. THE TWO OF YOU ARE ON YOUR OWN.
THIS SAYS "YOU ARE HERE" AND LOOK - IT'S A MAP OF STELLAR CITY.
WHAT ARE THOSE FLASHING ARROWS FOR?
THAT'S FOR WHEN YOU MOVE THE JOYSTICK.
IT SAYS "DEFEAT THREE LEVELS AND KAIRU THE KRUSHER IS YOUR TO COMMAND,"

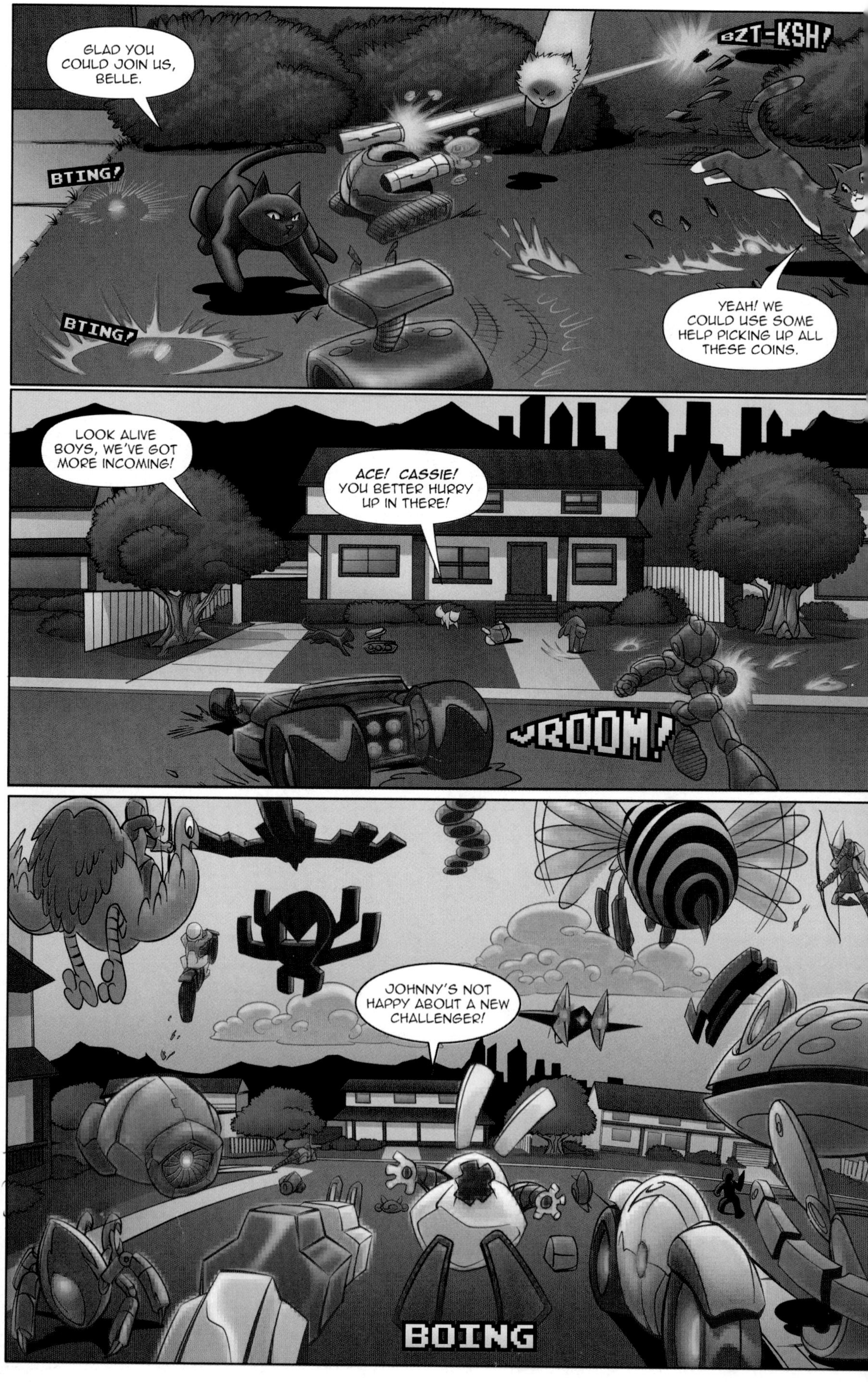
GLAD YOU COULD JOIN US, BELLE.
BZT-KSH!
BTING!
BTING!
YEAH! WE COULD USE SOME HELP PICKING UP ALL THESE COINS.
LOOK ALIVE BOYS, WE'VE GOT MORE INCOMING!
ACE! CASSIE! YOU BETTER HURRY UP IN THERE!
VROOM!
JOHNNY'S NOT HAPPY ABOUT A NEW CHALLENGER!
BOING

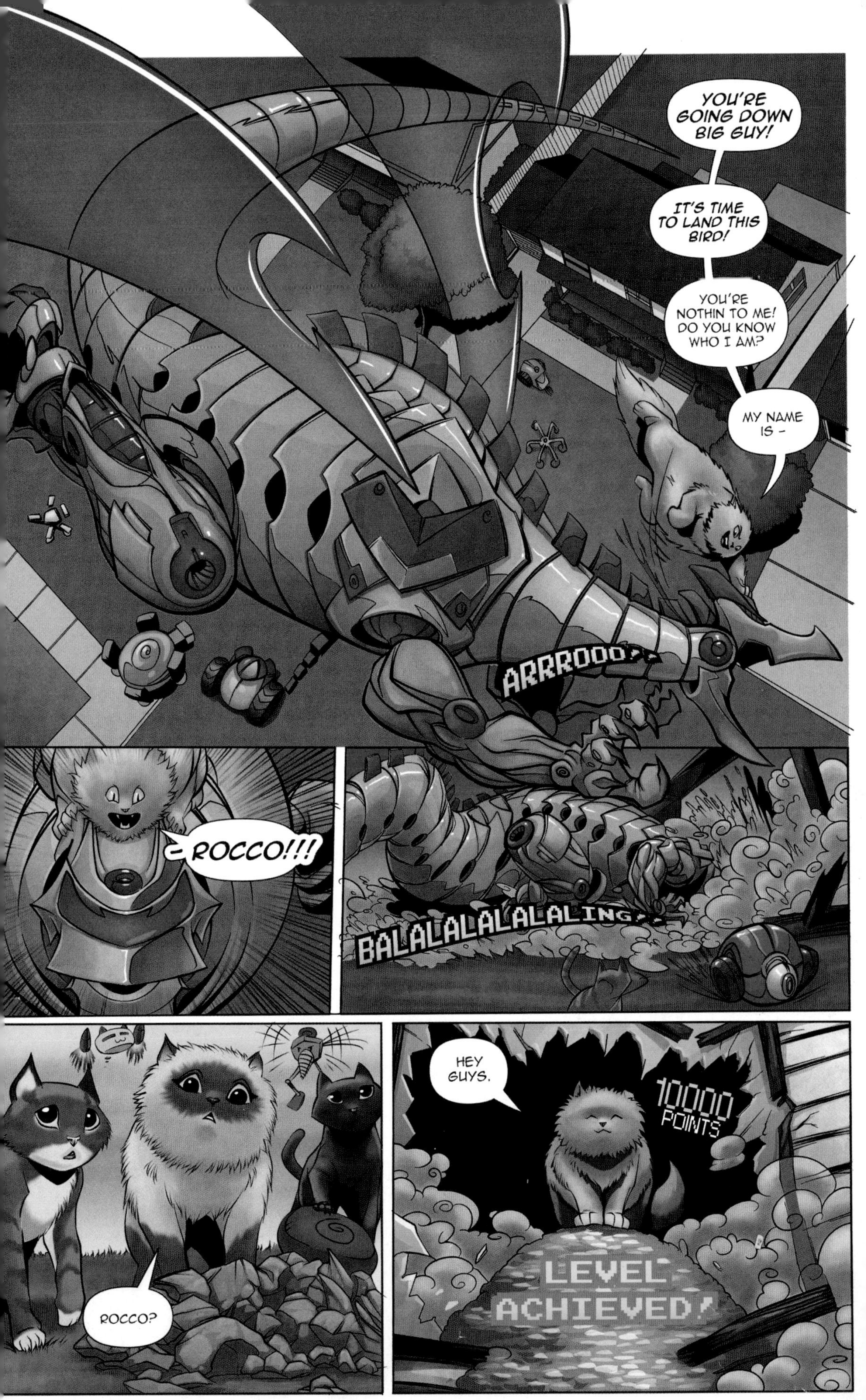

YOU'RE GOING DOWN BIG GUY!
IT'S TIME TO LAND THIS BIRD!
YOU'RE NOTHIN TO ME! DO YOU KNOW WHO I AM?
MY NAME IS -
ARRROOO!
- ROCCO!!!
BALALALALALALING!
ROCCO?
HEY GUYS.
10000 POINTS
LEVEL ACHIEVED!

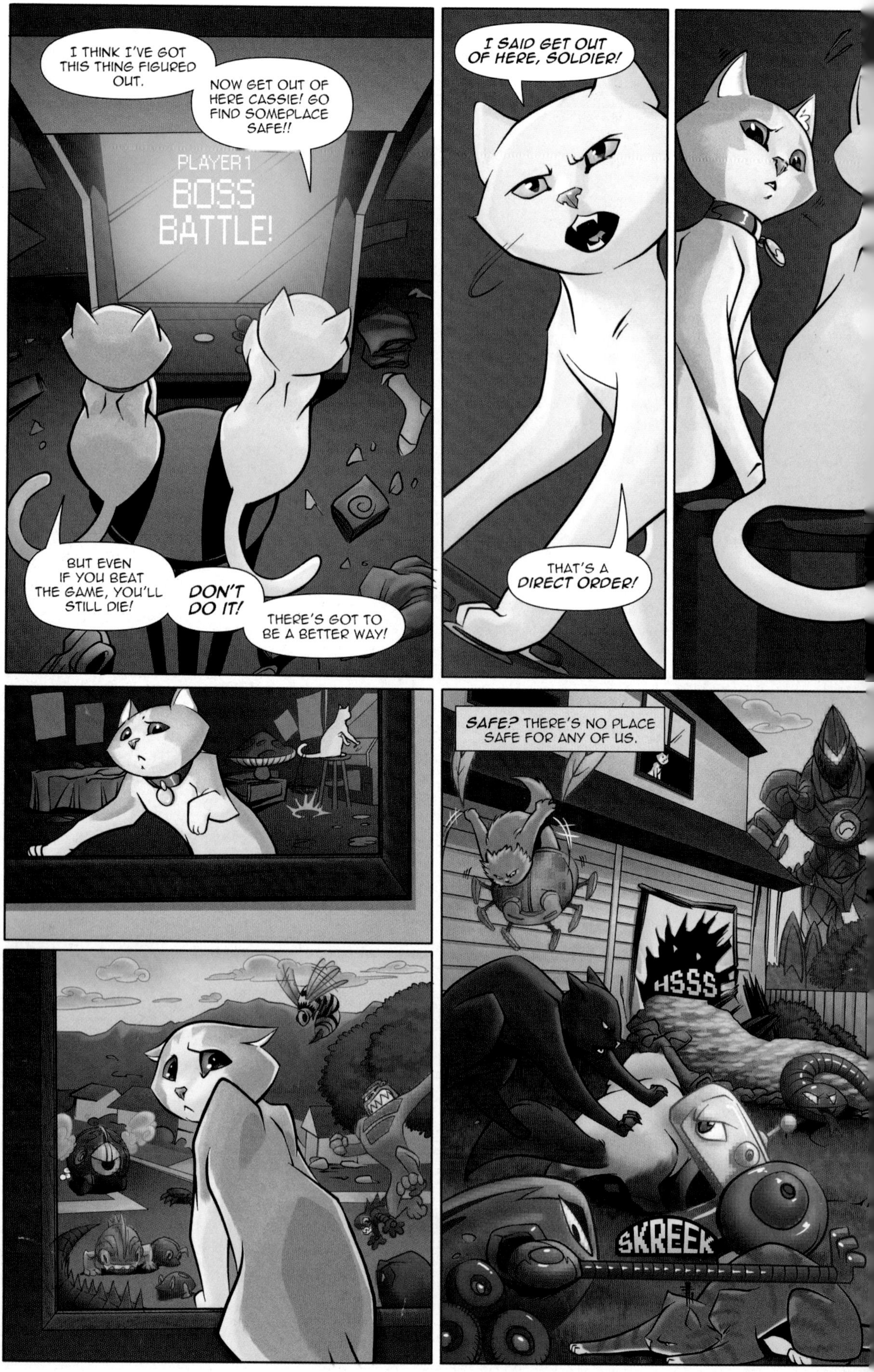
I THINK I'VE GOT THIS THING FIGURED OUT.
NOW GET OUT OF HERE CASSIE! GO FIND SOMEPLACE SAFE!!
PLAYER1
BOSS BATTLE!
BUT EVEN IF YOU BEAT THE GAME, YOU'LL STILL DIE!
DON'T DO IT!
THERE'S GOT TO BE A BETTER WAY!
I SAID GET OUT OF HERE, SOLDIER!
THAT'S A DIRECT ORDER!
SAFE? THERE'S NO PLACE SAFE FOR ANY OF US.
HSSS
SKREEK

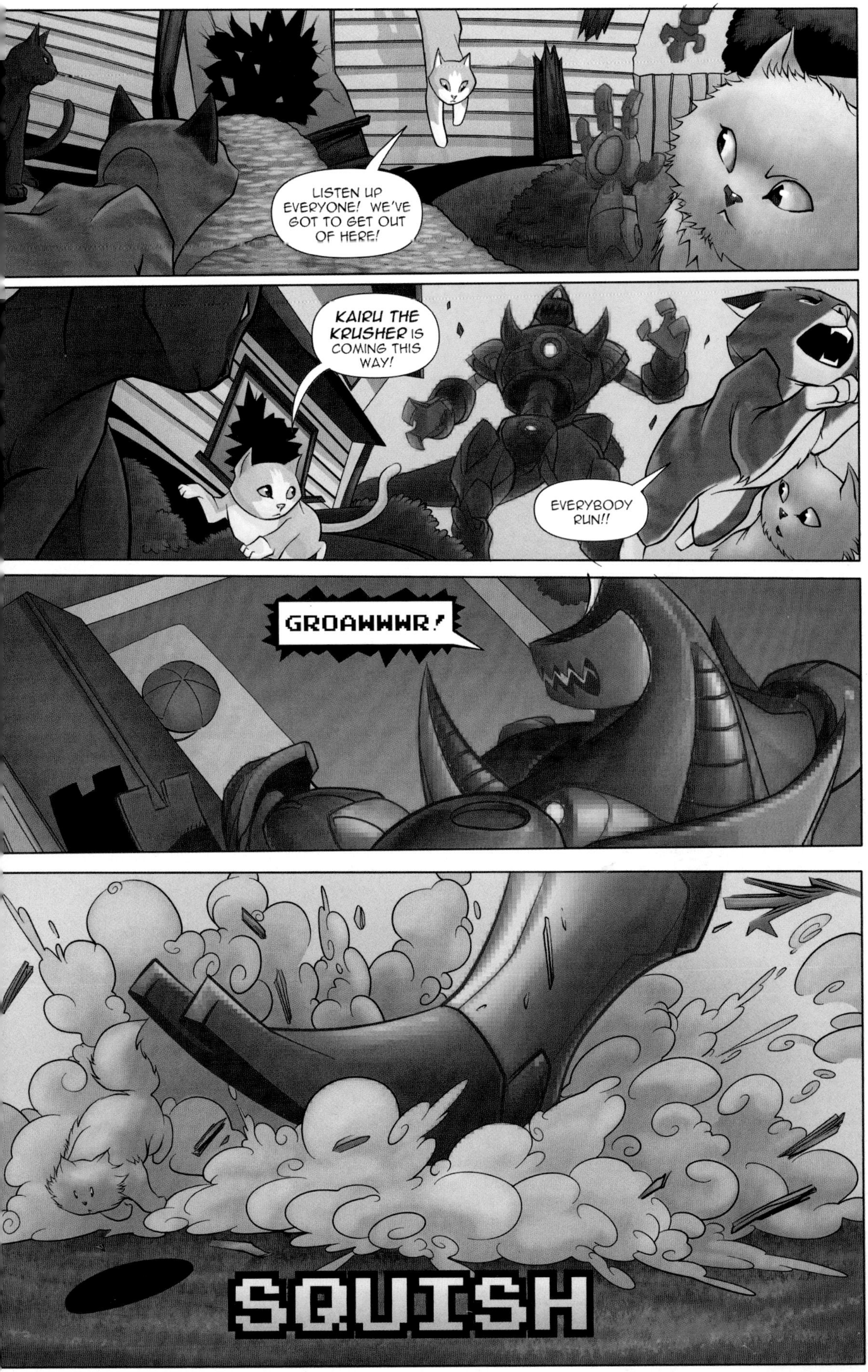
LISTEN UP EVERYONE! WE'VE GOT TO GET OUT OF HERE!
KAIRU THE KRUSHER IS COMING THIS WAY!
EVERYBODY RUN!!
GROAWWWR!
SQUISH

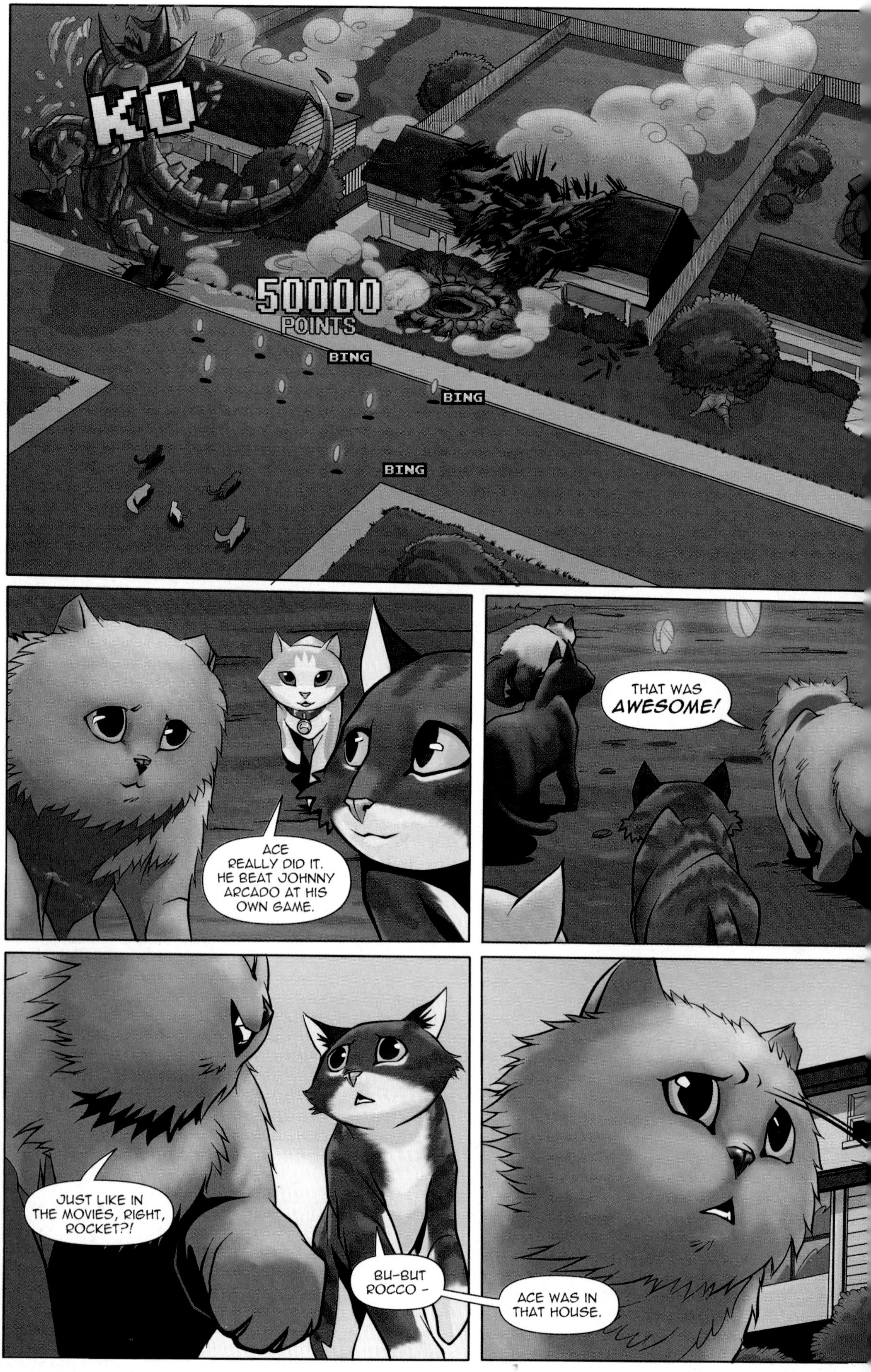
KO
50000 POINTS
BING
BING
BING
ACE REALLY DID IT. HE BEAT JOHNNY ARCADO AT HIS OWN GAME.
THAT WAS AWESOME!
JUST LIKE IN THE MOVIES, RIGHT, ROCKET?!
BU-BUT ROCCO -
ACE WAS IN THAT HOUSE.

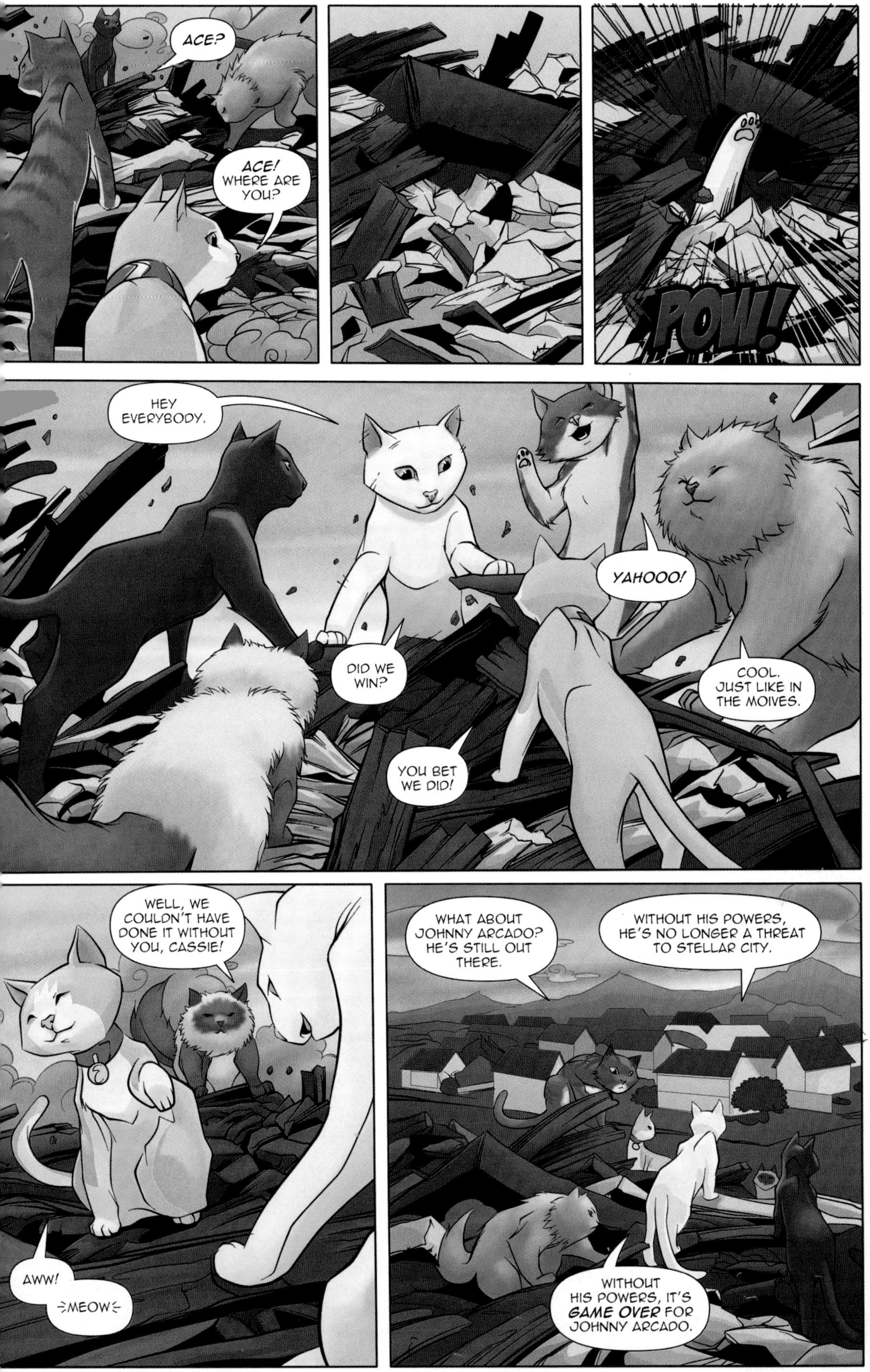
ACE?
ACE! WHERE ARE YOU?
POW!
HEY EVERYBODY.
YAHOOO!
DID WE WIN?
COOL. JUST LIKE IN THE MOIVES.
YOU BET WE DID!
WELL, WE COULDN'T HAVE DONE IT WITHOUT YOU, CASSIE!
AWW!
MEOW
WHAT ABOUT JOHNNY ARCADO? HE'S STILL OUT THERE.
WITHOUT HIS POWERS, HE'S NO LONGER A THREAT TO STELLAR CITY.
WITHOUT HIS POWERS, IT'S GAME OVER FOR JOHNNY ARCADO.

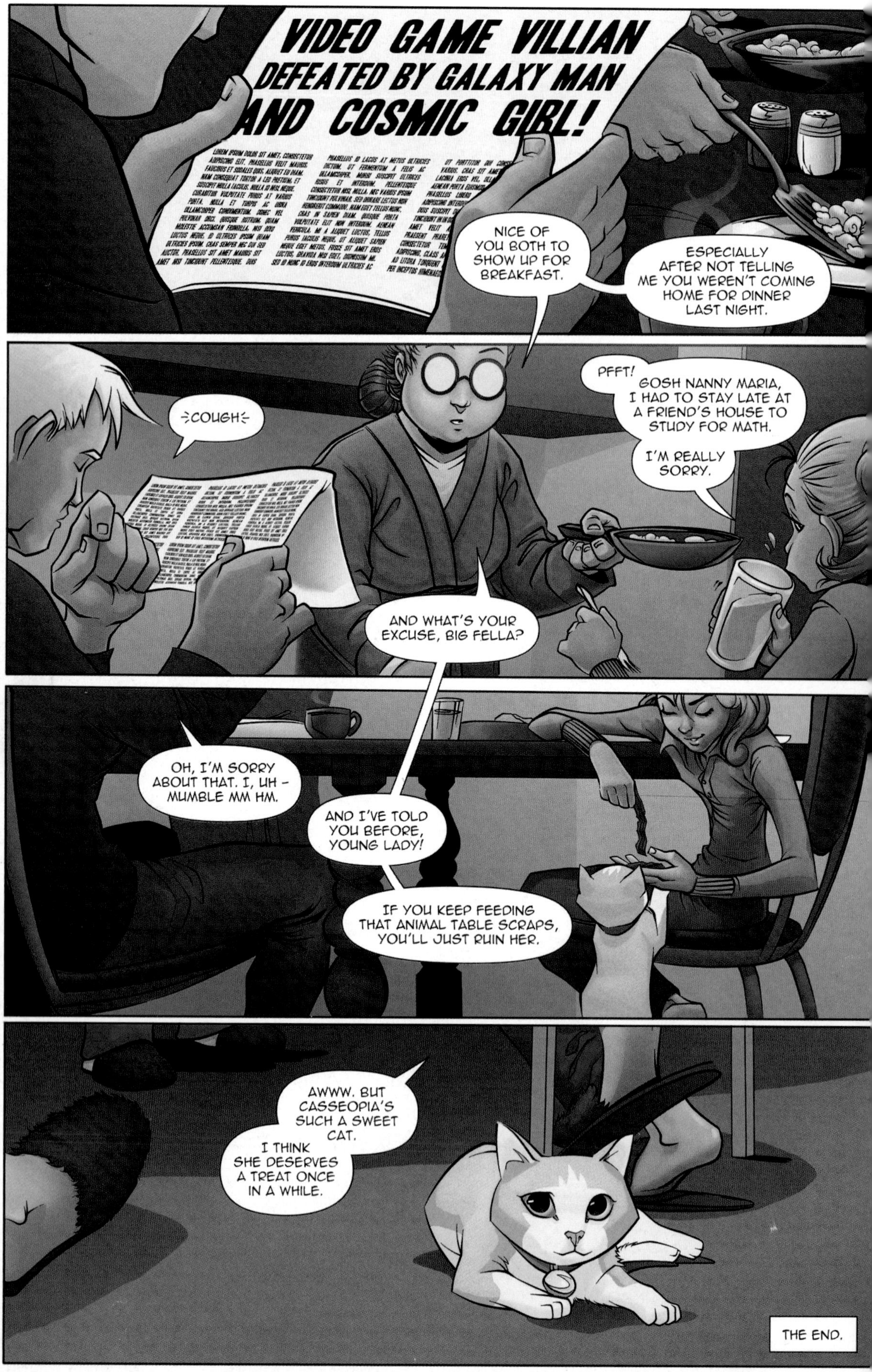
VIDEO GAME VILLIAN
DEFEATED BY GALAXY MAN
AND COSMIC GIRL!
NICE OF YOU BOTH TO SHOW UP FOR BREAKFAST.
ESPECIALLY AFTER NOT TELLING ME YOU WEREN'T COMING HOME FOR DINNER LAST NIGHT.
COUGH
PFFT!
GOSH NANNY MARIA, I HAD TO STAY LATE AT A FRIEND'S HOUSE TO STUDY FOR MATH.
I'M REALLY SORRY.
AND WHAT'S YOUR EXCUSE, BIG FELLA?
OH, I'M SORRY ABOUT THAT. I, UH - MUMBLE MM HM.
AND I'VE TOLD YOU BEFORE, YOUNG LADY!
IF YOU KEEP FEEDING THAT ANIMAL TABLE SCRAPS, YOU'LL JUST RUIN HER.
AWWW. BUT CASSEOPIA'S SUCH A SWEET CAT.
I THINK SHE DESERVES A TREAT ONCE IN A WHILE.
THE END.

HEROCHAT

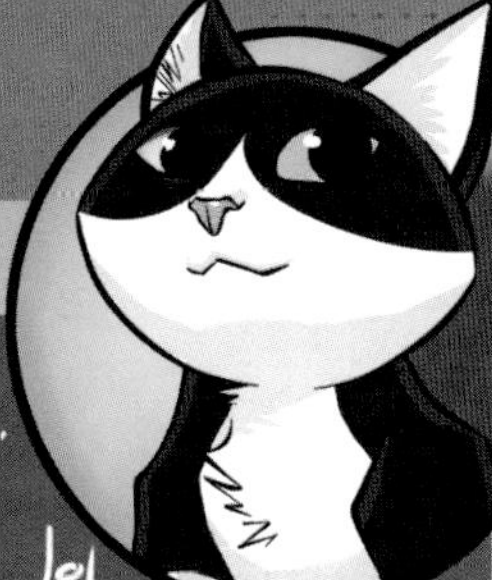

JOHNNY SURE DID CAUSE A LOT OF PROBLEMS! GOOD THING MY LITTLE SIS WAS THERE TO HELP. LOOKS LIKE ACE WILL NEED TO TEACH HER A FEW THINGS. TILL NEXT TIME CATS!

write to us @ kyle@galacticquest.com

-Bandit-

BONUS ART!

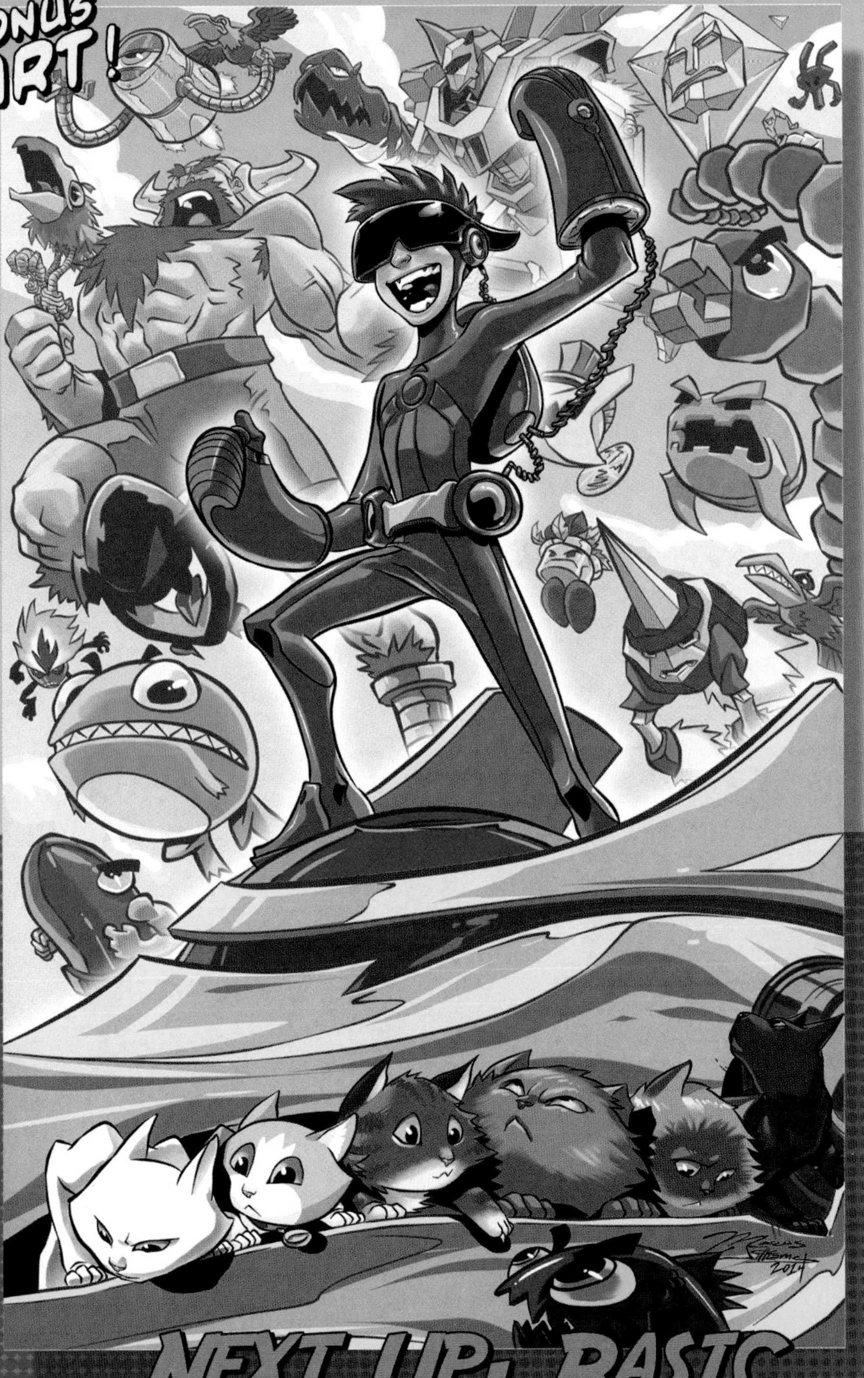

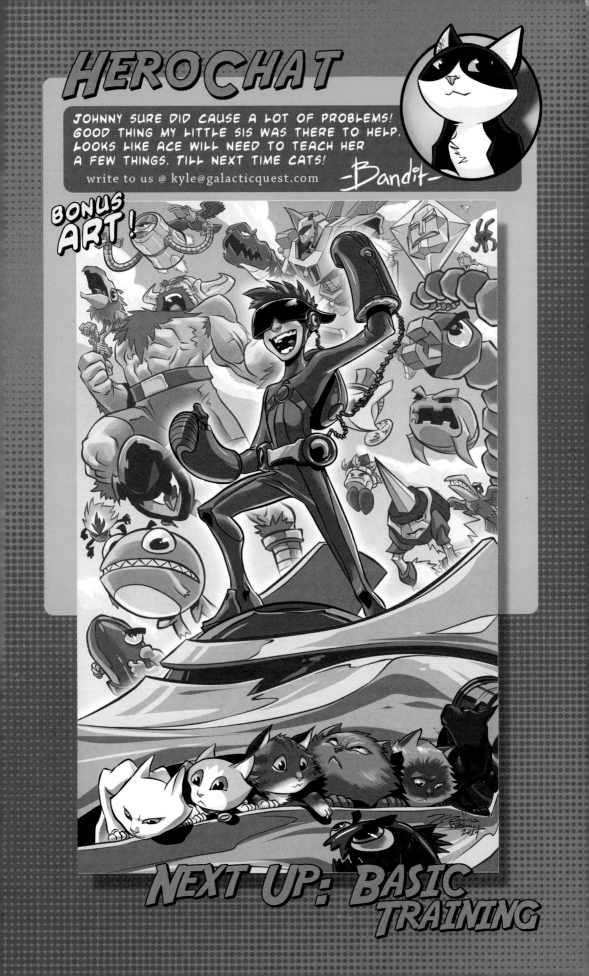

NEXT UP: BASIC TRAINING

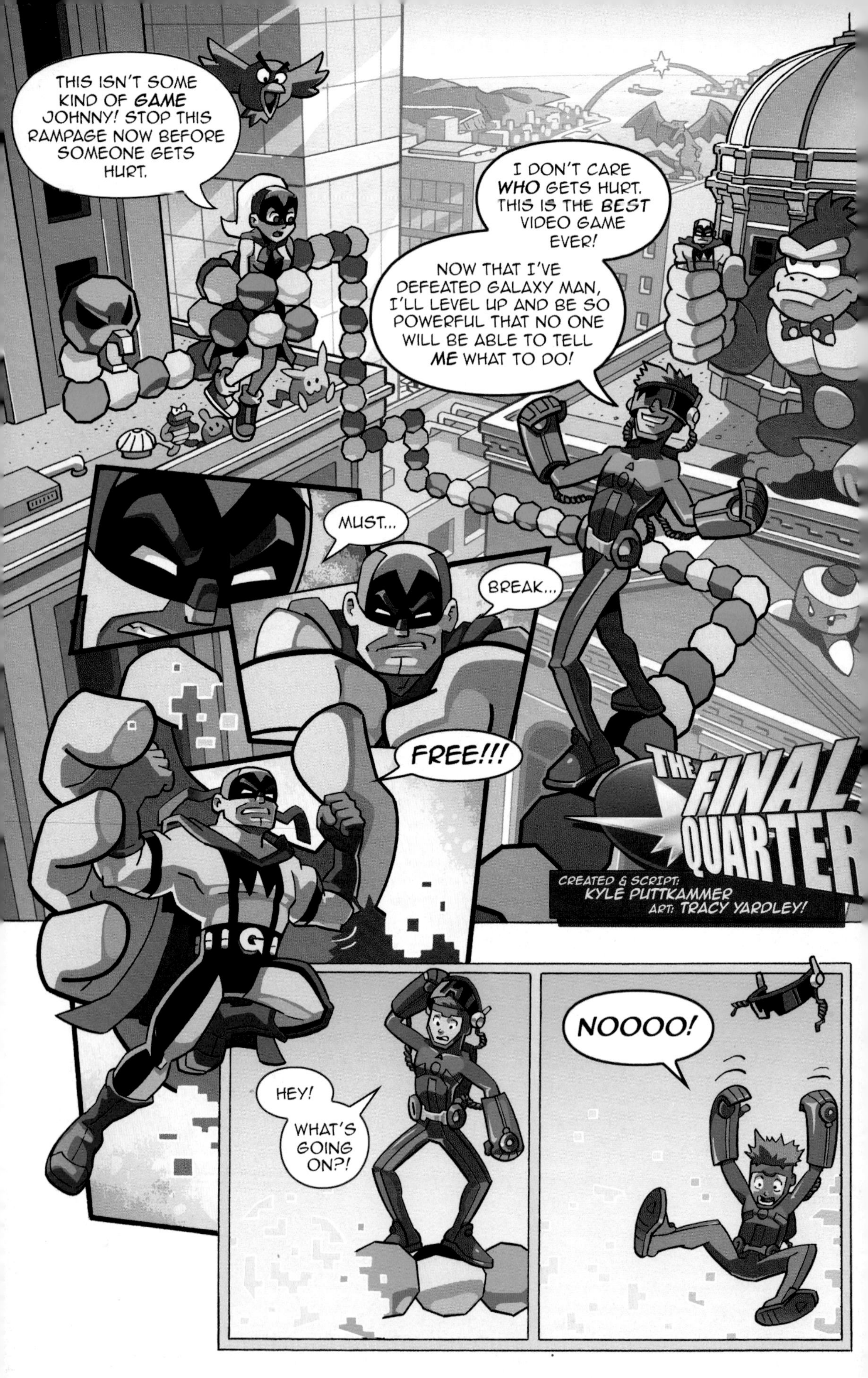
THIS ISN'T SOME KIND OF GAME JOHNNY! STOP THIS RAMPAGE NOW BEFORE SOMEONE GETS HURT.
I DON'T CARE WHO GETS HURT. THIS IS THE BEST VIDEO GAME EVER!
NOW THAT I'VE DEFEATED GALAXY MAN, I'LL LEVEL UP AND BE SO POWERFUL THAT NO ONE WILL BE ABLE TO TELL ME WHAT TO DO!
MUST...
BREAK...
FREE!!!
THE FINAL QUARTER
CREATED & SCRIPT: KYLE PUTTKAMMER
ART: TRACY YARDLEY!
HEY!
WHAT'S GOING ON?!
NOOOO!

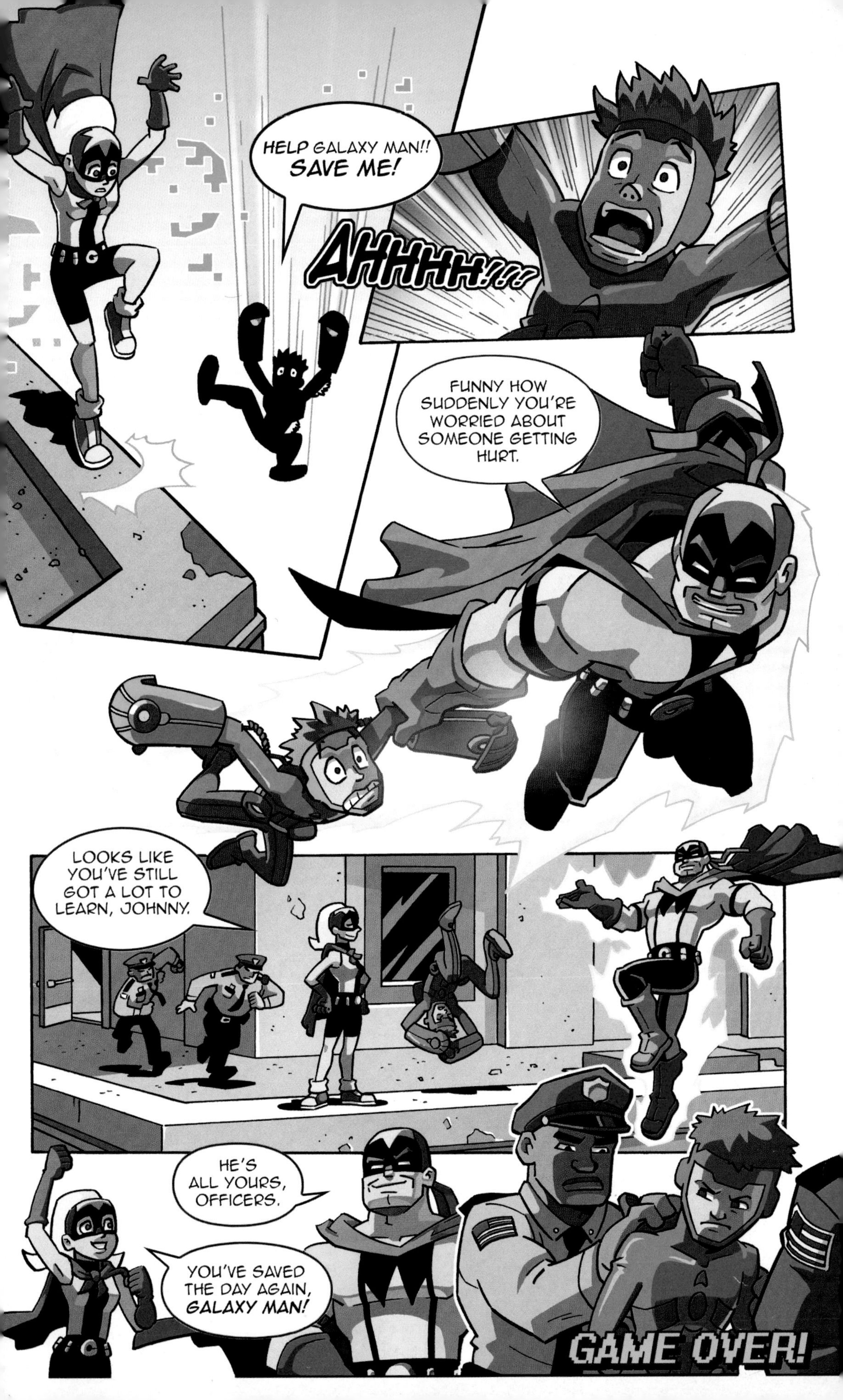

HELP GALAXY MAN!! SAVE ME!
AHHHH!?!?
FUNNY HOW SUDDENLY YOU'RE WORRIED ABOUT SOMEONE GETTING HURT.
LOOKS LIKE YOU'VE STILL GOT A LOT TO LEARN, JOHNNY.
HE'S ALL YOURS, OFFICERS.
YOU'VE SAVED THE DAY AGAIN, GALAXY MAN!
GAME OVER!

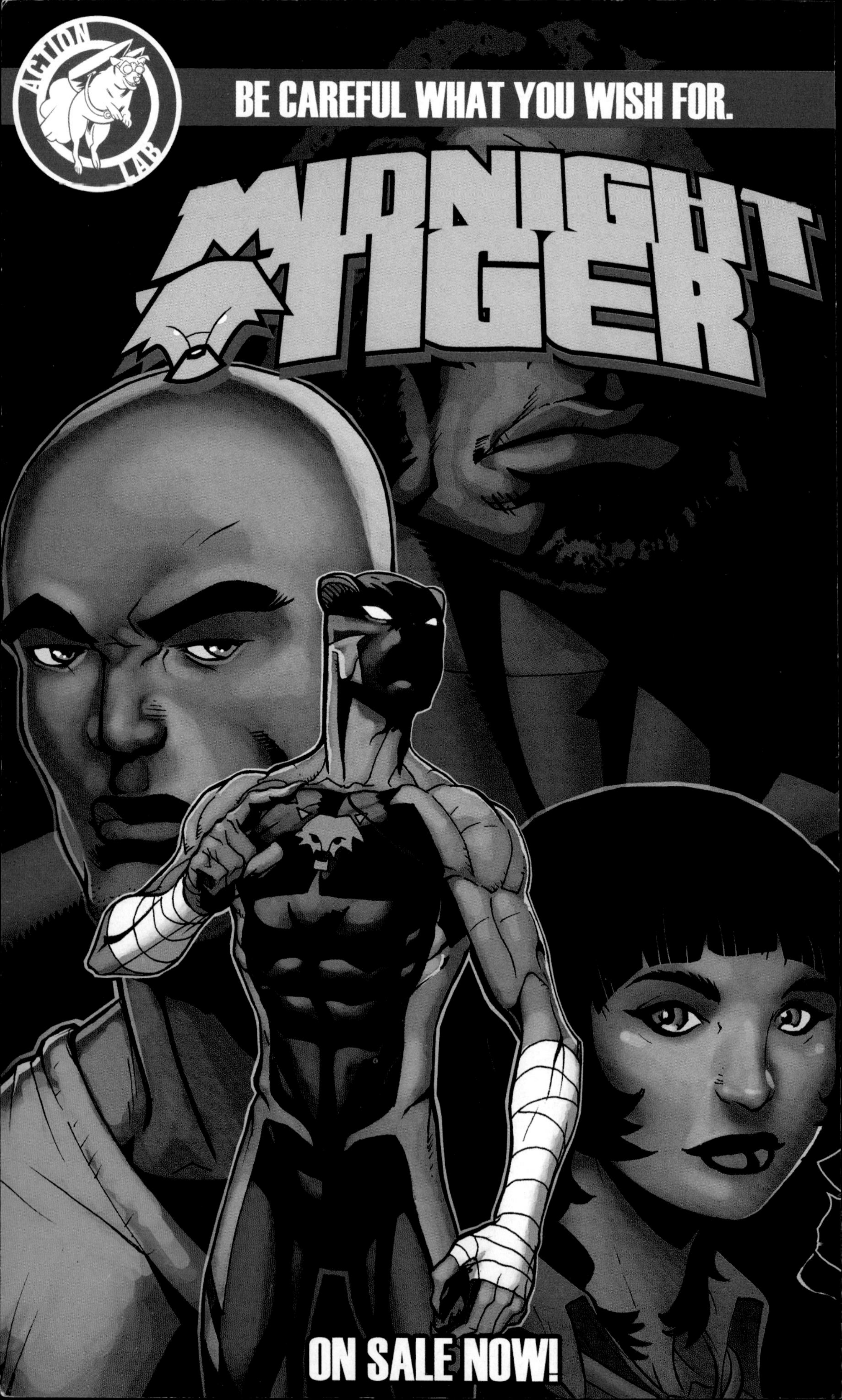

ACTION LAB
BE CAREFUL WHAT YOU WISH FOR.
MIDNIGHT TIGER
ON SALE NOW!

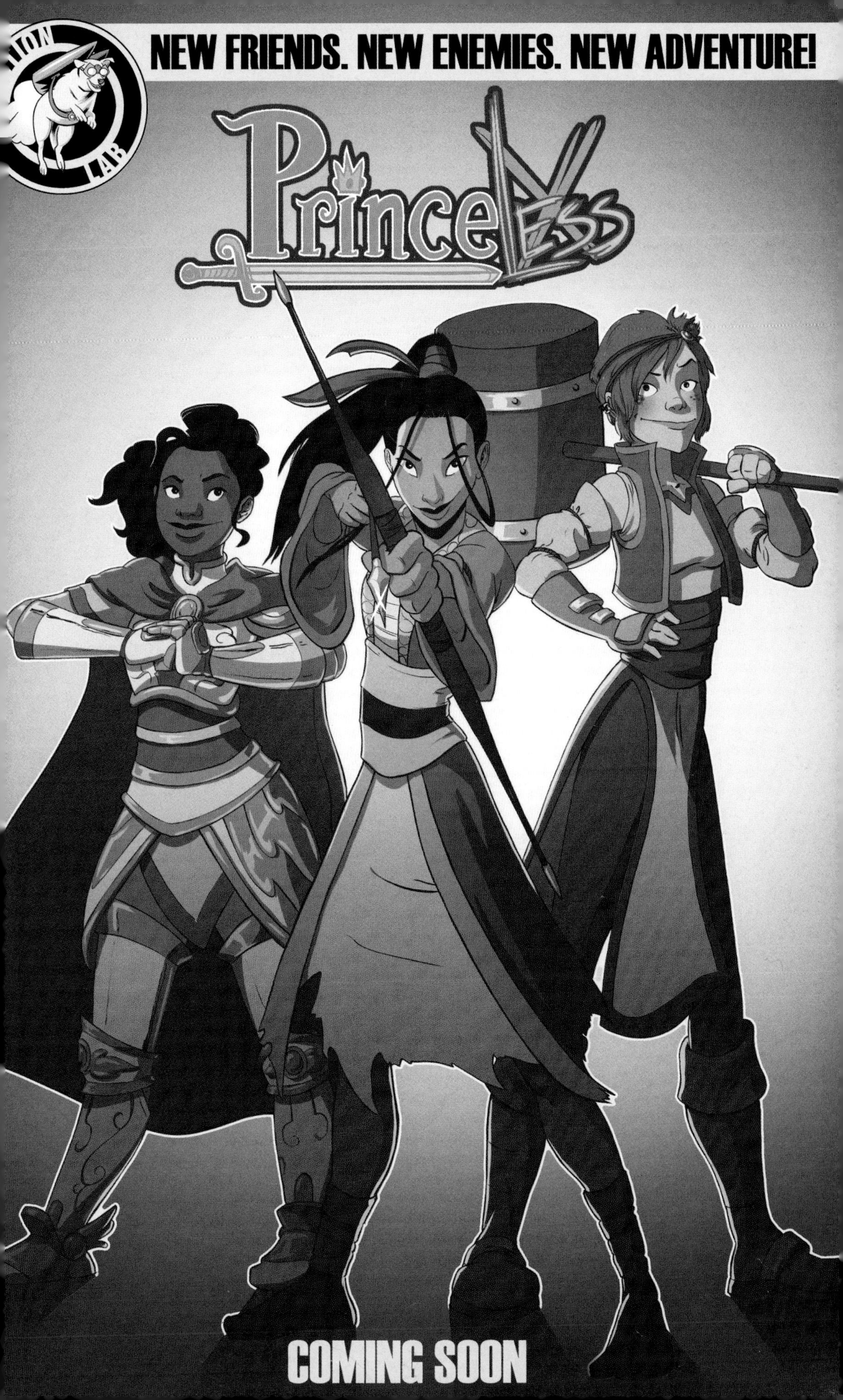
NEW FRIENDS. NEW ENEMIES. NEW ADVENTURE!
Princeless
COMING SOON

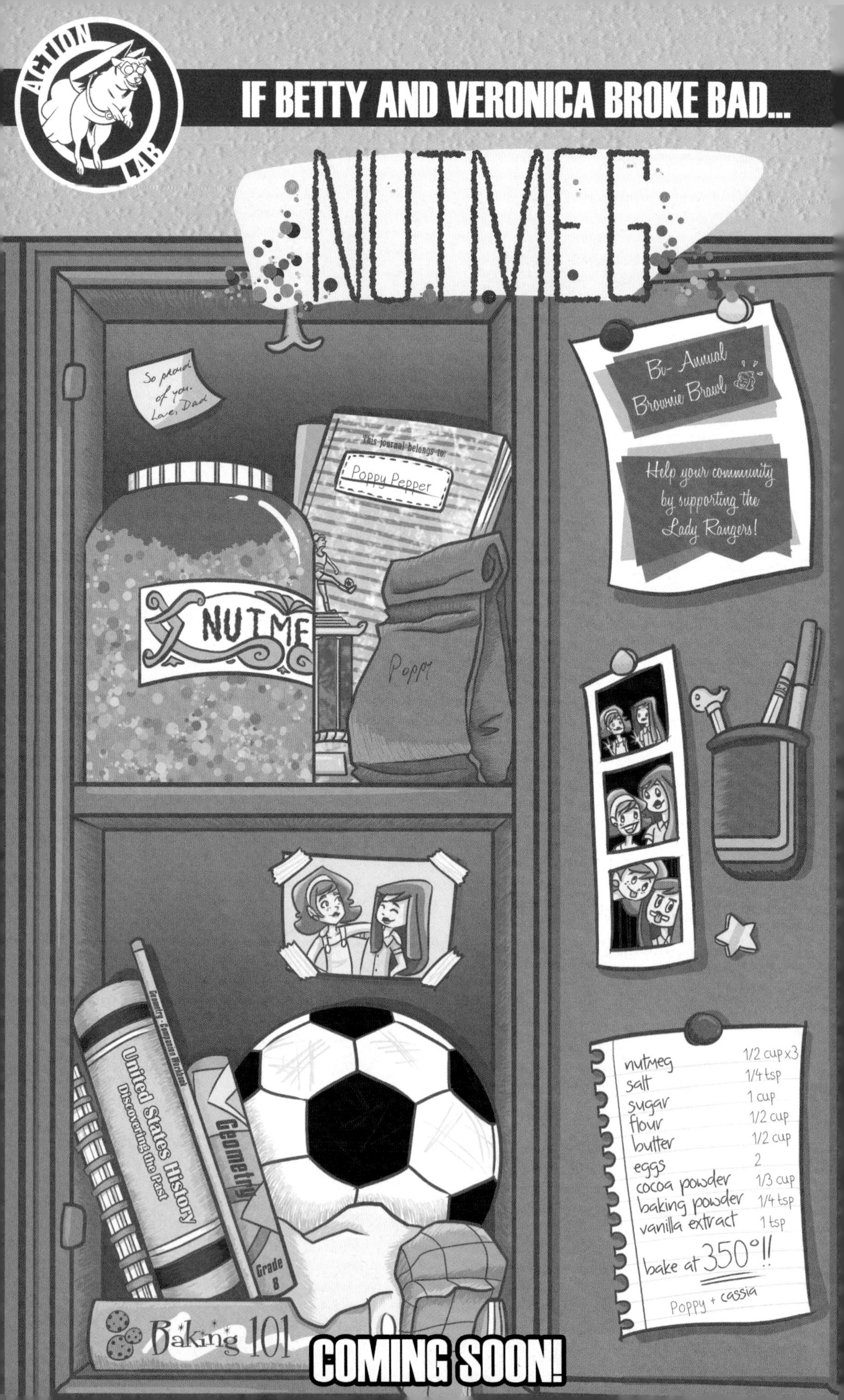
ACTION LAB
IF BETTY AND VERONICA BROKE BAD...
NUTMEG
So proud of you. Love, Dad
This journal belongs to:
Poppy Pepper
NUTME
Poppy
Bi-Annual Brownie Brawl
Help your community by supporting the Lady Rangers!
Geometry · Companion Workbook
United States History
Discovering the Past
Geometry
Grade 8
Baking 101
nutmeg 1/2 cup x3
salt 1/4 tsp
sugar 1 cup
flour 1/2 cup
butter 1/2 cup
eggs 2
cocoa powder 1/3 cup
baking powder 1/4 tsp
vanilla extract 1 tsp
bake at 350°!!
Poppy + cassia
COMING SOON!

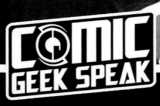

THE WORLD'S MIGHTIEST HERO.

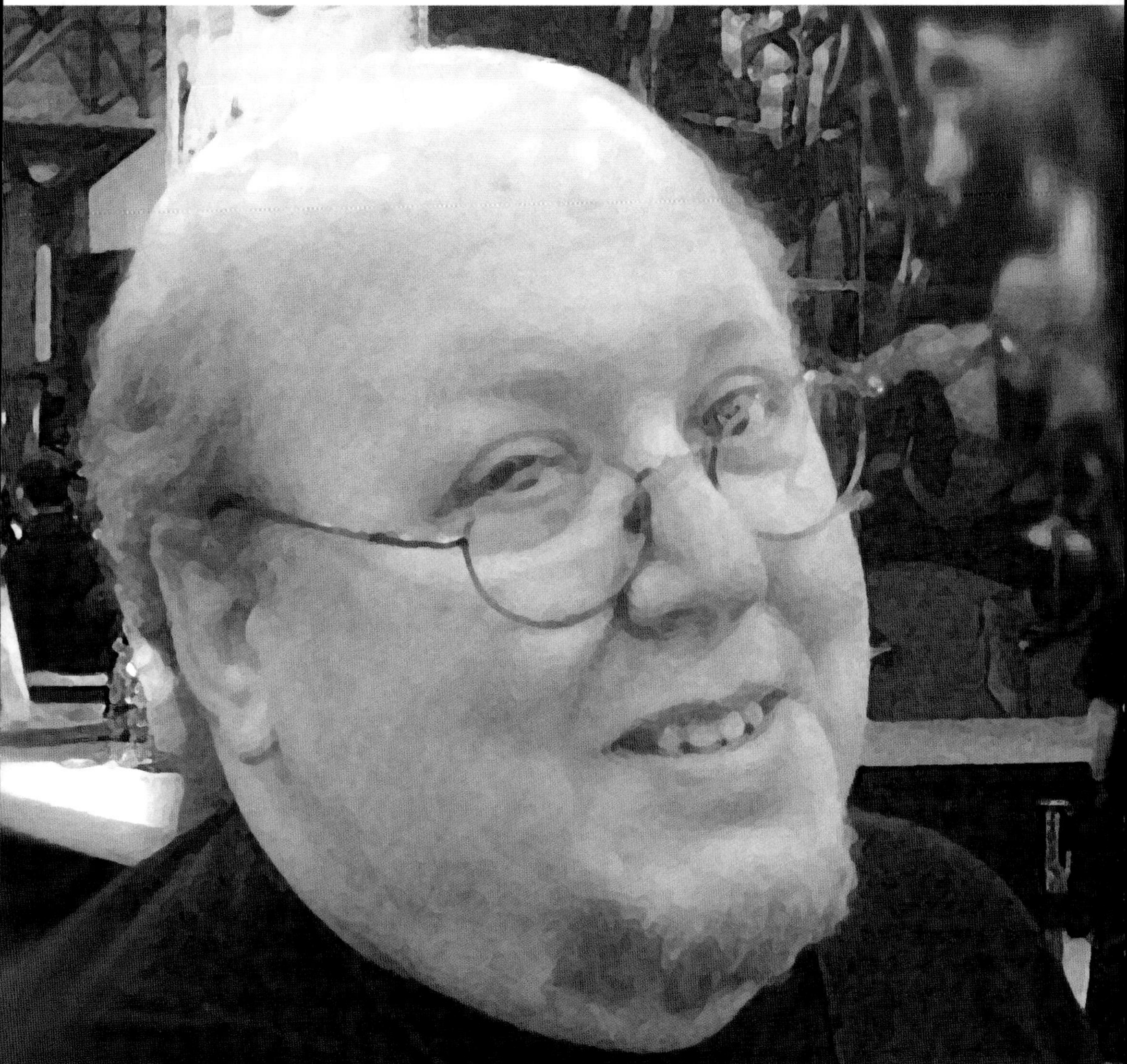

COMIC GEEK SPEAK

JAMIE DALLESSANDRO

1966 - 2014

READ MORE NOW

Hero Cats - Action Lab
www.actionlabcomics.com

00211

7 00465 77241 1

ACTIONLABCOMICS.COM

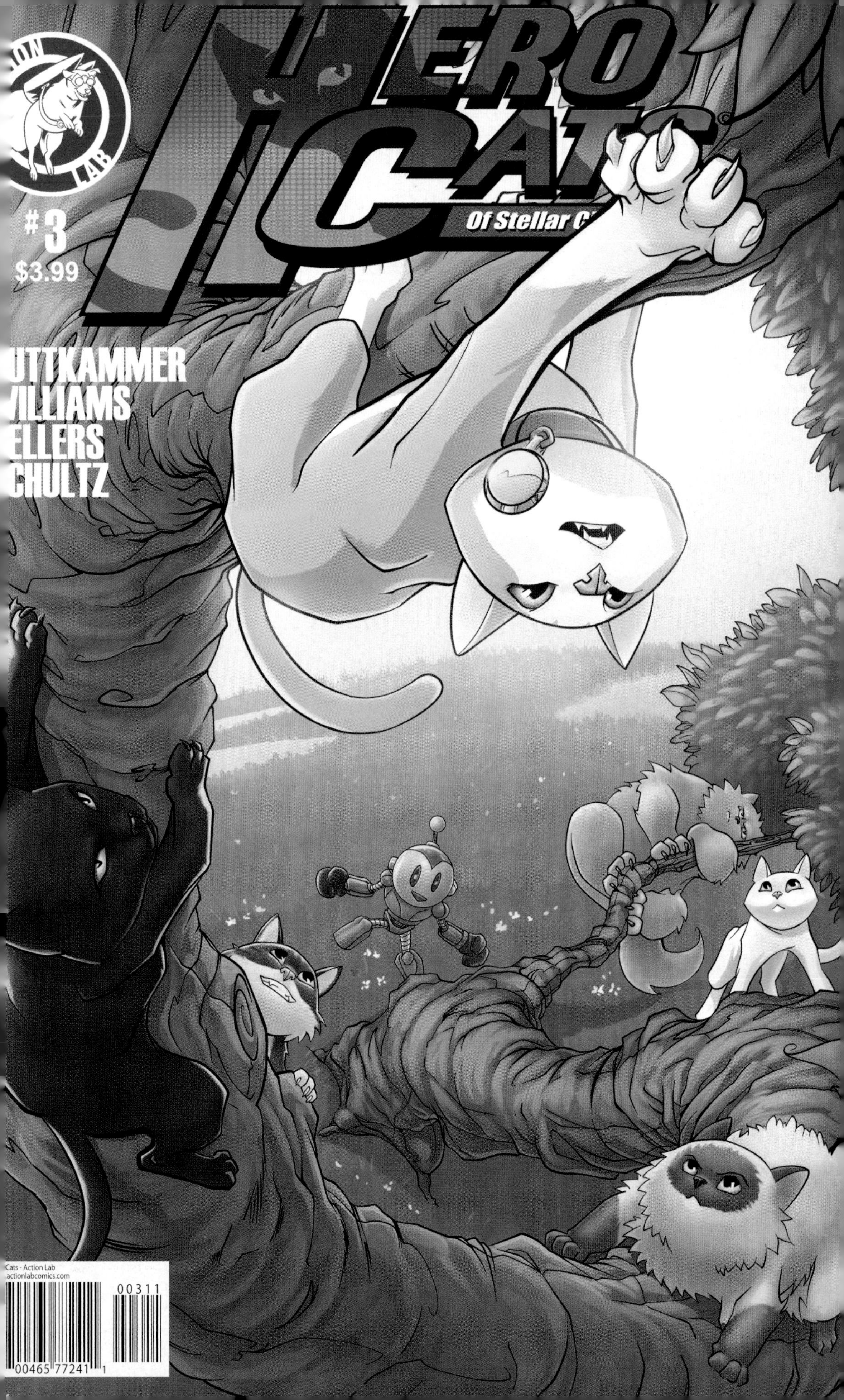

ERO
CAT
Of Stellar C
#3
$3.99
UTTKAMMER
VILLIAMS
ELLERS
CHULTZ
Cats - Action Lab
actionlabcomics.com
00311
00465 77241 1

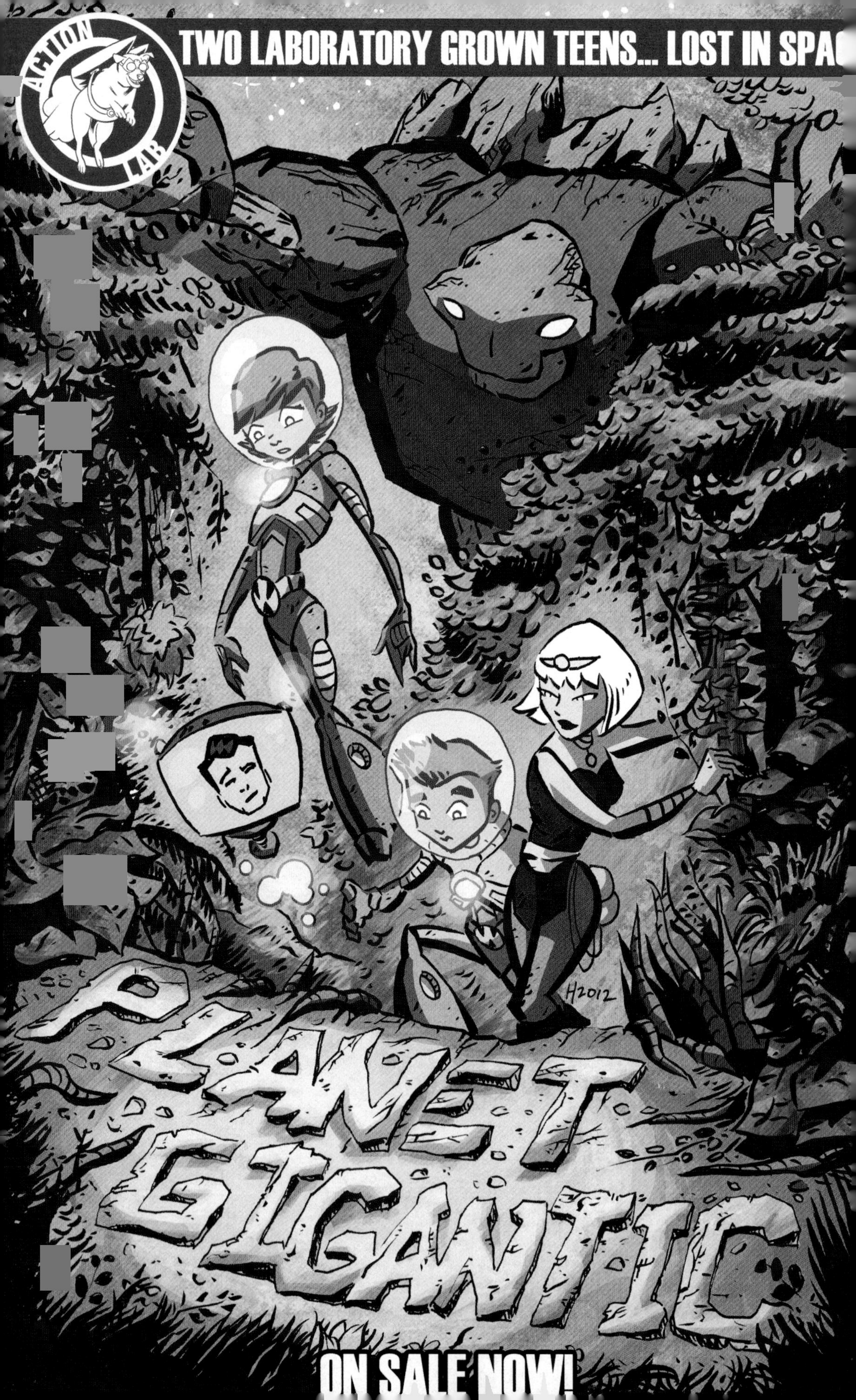
ACTION LAB
TWO LABORATORY GROWN TEENS... LOST IN SPAC
H2012
PLANET GIGANTIC
ON SALE NOW!

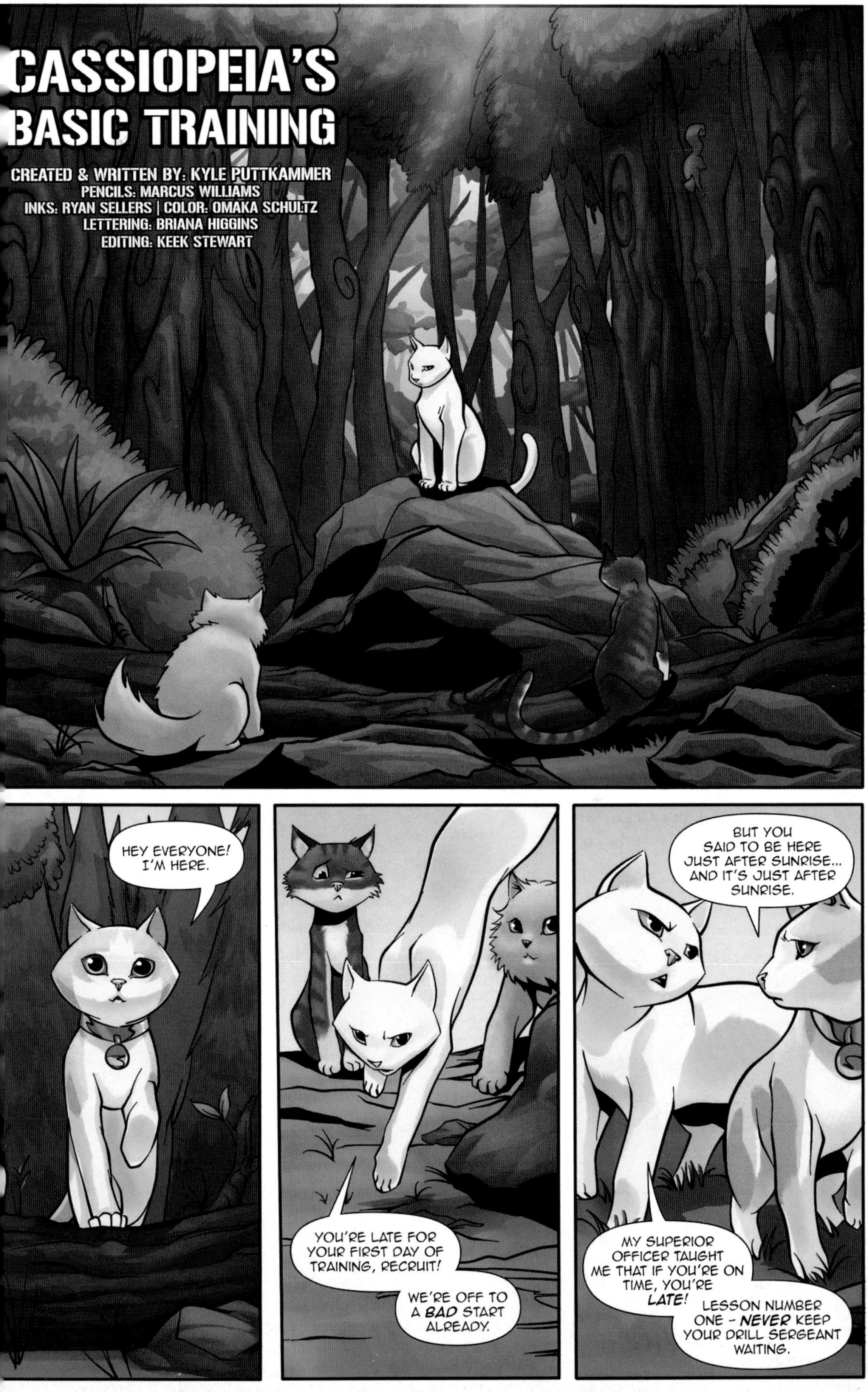
CASSIOPEIA'S BASIC TRAINING
CREATED & WRITTEN BY: KYLE PUTTKAMMER
PENCILS: MARCUS WILLIAMS
INKS: RYAN SELLERS | COLOR: OMAKA SCHULTZ
LETTERING: BRIANA HIGGINS
EDITING: KEEK STEWART
HEY EVERYONE! I'M HERE.
YOU'RE LATE FOR YOUR FIRST DAY OF TRAINING, RECRUIT!
WE'RE OFF TO A ***BAD*** START ALREADY.
BUT YOU SAID TO BE HERE JUST AFTER SUNRISE... AND IT'S JUST AFTER SUNRISE.
MY SUPERIOR OFFICER TAUGHT ME THAT IF YOU'RE ON TIME, YOU'RE ***LATE!***
LESSON NUMBER ONE - ***NEVER*** KEEP YOUR DRILL SERGEANT WAITING.

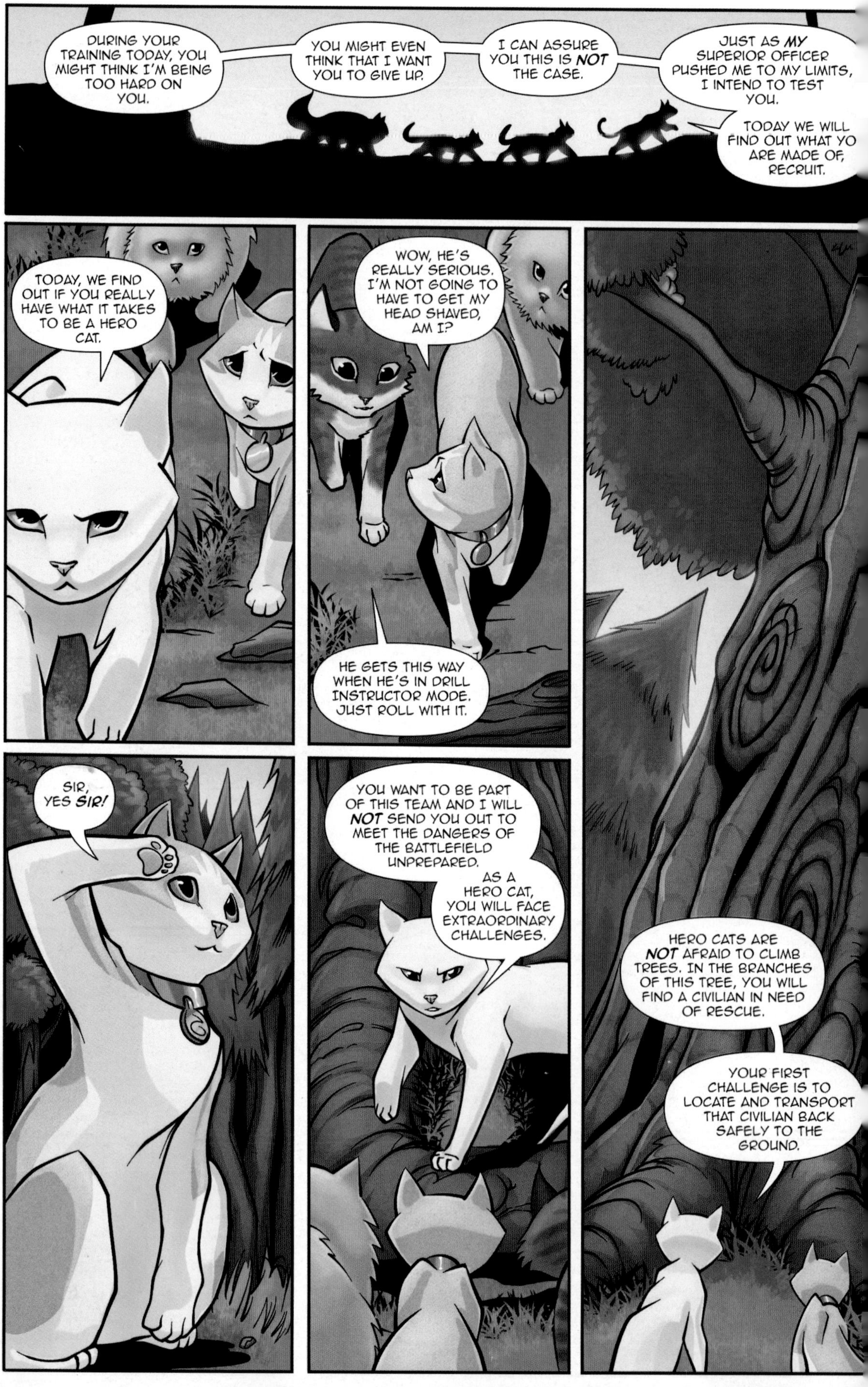
DURING YOUR TRAINING TODAY, YOU MIGHT THINK I'M BEING TOO HARD ON YOU.
YOU MIGHT EVEN THINK THAT I WANT YOU TO GIVE UP.
I CAN ASSURE YOU THIS IS NOT THE CASE.
JUST AS MY SUPERIOR OFFICER PUSHED ME TO MY LIMITS, I INTEND TO TEST YOU.
TODAY WE WILL FIND OUT WHAT YO ARE MADE OF, RECRUIT.
TODAY, WE FIND OUT IF YOU REALLY HAVE WHAT IT TAKES TO BE A HERO CAT.
WOW, HE'S REALLY SERIOUS. I'M NOT GOING TO HAVE TO GET MY HEAD SHAVED, AM I?
HE GETS THIS WAY WHEN HE'S IN DRILL INSTRUCTOR MODE. JUST ROLL WITH IT.
SIR, YES SIR!
YOU WANT TO BE PART OF THIS TEAM AND I WILL NOT SEND YOU OUT TO MEET THE DANGERS OF THE BATTLEFIELD UNPREPARED.
AS A HERO CAT, YOU WILL FACE EXTRAORDINARY CHALLENGES.
HERO CATS ARE NOT AFRAID TO CLIMB TREES. IN THE BRANCHES OF THIS TREE, YOU WILL FIND A CIVILIAN IN NEED OF RESCUE.
YOUR FIRST CHALLENGE IS TO LOCATE AND TRANSPORT THAT CIVILIAN BACK SAFELY TO THE GROUND.

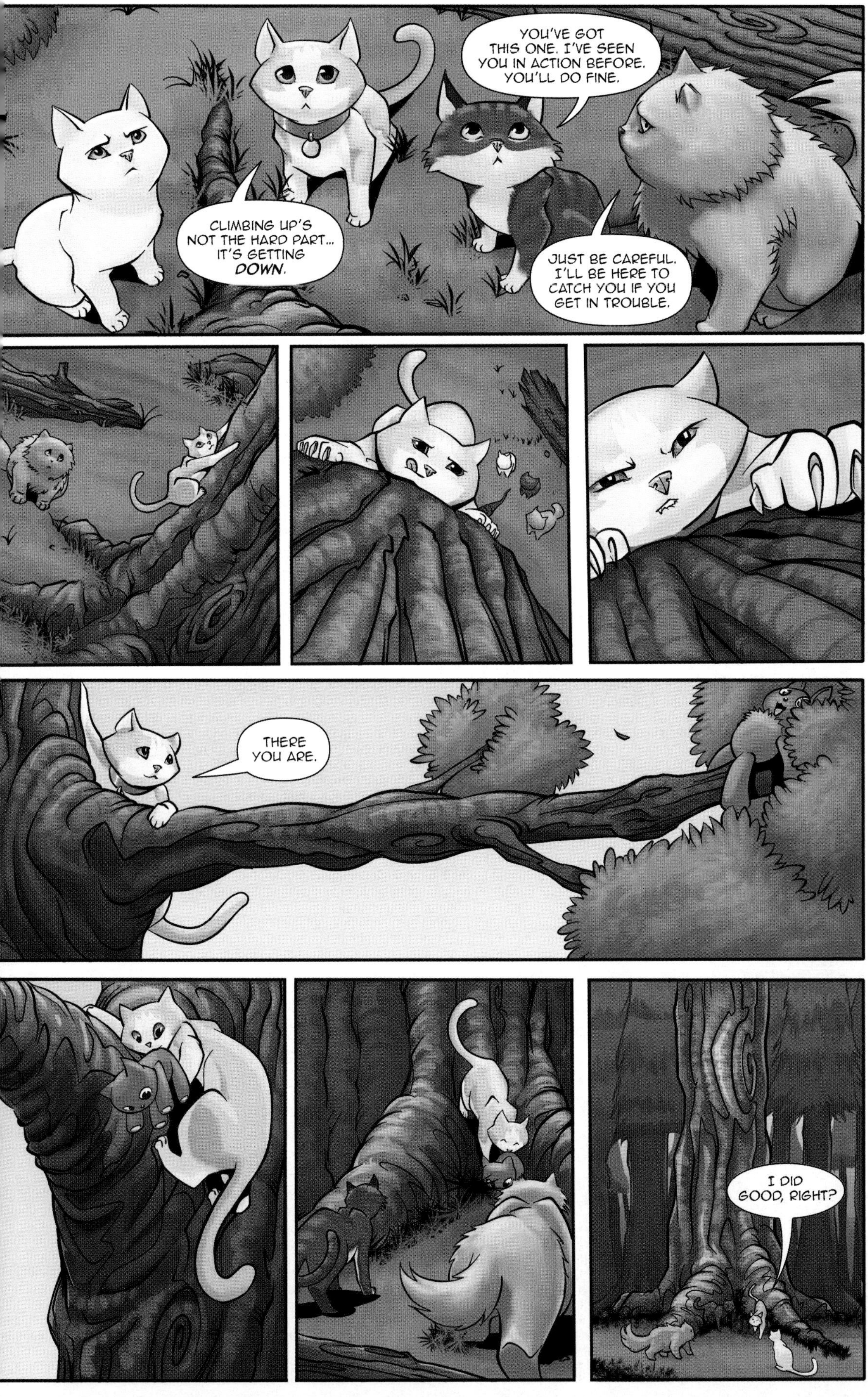
CLIMBING UP'S NOT THE HARD PART... IT'S GETTING DOWN.
YOU'VE GOT THIS ONE. I'VE SEEN YOU IN ACTION BEFORE. YOU'LL DO FINE.
JUST BE CAREFUL. I'LL BE HERE TO CATCH YOU IF YOU GET IN TROUBLE.
THERE YOU ARE.
I DID GOOD, RIGHT?

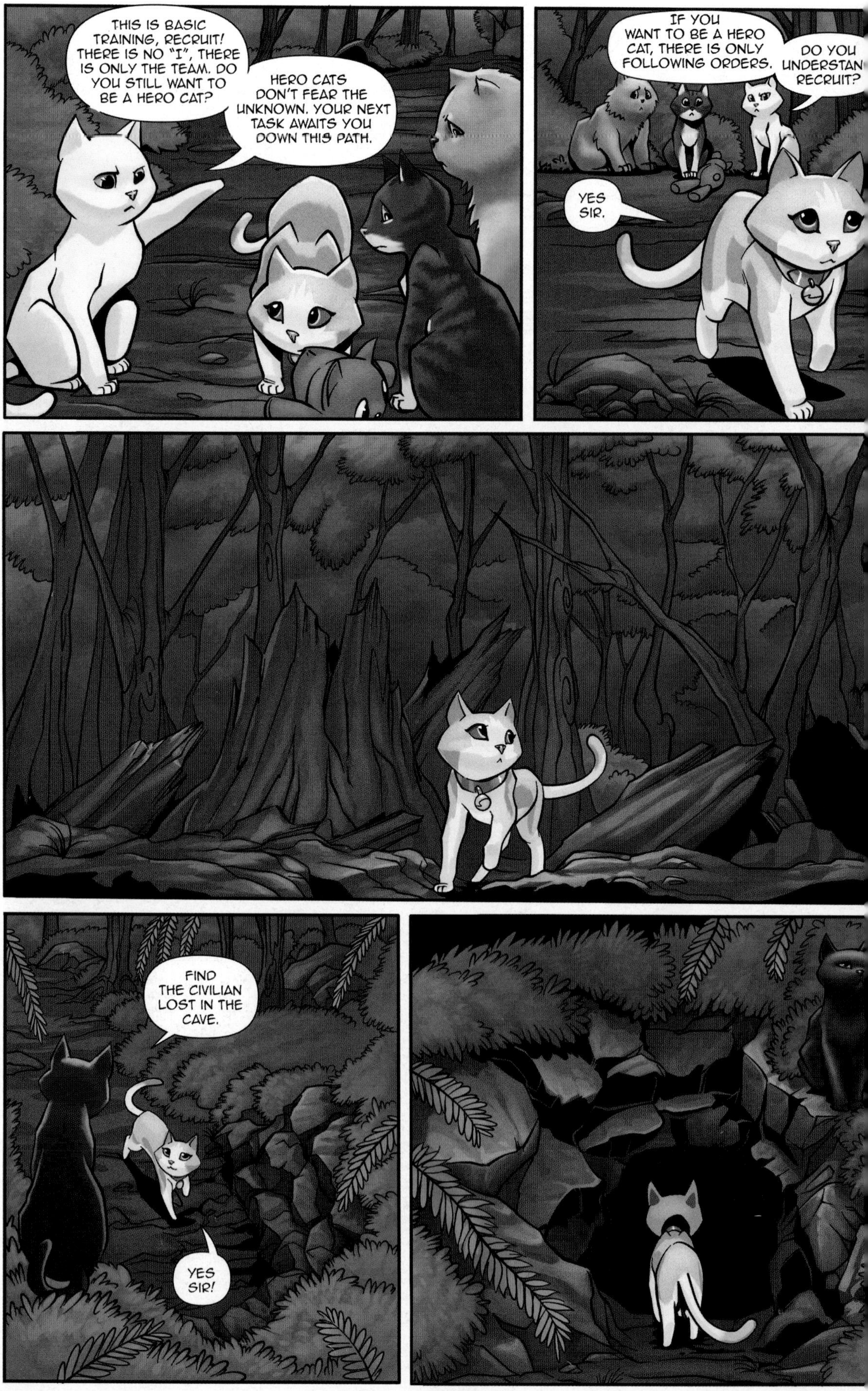

THIS IS BASIC TRAINING, RECRUIT! THERE IS NO "I", THERE IS ONLY THE TEAM. DO YOU STILL WANT TO BE A HERO CAT?
HERO CATS DON'T FEAR THE UNKNOWN. YOUR NEXT TASK AWAITS YOU DOWN THIS PATH.
IF YOU WANT TO BE A HERO CAT, THERE IS ONLY FOLLOWING ORDERS.
DO YOU UNDERSTAN RECRUIT?
YES SIR.
FIND THE CIVILIAN LOST IN THE CAVE.
YES SIR!

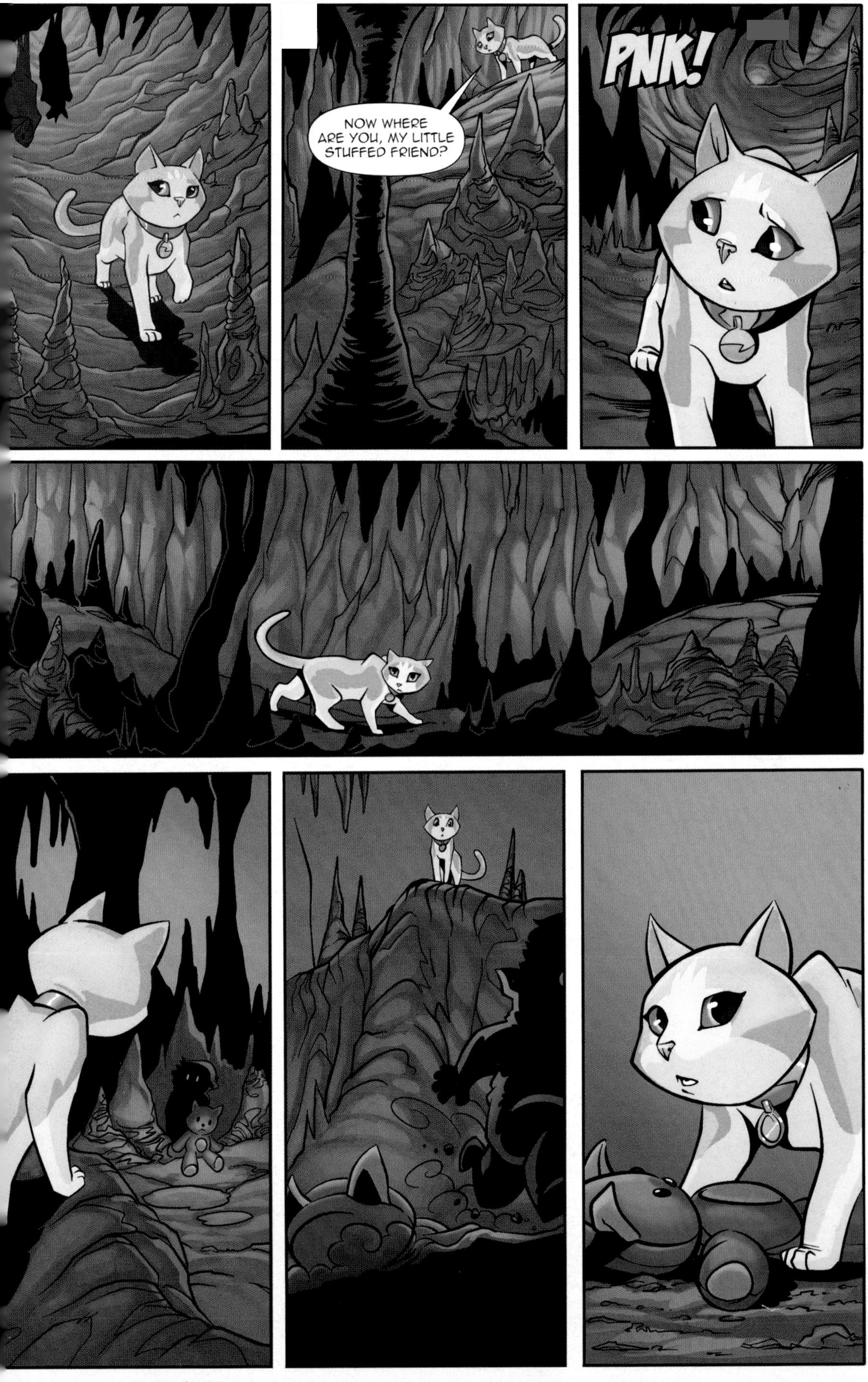
NOW WHERE ARE YOU, MY LITTLE STUFFED FRIEND?
PNK!

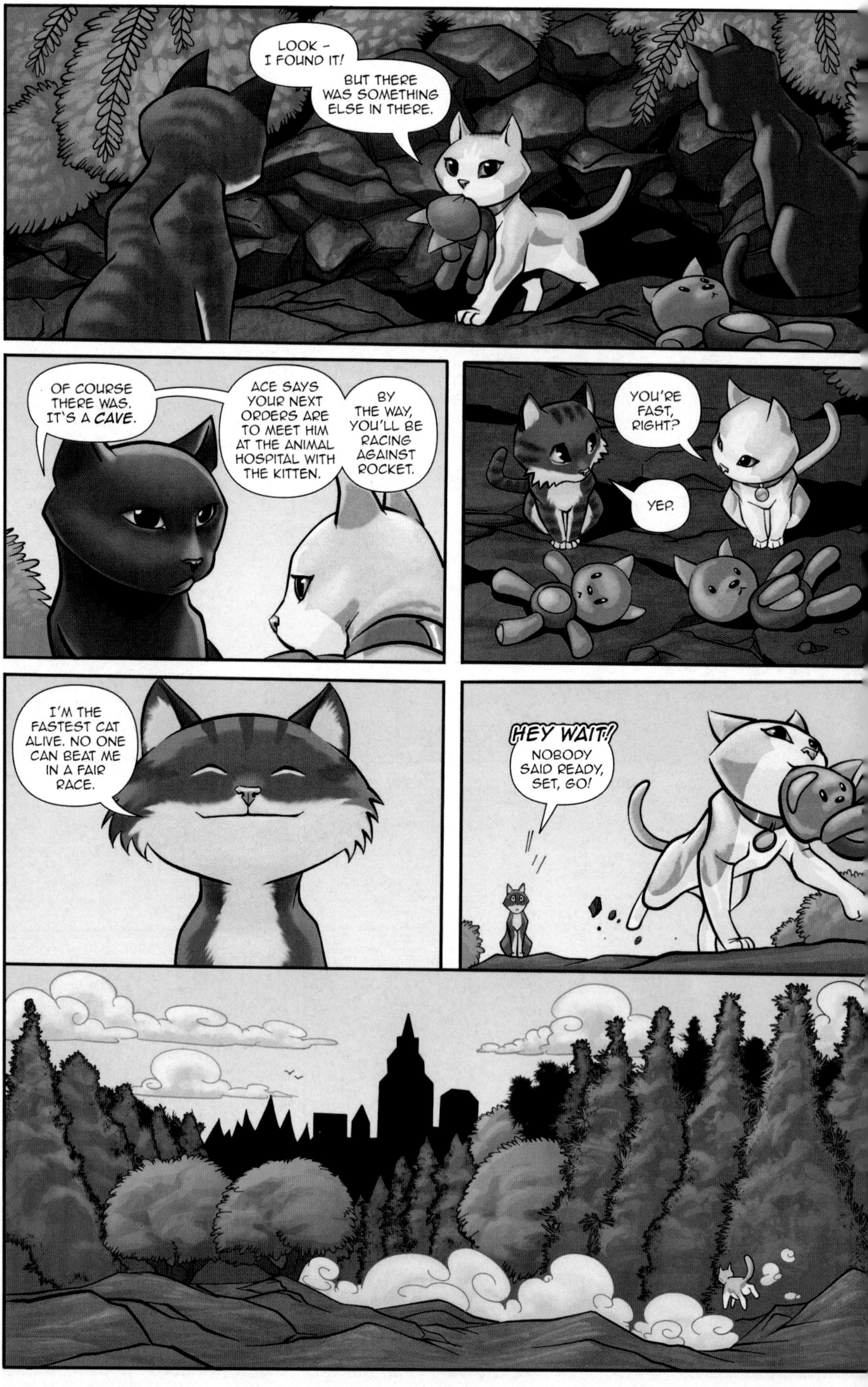
LOOK - I FOUND IT!
BUT THERE WAS SOMETHING ELSE IN THERE.
OF COURSE THERE WAS. IT'S A *CAVE*.
ACE SAYS YOUR NEXT ORDERS ARE TO MEET HIM AT THE ANIMAL HOSPITAL WITH THE KITTEN.
BY THE WAY, YOU'LL BE RACING AGAINST ROCKET.
YOU'RE FAST, RIGHT?
YEP.
I'M THE FASTEST CAT ALIVE. NO ONE CAN BEAT ME IN A FAIR RACE.
HEY WAIT!
NOBODY SAID READY, SET, GO!

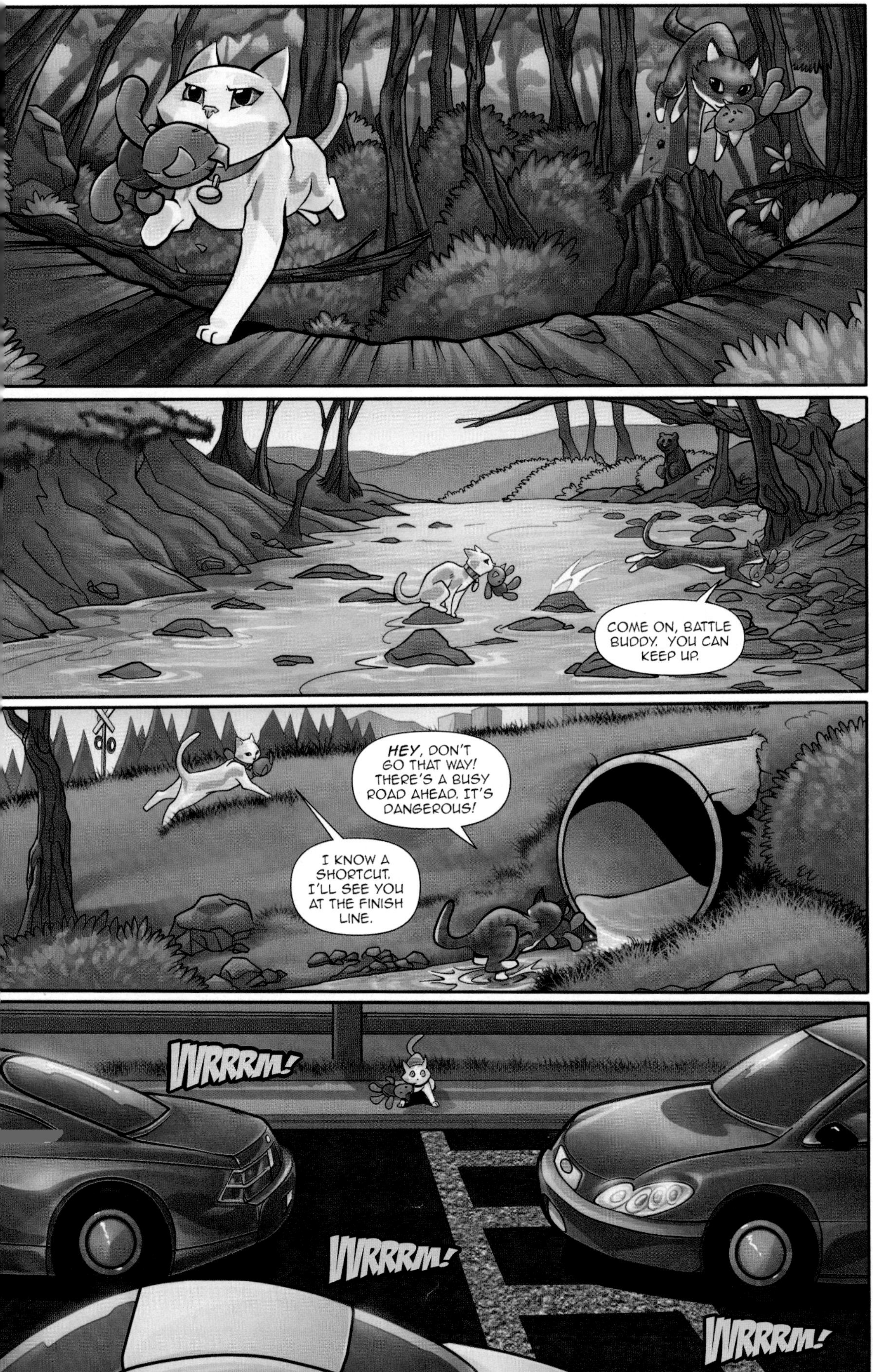
COME ON, BATTLE BUDDY. YOU CAN KEEP UP.
HEY, DON'T GO THAT WAY! THERE'S A BUSY ROAD AHEAD. IT'S DANGEROUS!
I KNOW A SHORTCUT. I'LL SEE YOU AT THE FINISH LINE.
VVRRRM!
VVRRRM!
VVRRRM!

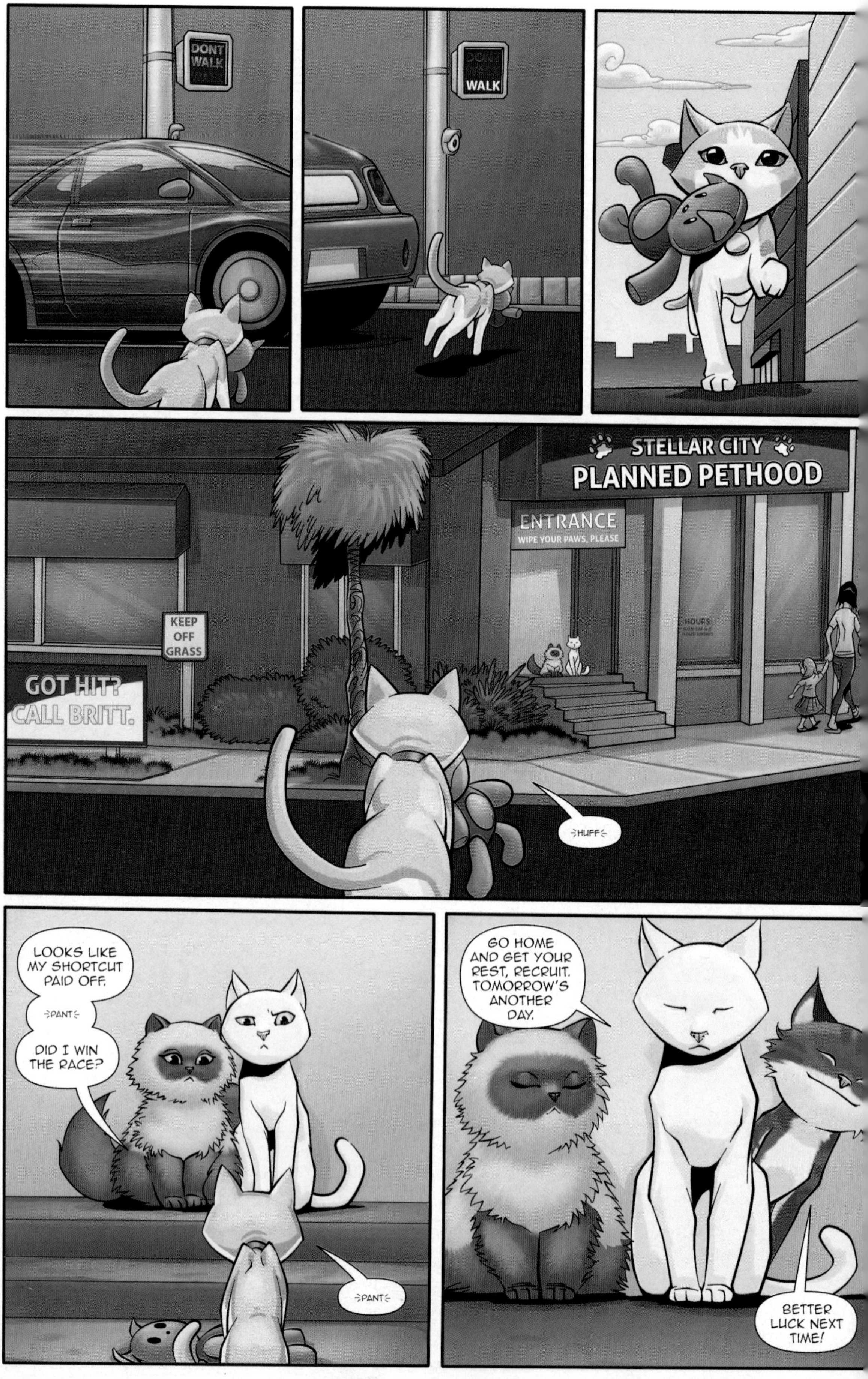
DONT WALK
WALK
STELLAR CITY
PLANNED PETHOOD
ENTRANCE
WIPE YOUR PAWS, PLEASE
KEEP OFF GRASS
GOT HIT? CALL BRITT.
HOURS
HUFF
LOOKS LIKE MY SHORTCUT PAID OFF.
PANT
DID I WIN THE RACE?
PANT
GO HOME AND GET YOUR REST, RECRUIT. TOMORROW'S ANOTHER DAY.
BETTER LUCK NEXT TIME!

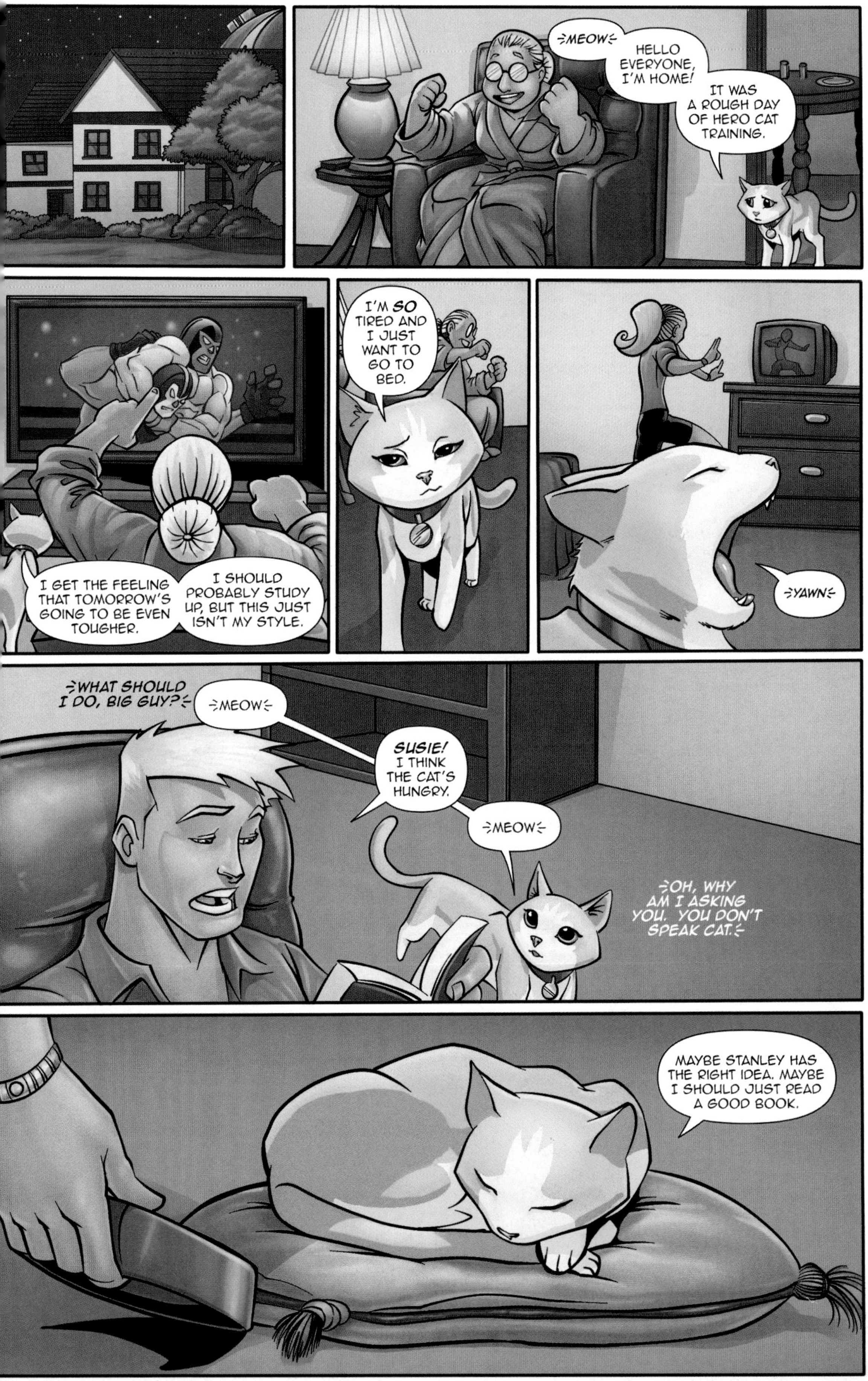

MEOW
HELLO EVERYONE, I'M HOME!
IT WAS A ROUGH DAY OF HERO CAT TRAINING.
I GET THE FEELING THAT TOMORROW'S GOING TO BE EVEN TOUGHER.
I SHOULD PROBABLY STUDY UP, BUT THIS JUST ISN'T MY STYLE.
I'M SO TIRED AND I JUST WANT TO GO TO BED.
YAWN
WHAT SHOULD I DO, BIG GUY?
MEOW
SUSIE! I THINK THE CAT'S HUNGRY.
MEOW
OH, WHY AM I ASKING YOU. YOU DON'T SPEAK CAT.
MAYBE STANLEY HAS THE RIGHT IDEA. MAYBE I SHOULD JUST READ A GOOD BOOK.

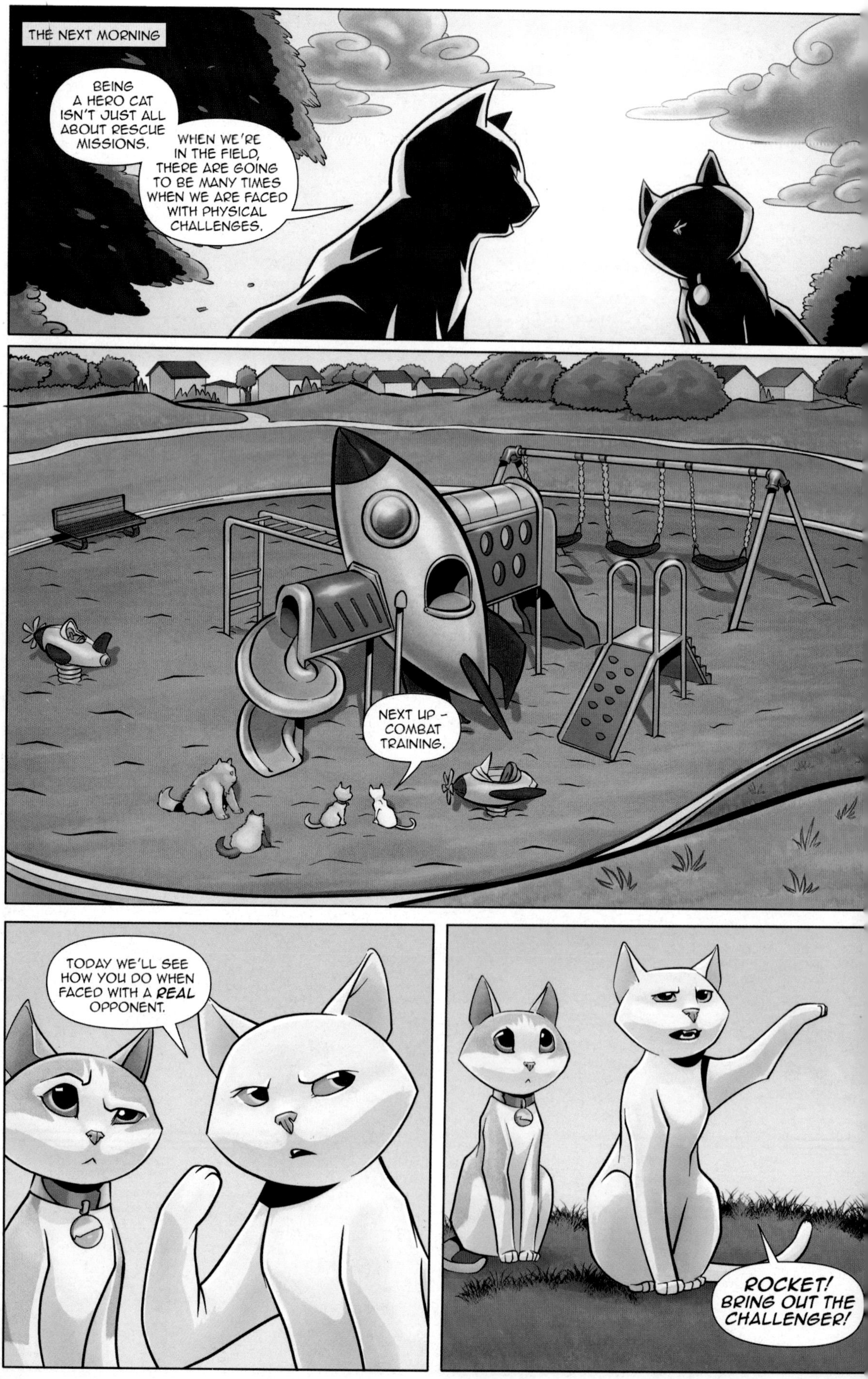
THE NEXT MORNING
BEING A HERO CAT ISN'T JUST ALL ABOUT RESCUE MISSIONS.
WHEN WE'RE IN THE FIELD, THERE ARE GOING TO BE MANY TIMES WHEN WE ARE FACED WITH PHYSICAL CHALLENGES.
NEXT UP - COMBAT TRAINING.
TODAY WE'LL SEE HOW YOU DO WHEN FACED WITH A *REAL* OPPONENT.
ROCKET! BRING OUT THE CHALLENGER!

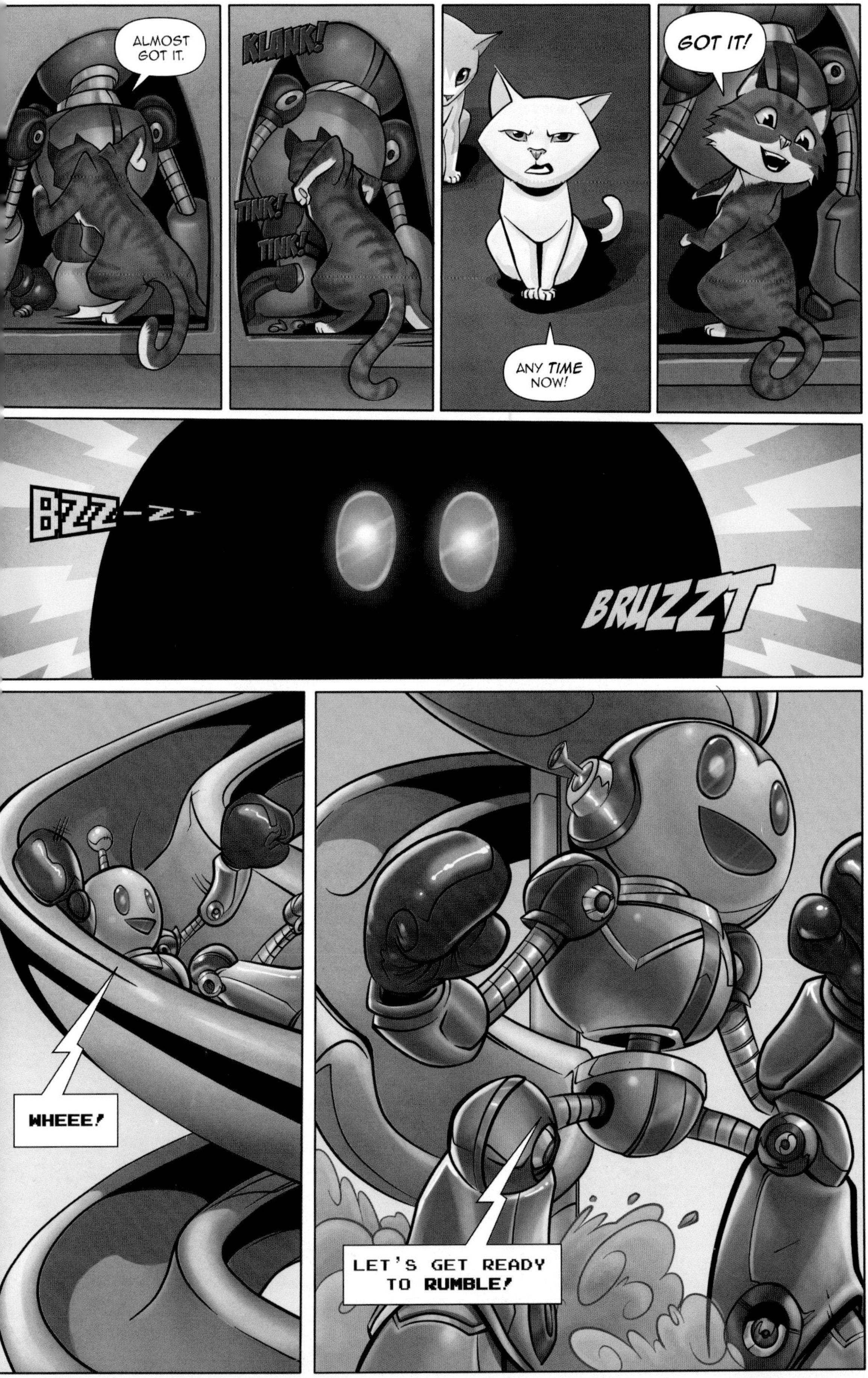
ALMOST GOT IT.
KLANK!
TINK! TINK!
ANY TIME NOW!
GOT IT!
BZZZ-Z-
BRUZZT
WHEEE!
LET'S GET READY TO RUMBLE!

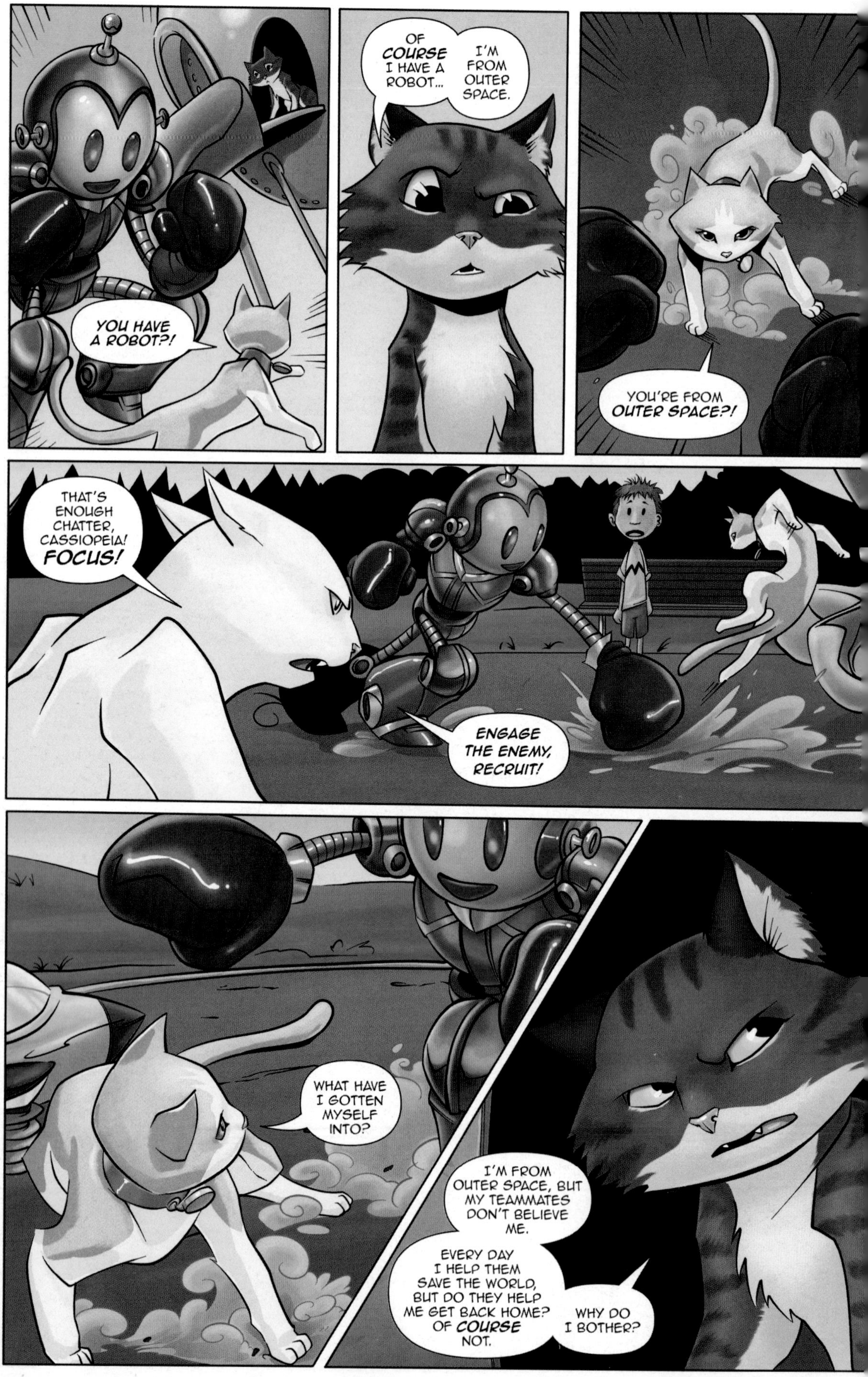

YOU HAVE A ROBOT?!
OF COURSE I HAVE A ROBOT...
I'M FROM OUTER SPACE.
YOU'RE FROM OUTER SPACE?!
THAT'S ENOUGH CHATTER, CASSIOPEIA! FOCUS!
ENGAGE THE ENEMY, RECRUIT!
WHAT HAVE I GOTTEN MYSELF INTO?
I'M FROM OUTER SPACE, BUT MY TEAMMATES DON'T BELIEVE ME.
EVERY DAY I HELP THEM SAVE THE WORLD, BUT DO THEY HELP ME GET BACK HOME? OF COURSE NOT.
WHY DO I BOTHER?

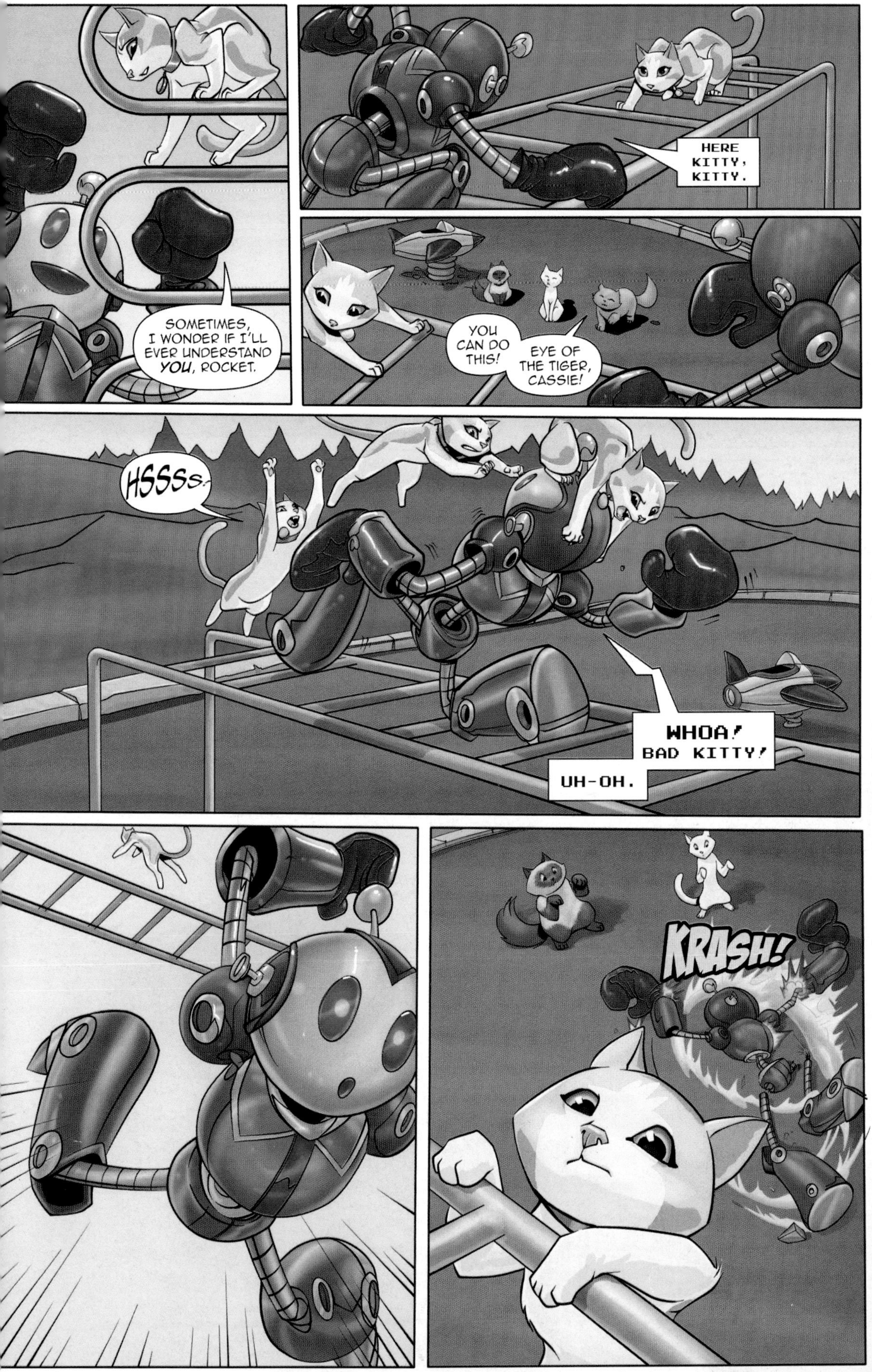
SOMETIMES, I WONDER IF I'LL EVER UNDERSTAND YOU, ROCKET.
HERE KITTY, KITTY.
YOU CAN DO THIS!
EYE OF THE TIGER, CASSIE!
HSSSs.
WHOA! BAD KITTY!
UH-OH.
KRASH!

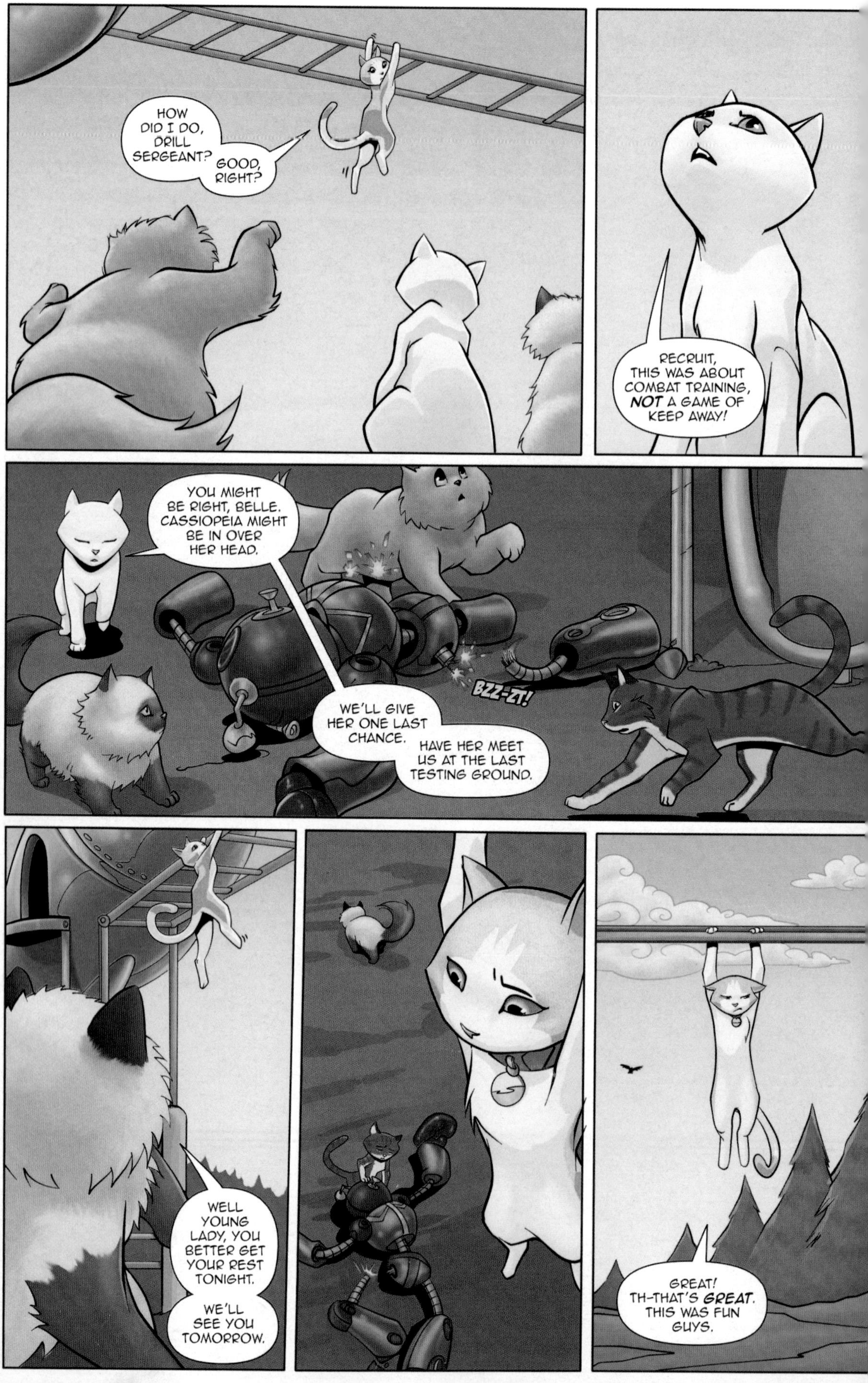
HOW DID I DO, DRILL SERGEANT?
GOOD, RIGHT?
RECRUIT, THIS WAS ABOUT COMBAT TRAINING, NOT A GAME OF KEEP AWAY!
YOU MIGHT BE RIGHT, BELLE. CASSIOPEIA MIGHT BE IN OVER HER HEAD.
BZZ-ZT!
WE'LL GIVE HER ONE LAST CHANCE.
HAVE HER MEET US AT THE LAST TESTING GROUND.
WELL YOUNG LADY, YOU BETTER GET YOUR REST TONIGHT.
WE'LL SEE YOU TOMORROW.
GREAT! TH-THAT'S GREAT. THIS WAS FUN GUYS.

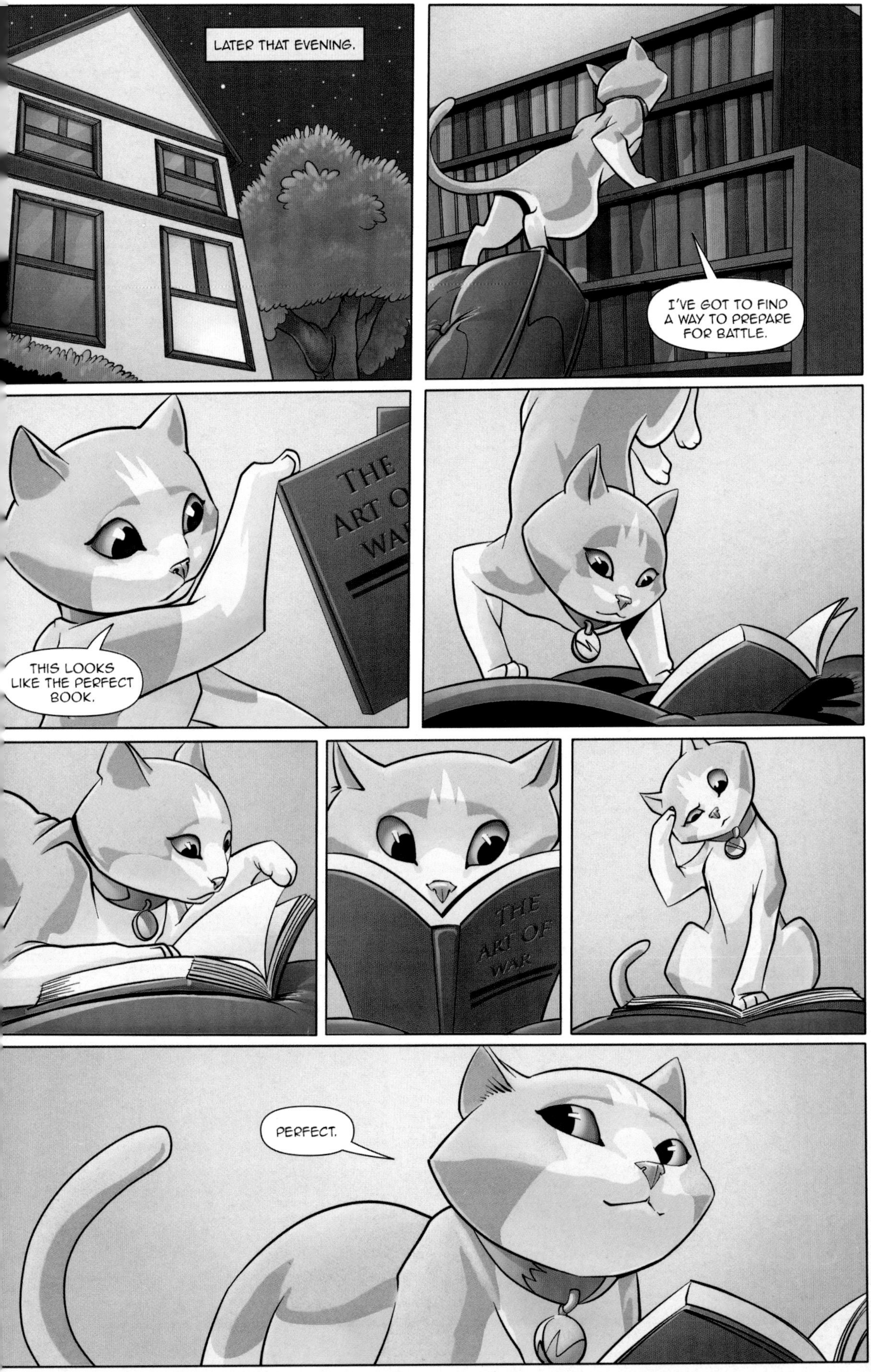
LATER THAT EVENING.
I'VE GOT TO FIND A WAY TO PREPARE FOR BATTLE.
THE ART OF WAR
THIS LOOKS LIKE THE PERFECT BOOK.
THE ART OF WAR
PERFECT.

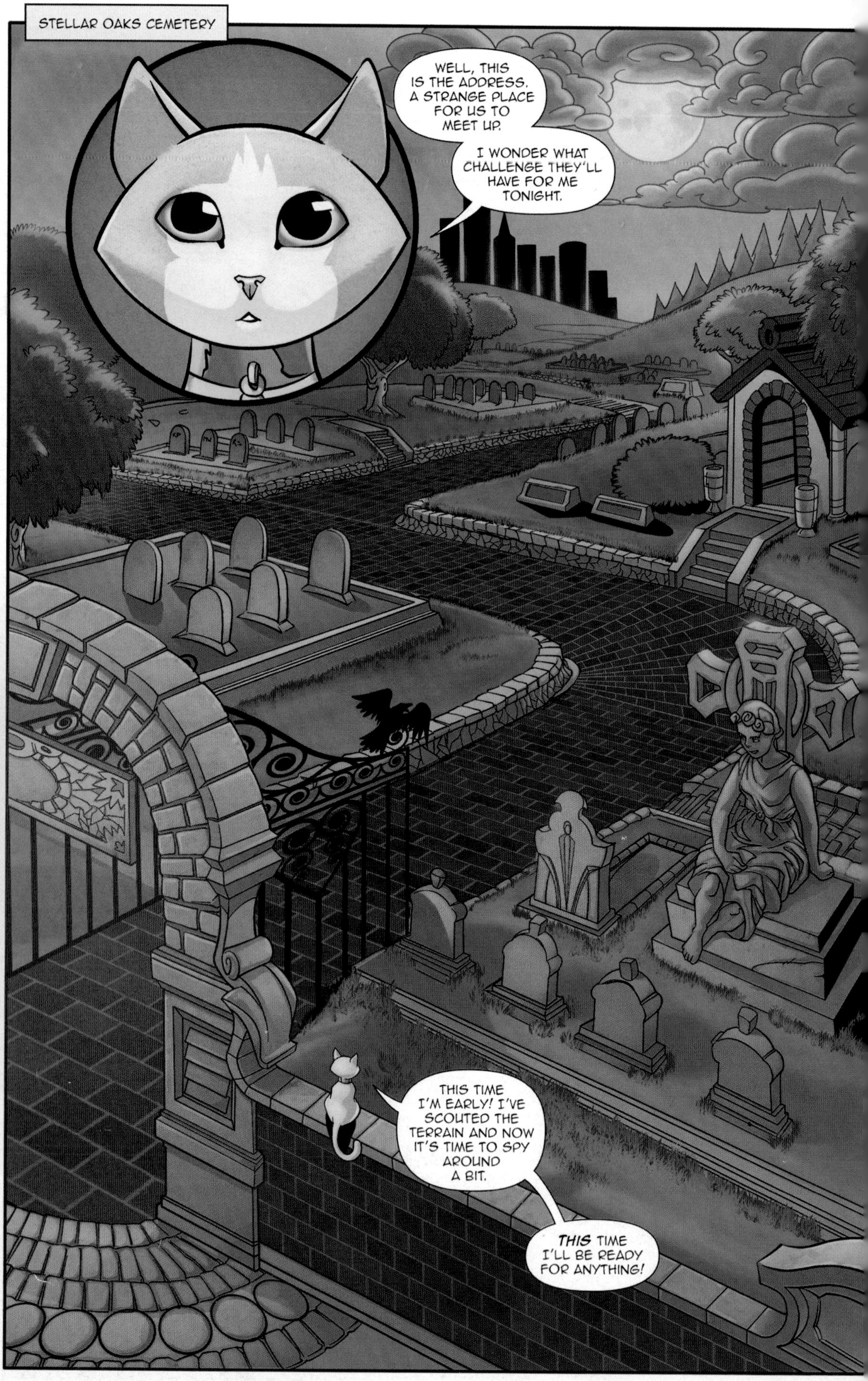
STELLAR OAKS CEMETERY
WELL, THIS IS THE ADDRESS. A STRANGE PLACE FOR US TO MEET UP.
I WONDER WHAT CHALLENGE THEY'LL HAVE FOR ME TONIGHT.
THIS TIME I'M EARLY! I'VE SCOUTED THE TERRAIN AND NOW IT'S TIME TO SPY AROUND A BIT.
THIS TIME I'LL BE READY FOR ANYTHING!

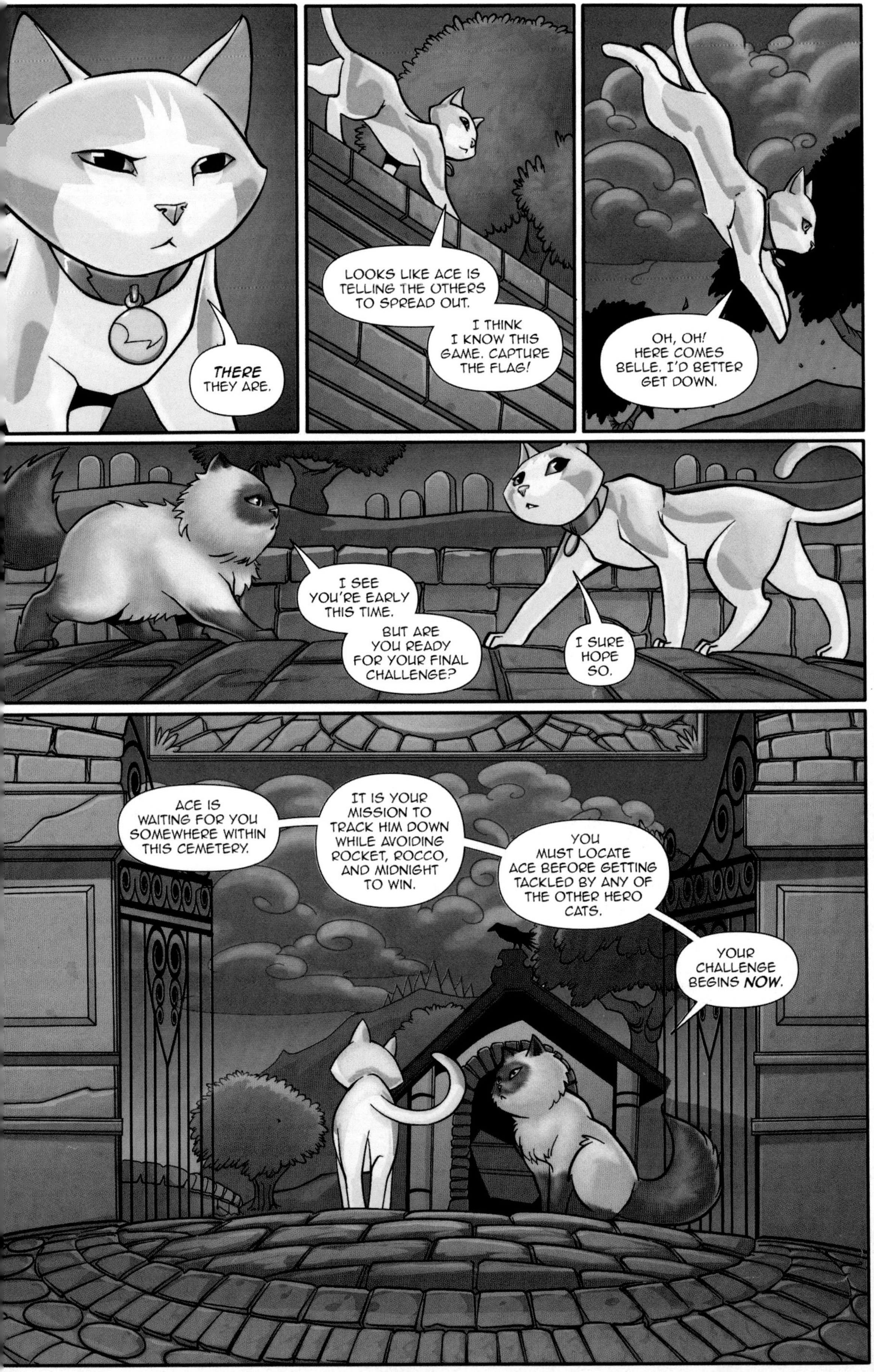
THERE THEY ARE.
LOOKS LIKE ACE IS TELLING THE OTHERS TO SPREAD OUT.
I THINK I KNOW THIS GAME. CAPTURE THE FLAG!
OH, OH! HERE COMES BELLE. I'D BETTER GET DOWN.
I SEE YOU'RE EARLY THIS TIME.
BUT ARE YOU READY FOR YOUR FINAL CHALLENGE?
I SURE HOPE SO.
ACE IS WAITING FOR YOU SOMEWHERE WITHIN THIS CEMETERY.
IT IS YOUR MISSION TO TRACK HIM DOWN WHILE AVOIDING ROCKET, ROCCO, AND MIDNIGHT TO WIN.
YOU MUST LOCATE ACE BEFORE GETTING TACKLED BY ANY OF THE OTHER HERO CATS.
YOUR CHALLENGE BEGINS NOW.

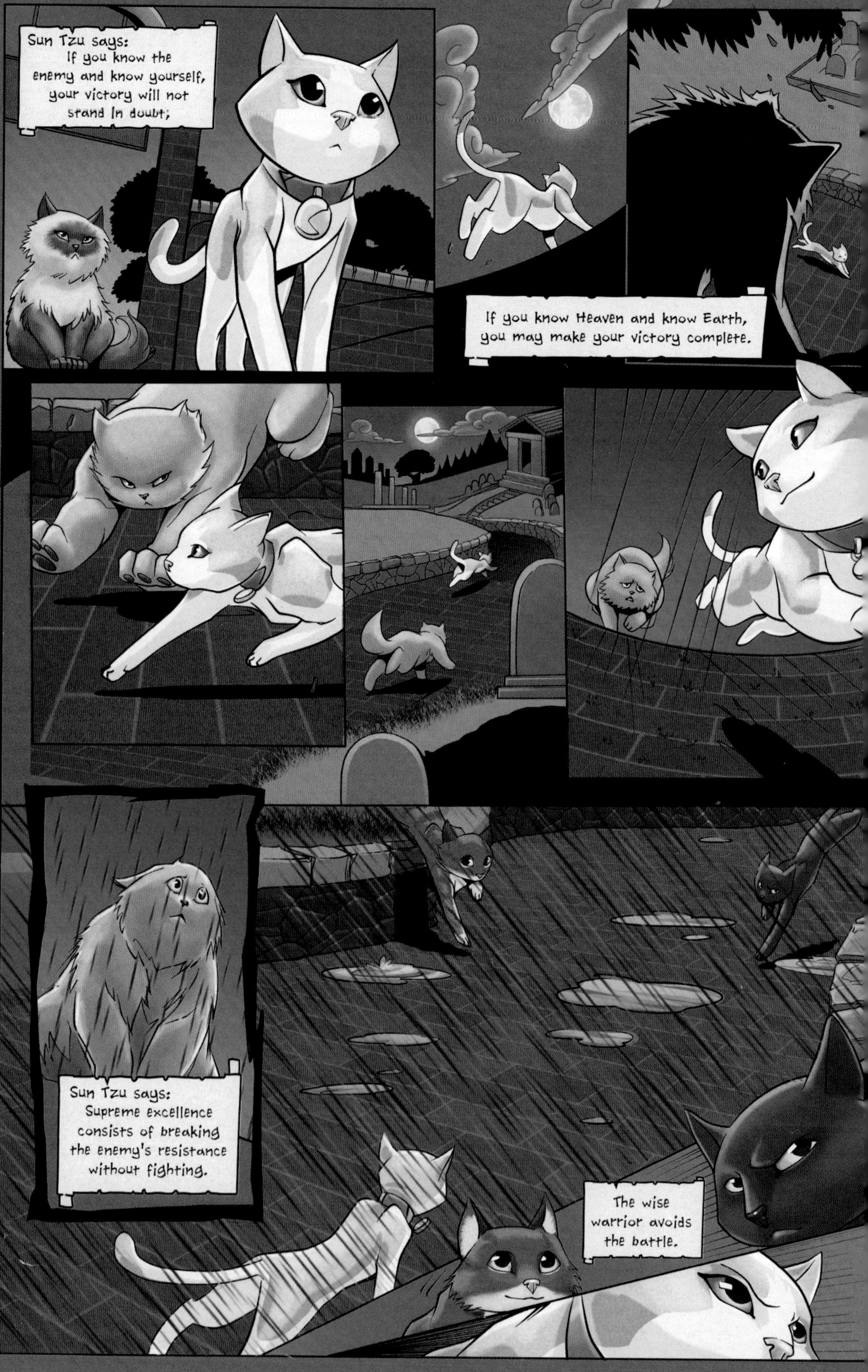
Sun Tzu says:
If you know the enemy and know yourself, your victory will not stand in doubt;
If you know Heaven and know Earth, you may make your victory complete.
Sun Tzu says:
Supreme excellence consists of breaking the enemy's resistance without fighting.
The wise warrior avoids the battle.

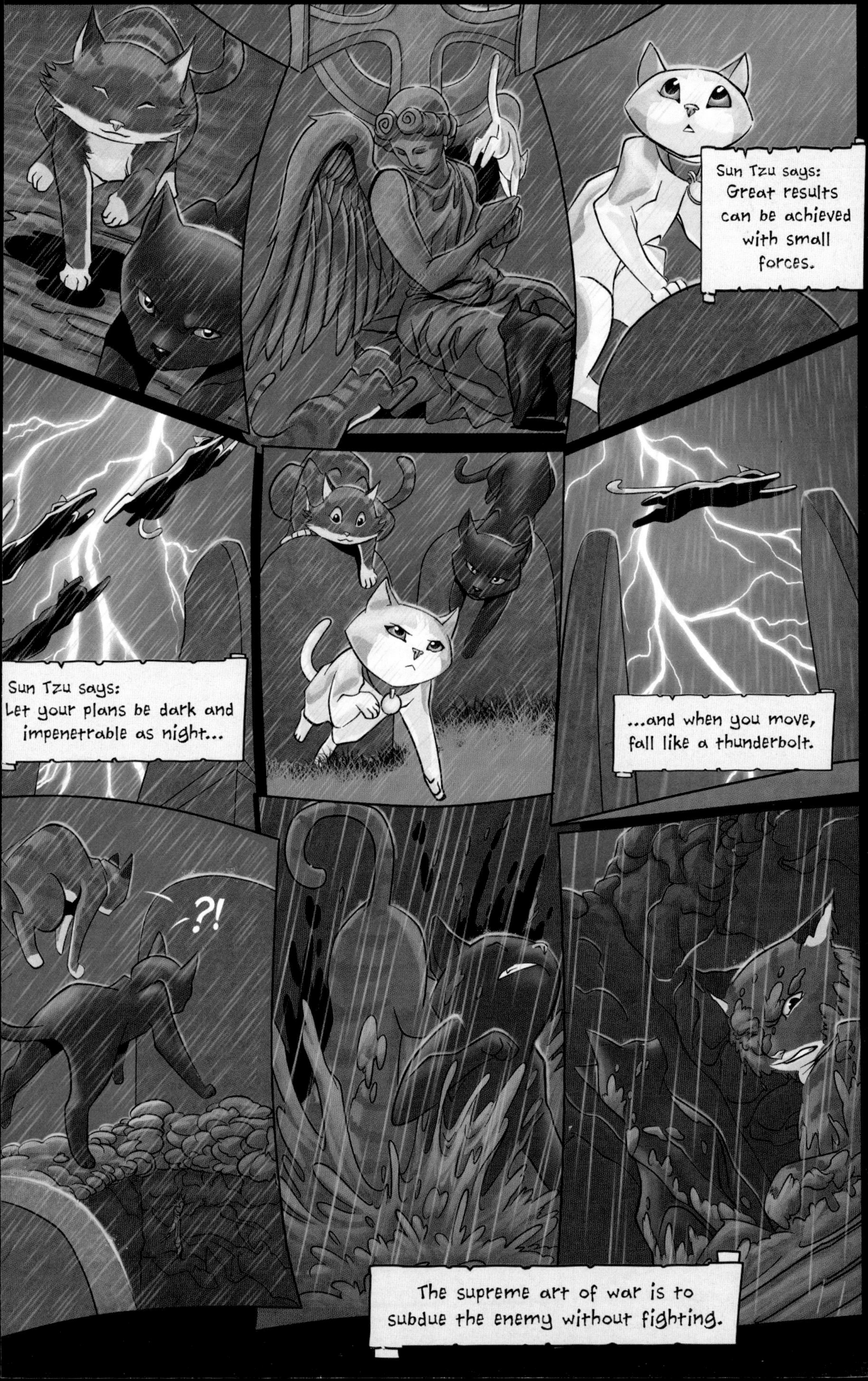
Sun Tzu says:
Great results can be achieved with small forces.
Sun Tzu says:
Let your plans be dark and impenetrable as night...
...and when you move, fall like a thunderbolt.
?!
The supreme art of war is to subdue the enemy without fighting.

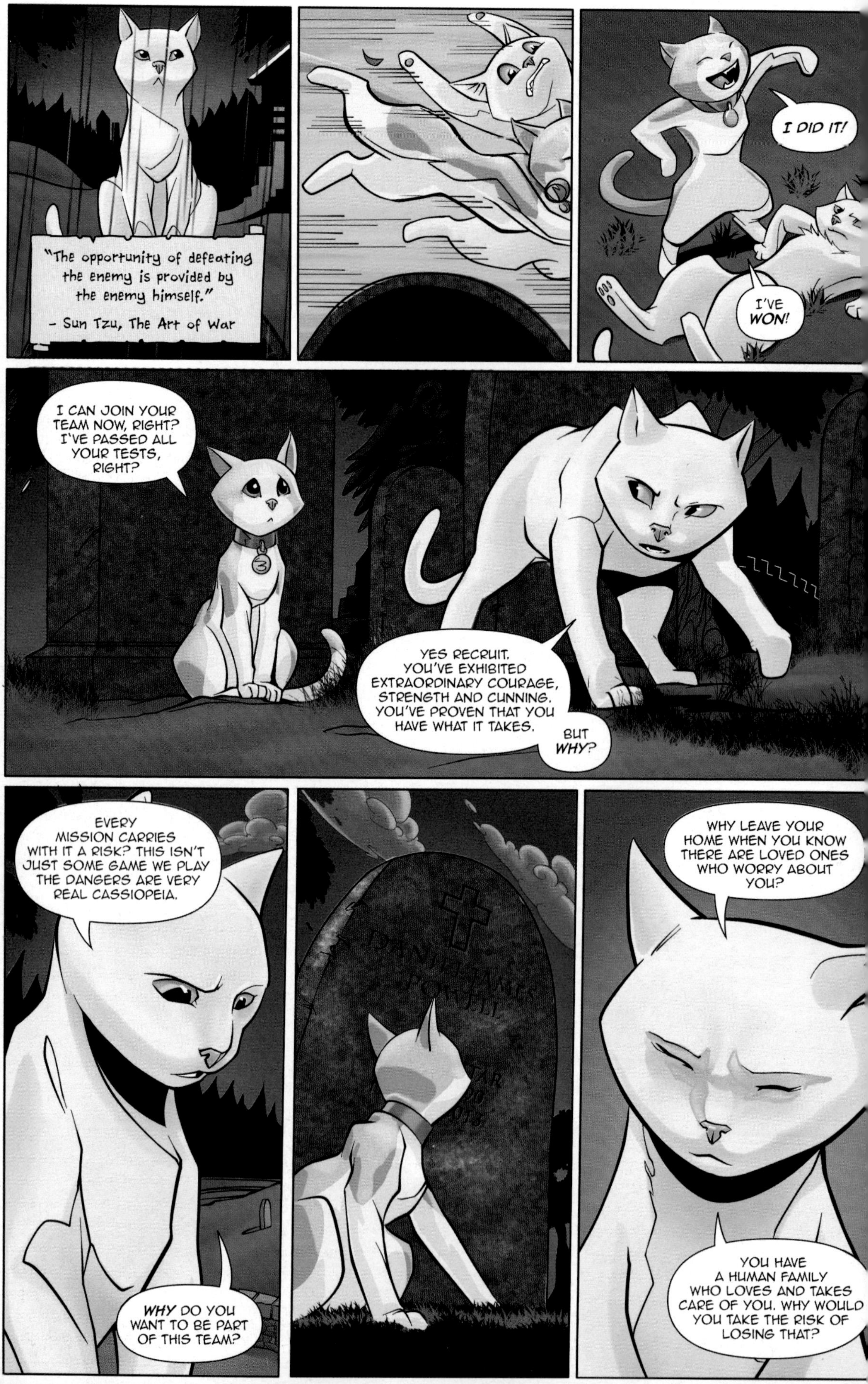
"The opportunity of defeating the enemy is provided by the enemy himself."
- Sun Tzu, The Art of War
I DID IT!
I'VE WON!
I CAN JOIN YOUR TEAM NOW, RIGHT? I'VE PASSED ALL YOUR TESTS, RIGHT?
YES RECRUIT. YOU'VE EXHIBITED EXTRAORDINARY COURAGE, STRENGTH AND CUNNING. YOU'VE PROVEN THAT YOU HAVE WHAT IT TAKES.
BUT WHY?
EVERY MISSION CARRIES WITH IT A RISK? THIS ISN'T JUST SOME GAME WE PLAY THE DANGERS ARE VERY REAL CASSIOPEIA.
WHY DO YOU WANT TO BE PART OF THIS TEAM?
WHY LEAVE YOUR HOME WHEN YOU KNOW THERE ARE LOVED ONES WHO WORRY ABOUT YOU?
YOU HAVE A HUMAN FAMILY WHO LOVES AND TAKES CARE OF YOU. WHY WOULD YOU TAKE THE RISK OF LOSING THAT?

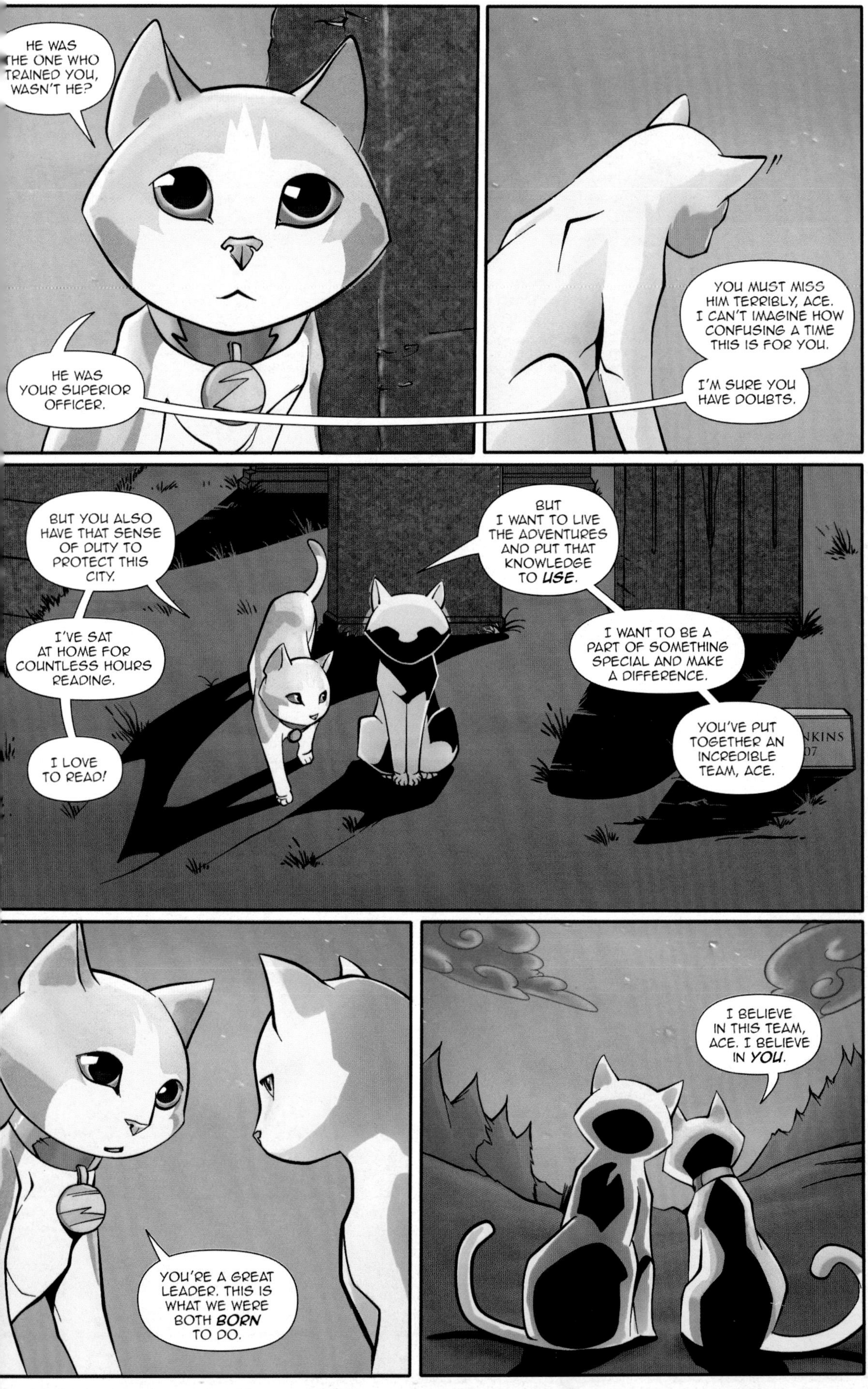
HE WAS THE ONE WHO TRAINED YOU, WASN'T HE?
HE WAS YOUR SUPERIOR OFFICER.
YOU MUST MISS HIM TERRIBLY, ACE. I CAN'T IMAGINE HOW CONFUSING A TIME THIS IS FOR YOU.
I'M SURE YOU HAVE DOUBTS.
BUT YOU ALSO HAVE THAT SENSE OF DUTY TO PROTECT THIS CITY.
I'VE SAT AT HOME FOR COUNTLESS HOURS READING.
I LOVE TO READ!
BUT I WANT TO LIVE THE ADVENTURES AND PUT THAT KNOWLEDGE TO USE.
I WANT TO BE A PART OF SOMETHING SPECIAL AND MAKE A DIFFERENCE.
YOU'VE PUT TOGETHER AN INCREDIBLE TEAM, ACE.
YOU'RE A GREAT LEADER. THIS IS WHAT WE WERE BOTH BORN TO DO.
I BELIEVE IN THIS TEAM, ACE. I BELIEVE IN YOU.

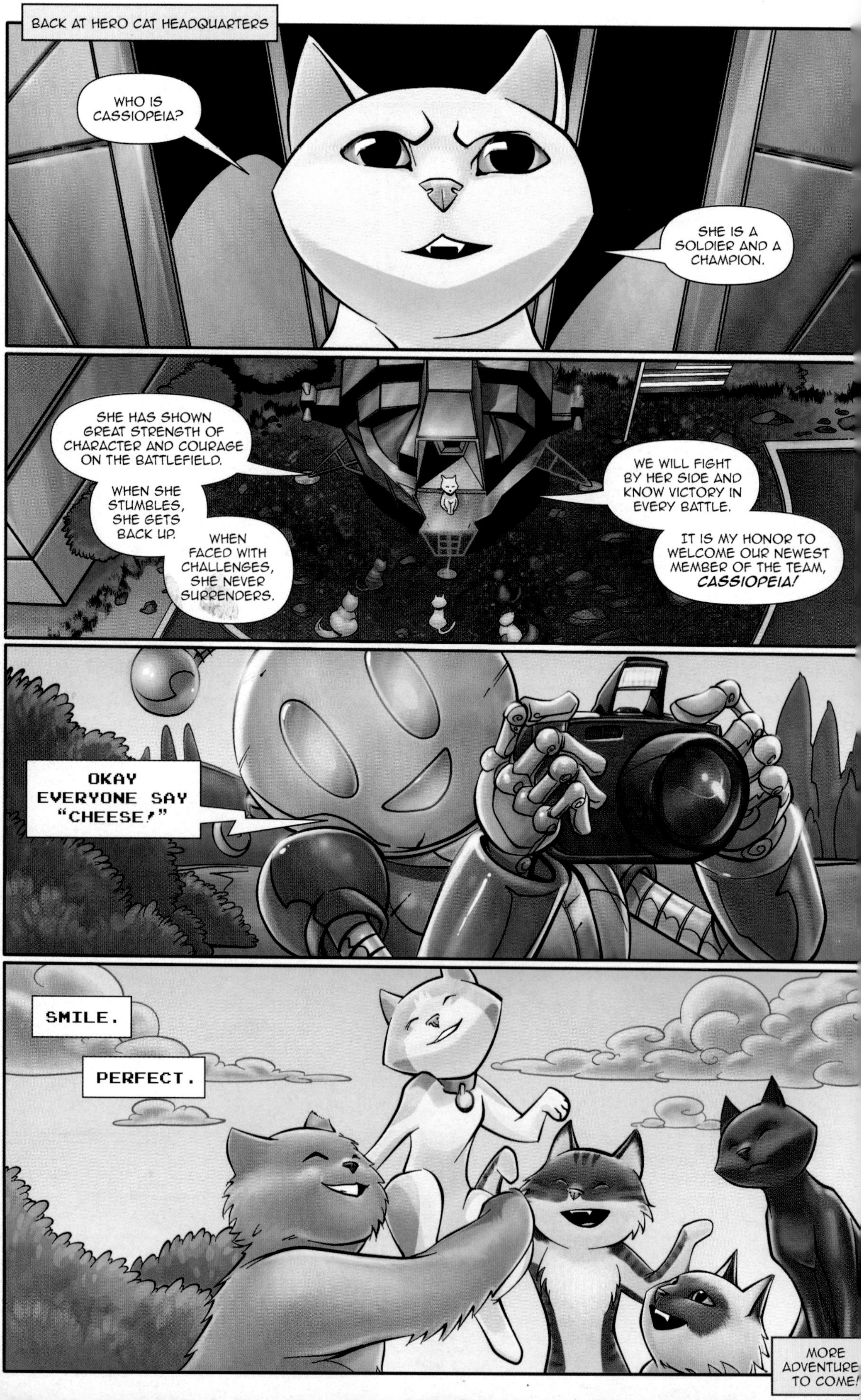
BACK AT HERO CAT HEADQUARTERS
WHO IS CASSIOPEIA?
SHE IS A SOLDIER AND A CHAMPION.
SHE HAS SHOWN GREAT STRENGTH OF CHARACTER AND COURAGE ON THE BATTLEFIELD.
WHEN SHE STUMBLES, SHE GETS BACK UP.
WHEN FACED WITH CHALLENGES, SHE NEVER SURRENDERS.
WE WILL FIGHT BY HER SIDE AND KNOW VICTORY IN EVERY BATTLE.
IT IS MY HONOR TO WELCOME OUR NEWEST MEMBER OF THE TEAM, CASSIOPEIA!
OKAY EVERYONE SAY "CHEESE!"
SMILE.
PERFECT.
MORE ADVENTURE TO COME!

HERO CHAT

EVERYONE'S TALKING ABOUT MY LITTLE SISTER'S ADVENTURES! BUT THERE'S SOMEONE ELSE I'D LIKE YOU TO MEET. HERE'S A FEW WORDS FROM THE WRITER OF HERO CATS.

UNTIL NEXT TIME CATS!

-Bandit-

GREETING CITIZENS OF STELLAR CITY,

WHAT AN INCREDIBLE JOURNEY WE'RE ON! I'M GLAD YOU HAVE JOINED US.

YEARS AGO MY FAMILY WANTED TO READ MORE "ALL AGES" BOOKS. WE WENT TO COMIC CONVENTIONS AND MET AN AMAZING ARTIST NAMED HUMBERTO RAMOS WHO DID A QUICK SKETCH OF A CHARACTER I WAS WORKING ON. IT WAS SO COOL THAT I JUST HAD TO GIVE HIM A NEW NAME. THUS GALAXY MAN WAS BORN.

AS A HOBBY, I TEACH "HOW TO DRAW" CLASSES AT LIBRARIES THROUGHOUT GEORGIA. THE KIDS REALLY LOVED GALAXY MAN, SO WE CREATED FOUR SELF PUBLISHED ISSUES. THAT'S WHEN I MET MARCUS WILLIAMS. I KNEW HIS ART NEEDED A SERIES OF ITS OWN, SO COSMIC GIRL'S CAT TOOK CENTER STAGE. OF COURSE CASSIOPEIA COULDN'T SAVE THE DAY ALL BY HERSELF, SO THE TEAM WAS ASSEMBLED.

MY FAMILY LOVES THE HERO CATS. FROM THE FEEDBACK WE GET, YOU LOVE HERO CATS TOO. WITH YOUR SUPPORT, WE CAN KEEP THIS CREATIVE TEAM INSPIRED. SO, PLEASE KEEP POSTING ONLINE AND ASKING YOUR LOCAL RETAILER FOR MORE. LET'S MAKE THIS A LONG, WONDERFUL AND REWARDING JOURNEY TOGETHER. IT IS OUR GOAL TO INSPIRE THE NEXT GENERATION OF COMIC READERS.

STAY STELLAR!

email Kyle Puttkammer
@ kyle@galacticquest.com

NEXT UP: THE WORLD BENEATH OUR FEET!

Bryan Seaton - Publisher
Kevin Freeman - President
Dave Dwench - Creative Director
Shawn Gabborin - Editor in Chief
Jamal Igle & Kelly Dale - Co-Directors of Marketing
Jim Dietz - Social Media Director
Jeremy Whitley - Education Outreach Director
Chad Cicconi & Colleen Boyd - Associate Editors

HERO CATS #3, December 2014. Copyright Kyle Puttkammer, 2014
Published by Action Lab Entertainment. All rights reserved. All characters
are fictional. Any likeness to anyone living or dead is purely coincidental. No
part of this publication may be reproduced or transmitted without permission,
except for small excerpts for review purposes. Printed in Canada. First Printing.

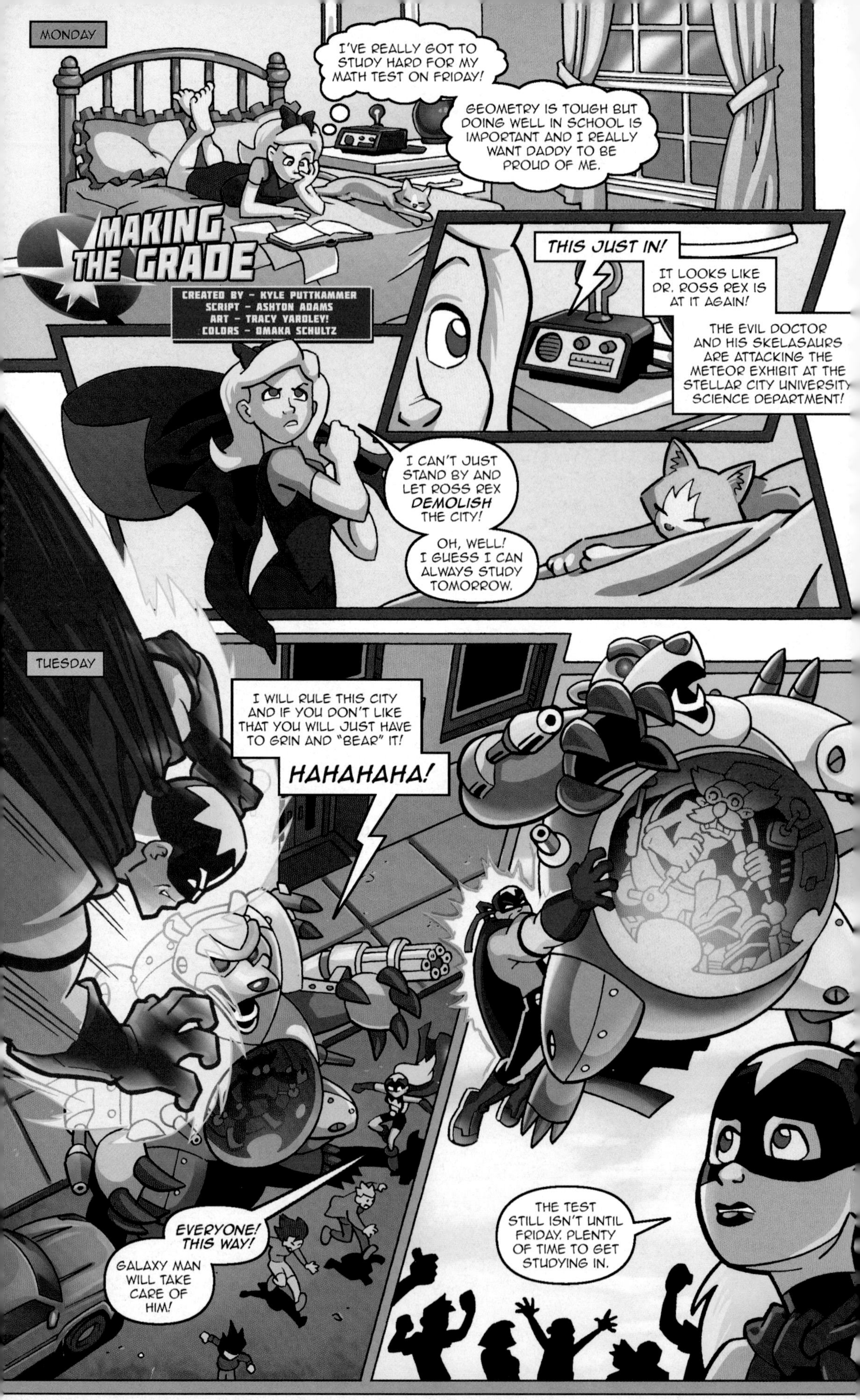
MONDAY
I'VE REALLY GOT TO STUDY HARD FOR MY MATH TEST ON FRIDAY!
GEOMETRY IS TOUGH BUT DOING WELL IN SCHOOL IS IMPORTANT AND I REALLY WANT DADDY TO BE PROUD OF ME.
MAKING THE GRADE
CREATED BY - KYLE PUTTKAMMER
SCRIPT - ASHTON ADAMS
ART - TRACY YARDLEY!
COLORS - OMAKA SCHULTZ
THIS JUST IN!
IT LOOKS LIKE DR. ROSS REX IS AT IT AGAIN!
THE EVIL DOCTOR AND HIS SKELASAURS ARE ATTACKING THE METEOR EXHIBIT AT THE STELLAR CITY UNIVERSITY SCIENCE DEPARTMENT!
I CAN'T JUST STAND BY AND LET ROSS REX DEMOLISH THE CITY!
OH, WELL! I GUESS I CAN ALWAYS STUDY TOMORROW.
TUESDAY
I WILL RULE THIS CITY AND IF YOU DON'T LIKE THAT YOU WILL JUST HAVE TO GRIN AND "BEAR" IT!
HAHAHAHA!
EVERYONE! THIS WAY!
GALAXY MAN WILL TAKE CARE OF HIM!
THE TEST STILL ISN'T UNTIL FRIDAY. PLENTY OF TIME TO GET STUDYING IN.

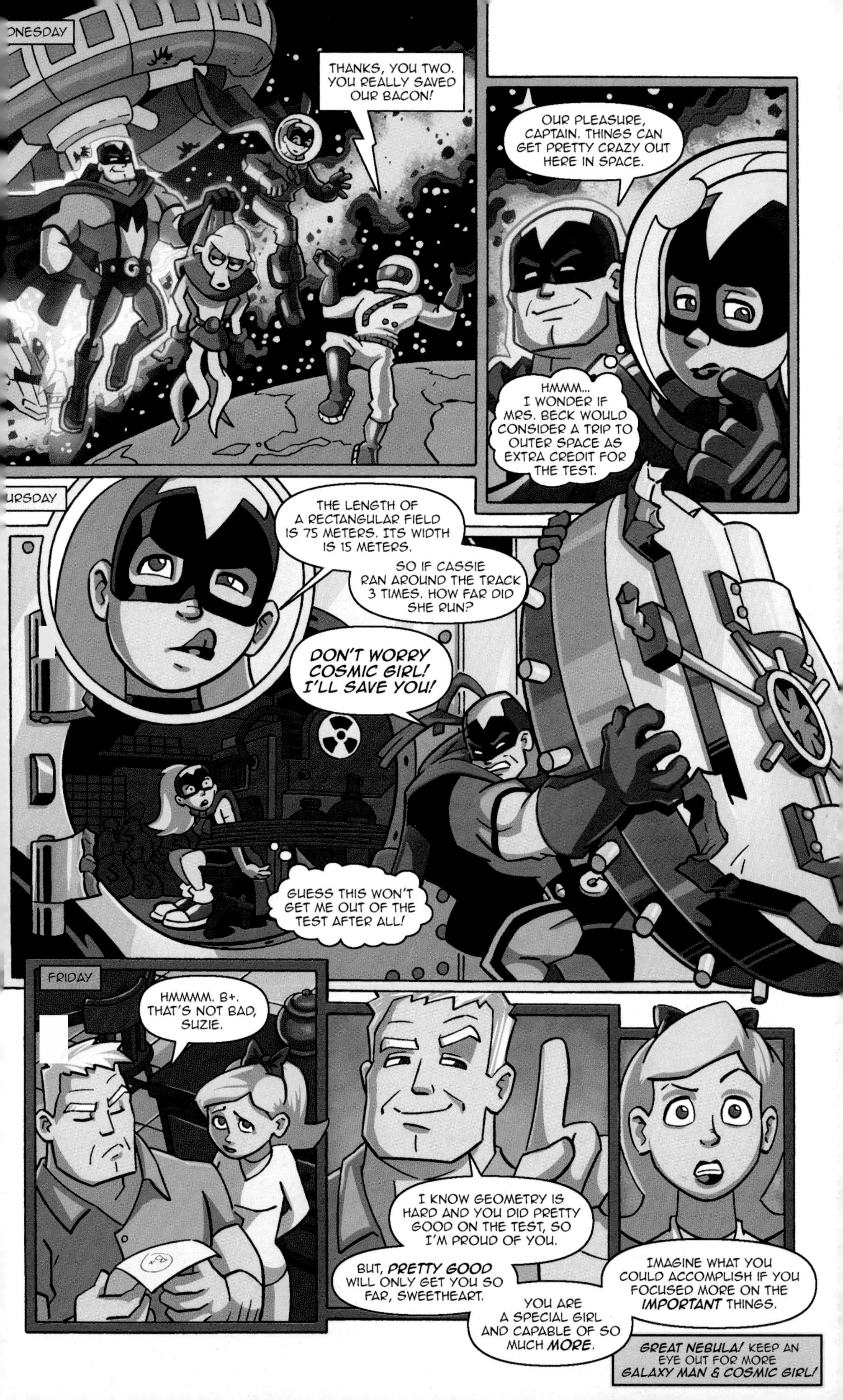
ONESDAY
THANKS, YOU TWO. YOU REALLY SAVED OUR BACON!
OUR PLEASURE, CAPTAIN. THINGS CAN GET PRETTY CRAZY OUT HERE IN SPACE.
HMMM... I WONDER IF MRS. BECK WOULD CONSIDER A TRIP TO OUTER SPACE AS EXTRA CREDIT FOR THE TEST.
URSDAY
THE LENGTH OF A RECTANGULAR FIELD IS 75 METERS. ITS WIDTH IS 15 METERS.
SO IF CASSIE RAN AROUND THE TRACK 3 TIMES, HOW FAR DID SHE RUN?
DON'T WORRY COSMIC GIRL! I'LL SAVE YOU!
GUESS THIS WON'T GET ME OUT OF THE TEST AFTER ALL!
FRIDAY
HMMMM. B+. THAT'S NOT BAD, SUZIE.
B+
I KNOW GEOMETRY IS HARD AND YOU DID PRETTY GOOD ON THE TEST, SO I'M PROUD OF YOU.
BUT, PRETTY GOOD WILL ONLY GET YOU SO FAR, SWEETHEART.
YOU ARE A SPECIAL GIRL AND CAPABLE OF SO MUCH MORE.
IMAGINE WHAT YOU COULD ACCOMPLISH IF YOU FOCUSED MORE ON THE IMPORTANT THINGS.
GREAT NEBULA! KEEP AN EYE OUT FOR MORE GALAXY MAN & COSMIC GIRL!

MONSTERS HAVE NEVER BEEN THIS ADORABI

VAMPLETS

ON SALE NOW!